PHYLLIS HALLDORSON
My Heart's Undoing

Silhouette Special Edition

Published by Silhouette Books New York

America's Publisher of Contemporary Romance

For Leslie Wainger,
who pulled *Temporary Bride* from the slush pile
and made all my dreams come true.
Many thanks and much love.

SILHOUETTE BOOKS
300 E. 42nd St., New York, N.Y. 10017

ISBN: 0-373-09290-3

First Silhouette Books printing February 1986

America's Publisher of Contemporary Romance

Printed in the U.S.A.

PHYLLIS HALLDORSON,

like all her heroines, is as in love with her husband today as on the day they met. It is because she has known so much love in her own life that her characters seem to come alive as they, too, discover the joys of romance.

Chapter One

The column of figures blurred before Colleen's misty blue eyes, and with a sigh of disgust she slammed the ledger shut and pushed it aside. She might as well accept the fact that the next two days were going to be pure agony and stop trying to convince herself that she could endure them and still carry on with business as usual. She realized now that she should never have allowed herself to be persuaded to take part in the wedding.

The wedding. She winced, an automatic reaction that occurred every time it was mentioned. In just forty-eight hours she was going to have to stand by with a bright smile and watch the man she'd loved for sixteen years, since she was eight, marry another woman. And not just any other woman. Erik was marrying her cousin, Brett Kendrick, who, though four years older than Colleen, had always been one of her best friends.

She closed her eyes and the picture that seemed to be engraved on the inside of her lids came to life. Erik Johansen, all six feet two inches of him. A blond, green-eyed Viking who still looked like the football star he'd been in college, with his wide shoulders that tapered down to a proportionately slender waist and hips, every inch muscle.

He'd been her older brother Devin's roommate during their four undergraduate years at Michigan State, and she'd been captivated from the first time Devin brought him home. In the intervening years her feelings had progressed from childish hero worship, to adolescent infatuation, to a deep and abiding love, all without his knowledge, consent or participation.

A voice speaking to her startled her out of her reverie, and her eyelids flew open as her gaze focused on a buxom woman with strawberry blond hair, brown eyes and freckles sprinkled across her pert nose. Her sister-in-law and business partner, April O'Farrell. The expression on April's pretty face was one of concern. "Colleen, are you all right? You looked so—oh honestly, you never should have agreed to be Brett's maid of honor. If she'd had a shred of sensitivity she wouldn't have asked you."

April was the only other person on earth who knew about Colleen's misplaced love for Erik Johansen, and then only because Colleen had become overconfident the year before when Erik had finally discovered that she'd grown into an attractive young woman and had begun taking her out. Not that the relationship had ever developed into much of a romance, but after several months of dating with the inevitable good-night kisses and a few sessions of making out, she'd developed a glow of happiness that could no longer be hidden from

April when they worked so closely together in the boutique every day. April had teased her gently and she'd confessed her longtime passion for her brother's friend. She'd sworn April to silence and April had honored her vow. She hadn't even told Devin, her husband.

So it was to April that Colleen had turned for comfort when Brett returned to Detroit from New York City three months before and ignited the fires of passion in Erik that made him forget everything but his desire for the tall willowy photographer's model with honey-blond hair, brown eyes flecked with green and a golden tan complexion. It was April whose shoulder bore the brunt of Colleen's tears, and April who had kept Colleen's humiliating secret.

Now Colleen found it necessary to defend Brett. "April, I appreciate your loyalty, but that's really not fair. Brett has no idea how I feel about Erik. I don't think she even realizes that we were dating on a fairly regular basis before she came back. She's been living in New York for the past ten years, ever since she graduated from high school. She didn't even know Erik until I introduced them. When she asked me to be her maid of honor there was no way I could refuse without arousing suspicion. Brett and I were very close all the time we were growing up, even though she was older. She hasn't any sisters, so I was a natural choice for the position of honor in her wedding."

April shook her head. "I don't agree. You don't owe Brett or Erik anything. Brett's too self-centered to think of anyone but herself, and Erik's an idiot. How he could possibly prefer her to you is beyond me. She'll never settle down and be the kind of wife he's looking for."

Colleen picked up a pencil and tapped the eraser end on the desk. "Erik's thirty-four years old," she said impatiently. "He knows what he wants, and he wants Brett. Sure she has flaws, but so does he. So do I. None of us is perfect, so they'll learn to live with each other's imperfections." She managed a weak smile. "I'm sure you found out that Devin has a nasty temper."

April laughed. "I sure did, and he discovered that I have one to match it, but we love each other enough to control our tantrums and not let them leave scars. I doubt that Brett will ever love anyone enough to give up her selfish ways. She always gets what she wants no matter who gets hurt in the process. Eventually, she'll hurt Erik."

Colleen shivered. April was right. Brett, an only child, had been the center of her parents' universe, the sun around which they revolved. They had been so anxious for her to be happy that they had never denied her anything. She'd been a willful, spoiled but captivating youngster, and she'd grown up to be a willful, spoiled but incredibly beautiful woman who never doubted that anything she wanted was hers for the taking. "I hope you're wrong," Colleen said. "She really seems to love Erik. Maybe now that she's getting married she'll settle down and be a good wife and mother."

April snorted. "Settle down? I've been a member of your family for eight years now and Brett's never been in love with anyone but herself. She's not in love, she's getting old and scared and has headed for the nearest shelter, which happens to be Erik."

"Old!" Colleen laughed mirthlessly. "She's only twenty-eight."

"That's old for a photographer's model. She's been modeling for ten years, and she's never lived up to her early potential. Oh, she's worked steady enough, but she never hit it really big, and now her time's running out and she knows it."

Colleen's shoulders slumped. This conversation was getting too painful to continue. She looked at her watch. "Didn't you say something about needing part of the morning off to take my two baby nieces to the dentist for their checkup?"

April glanced at the clock. "Baby nieces! You'd better start looking at them a little closer, Aunt Colleen. Mackenzie's seven and Shana's six, and they grow out of their clothes on an average of every two weeks. You're right, though, I'll have to hurry in order to pick them up at school and get them to their appointment on time."

It was almost noon when Brett phoned Colleen at the boutique. She never identified herself when starting a telephone conversation. There was no need; no one else had such a husky, sexy voice. Only this time it was more harsh than sexy. "Colleen, I need to see you at once. Meet me at your apartment in an hour, and for God's sake don't be late. This is important."

She hung up without giving Colleen a chance to answer.

Fifty minutes later Colleen stepped off the bus on East McNichols Road and started to walk the two blocks to her apartment house. The noonday sun was shining brightly, but the January breeze was frosty and penetrated even through her gray wool slacks, long-sleeved sweater and heavy, quilted, full-length brown coat. She wore a cream-colored knit cap pulled over her ears and her shoulder-length black hair, matching knitted gloves and knee-high boots to make walking in the hard-packed snow less hazardous.

Colleen didn't own a car. It was too great a luxury in a city the size of Detroit, where it could cost more to park for a month than to rent an apartment. The public transportation was excellent in her part of the city, and on stormy days she and the other three working women in her apartment house shared a taxi. Also, her parents lived less than a mile from her and were always willing to transport her on errands if necessary.

As she turned the corner she noticed Brett's new red Thunderbird, a gift from Erik, parked at the curb of the big old house that had been converted into four small apartments, one of them Colleen's. Brett was never bothered by trivial things such as premium parking rates or the lack of a steady income. She always assumed that everything would work out, and somehow for her it always did.

As Colleen walked toward the car, the door on the driver's side opened and Brett stepped out. Colleen felt the familiar stab of envy at the graceful way she moved all five feet nine inches of her. It was the result of the ballet and acrobatic dancing lessons she'd had as a child and teenager, and Colleen always felt coltish beside her.

Brett called to her cousin, and her tone was impatient. "If you'd buy a car like everybody else it wouldn't take you forever to get places. Hurry up, I've got a lot to say and not much time in which to say it."

Colleen joined her, and together they went into the house and up the stairs to Colleen's apartment. She turned up the thermostat and took Brett's silver-fox fur coat to hang in the closet, then went into the kitchen to make coffee. Brett paced around the three small rooms, and Colleen knew that this was more than just a case of bridal nerves. Brett looked tense, strained, but there was also an air of suppressed excitement about her that seemed at war with her anxiety.

Colleen's anger at being summoned so regally and then left with no means of refusing began to wane. This wasn't like Brett. Brett was always cool and in control. She knew at all times where she was headed, how she would get there and what would be waiting for her at the end of the journey. What could have happened to upset her so?

"Brett," Colleen said as she poured the hot, freshly brewed liquid into thick mugs, "for heaven's sake calm down and tell me what's happened. It can't be too much of a disaster—the dressmaker has your dress finished, pressed and ready to put on, the caterers are preparing the buffet luncheon for the reception, and you'll never convince me that Erik has changed his mind. So what's the problem that couldn't wait until we see each other tonight at the rehearsal?"

Brett opened the cupboard door, found a bottle of whiskey and liberally laced her coffee with it, then took a swallow before she spoke. "I had a call from my agent in New York this morning," she said, and the excitement Colleen had sensed vibrated in her voice. "Colleen, I've been offered the Monique St. Amour assignment."

Colleen blinked. "The what? I don't understand."

"The Monique St. Amour assignment. You know, the cosmetic company. They're starting a new ad campaign featuring a St. Amour girl. Sort of the all-American glamour girl type that every woman dreams of being. Well, I'm it! The head of the ad agency called my agent and offered me a contract. It's to be a worldwide promotion, and they'll be photographing me at all the exciting and glamorous landmarks. The Eiffel Tower in Paris, St. Peter's Basilica in Rome, the Parthenon in Greece—"

Colleen was struggling to keep up with her cousin's rambling and had only just begun to understand the implications of what she was saying. "Now just a minute," she interrupted, "you're marrying Erik on Saturday. How are you going to juggle an around-the-world modeling assignment and your responsibilities as Erik's wife?"

Brett took another long swig of her whiskey-laced coffee. "That's what I had to talk to you about. I'm not going to marry Erik, Colleen."

Colleen could only stare, openmouthed and disbelieving. "You're what?" she finally gasped, convinced she'd misunderstood.

Brett looked away. "I can't marry Erik. He'd never agree to my taking this assignment, but it's the shot of adrenaline that will save my career. Oh, don't you see, this one assignment will open doors for me for years to come. To say nothing of the money. You wouldn't believe how lucrative something like this can be. I'll be a celebrity. Everyone will recognize the Monique St. Amour girl."

"But what about Erik?" Colleen couldn't believe what she was hearing.

Brett's expression changed to one of distress. "You know it breaks my heart to call off our wedding plans. I love Erik. That's why I've decided against marrying him. He'd never be happy with a dedicated career woman for a wife, and we both know that's what I'll always be. Now that I have this chance I couldn't possibly turn it down. It's what I've been working for all my life."

For just a moment Colleen felt an overwhelming sense of relief. Brett wasn't going to marry Erik after all. Was there still a chance for her?

She banished the selfish thought and realized that she was trembling. She took the few steps to the yellow Formica table and sank down on one of the chairs. April had been right. Brett was totally self-centered and incapable of loving anyone. A blind anger replaced her stunned incredulity. "How could you?" she hissed. "Dammit, Brett, how can you do this to Erik?" Her voice was rising. "He loves you. I've never seen a man so much in love. If you walk away from him he'll be shattered."

Brett took another swig of her spilled coffee. "Do you think this is easy for me? I know he loves me. I know he'll be hurt, but there's nothing else I can do. I'm just glad the offer came before we were married. At least we won't have to go through the mess of a divorce. He'll get over it, Colleen, and some day he'll find a sweet, submissive woman who will clean his house and give him babies and be the perfect corporate wife. Then he'll be thankful that I had the good sense to walk away and leave him."

"I just don't believe this," Colleen raged. "The wedding is only two days away. The gifts have been received and acknowledged. The caterers will have to be paid whether the food is served or not. It's too late to cancel the flowers—Brett, how can you be so heartless?"

Brett slammed her cup down on the counter. "Oh, come off it, Colleen. I'm not Cinderella and Erik's not Prince Charming. You always did believe in fairy tales, but you've got to grow up sometime. Erik and I haven't exactly been waiting for the marriage vows to start the honeymoon. Actually, we've already sated a lot of the passion we felt for each other. I'm not cheating him— he got what he wanted from me.''

For the first time since she'd learned to talk, Colleen was speechless. How could you appeal to the compassion of someone who had none? Brett didn't even comprehend what Colleen was talking about. She thought sexual desire and love were indistinguishable. She couldn't fathom the deep and abiding love that Erik had so trustingly offered her, and there was no way she ever could have returned it.

Colleen felt a wave of sympathy for Erik that was agonizing in its intensity. He'd been instantly and totally captivated by Brett. Swept off his feet, as her mother would say. He'd showered her with expensive gifts and taken her to glamorous and exciting places where they were spotlighted and talked about. The beautiful model and the handsome former Michigan State football star. When she'd finally agreed to marry him he'd positively glowed with happiness. It would devastate him to lose her now.

She closed her eyes to try to shut out the painful thoughts. ''Have you told Erik yet?'' she asked.

''Well—uh—no, not yet.'' Something in Brett's tone made Colleen open her eyes. ''That's another thing I wanted to talk to you about, Colleen. I was hoping maybe...I mean, you and Erik have known each other so long and are such good friends. What I'm trying to say is I...I want you to tell him for me.''

Chapter Two

Brett's words seemed to vibrate inside Colleen's skull. *I want you to tell him for me.* That did it! She jumped to her feet and clutched the back of the metal chair to keep from rearranging that perfect oval face with her bare fists.

"Who in hell do you think you are?" Colleen's voice was low and furious. "You come back to Detroit after ten years and announce to anyone who will listen that you're ready to settle down; you turn all that practiced charm on Erik, who's the sweetest, most thoughtful man in the whole world, until he's crazy in love with you; you accept a diamond from him that must have put him in hock for years, and set the wedding date, and now you're just going to walk away, break the poor guy's heart and leave me to do the dirty work of telling him 'sorry, I've changed my mind, something better has come along.' No way. The very least you owe him is to face him and tell him yourself.''

She was thankful for the chair she was gripping so tightly. Without it she doubted that her quaking knees would hold her up.

Brett tipped her head to one side and looked at Colleen. "You know, if you're not careful I'm going to suspect that you're in love with Erik.'' Her voice was calm and cool and remained so as she continued. ''I've neither the time nor the inclination to tell him in person; my plane leaves for New York in two hours. Besides, you know I hate scenes. If you won't tell him then I'll just write him a letter and have it delivered by messenger service.''

''You wouldn't. You couldn't. Even you couldn't be that cruel.''

''Oh, for heaven's sake, Colleen, Erik's a grown man. He may hurt for a while, but he'll survive. Now, are you going to tell him or do I have to put it all in a note?''

Colleen knew she couldn't let him get the shattering news that way. She suddenly envied Brett her inability to care. It was so much easier than caring too much. She'd always felt the pain of others to a degree, but with Erik, his agony became her own. She felt dizzy, and nausea cramped her stomach muscles. In that moment she hated Brett, and she was determined not to let her cousin profit from the shambles she was making of Erik's life.

She took a deep breath and squared her shoulders. Her voice was cold and steady. ''All right, Brett, I'll tell him, and I hope he'll see you for just what you are—a sadistic bitch who doesn't give a damn about anybody but herself.''

Brett opened her mouth to protest but Colleen held out her hand. "Give me the ring."

Brett looked puzzled. "The ring?"

Colleen nodded. "The diamond engagement ring Erik gave you. It's customary to return it if the engagement is broken, you know."

"Oh. Oh yes." She began to toy with the expensive stone. "I—I'm sure Erik would want me to keep it. He had it designed especially for me."

Colleen didn't so much as blink, and her tone was icy. "Give it to me, Brett."

Slowly Brett slipped it off her finger and deposited it in Colleen's palm. "I suppose you're right," she said sadly, "it should be returned."

Colleen transferred the ring from her right hand to the left, and then held the right one out again. "Now give me the keys to the car."

"The keys—" Brett screeched. "Now look here, the Thunderbird was a gift, free and clear—"

"Give me the keys," Colleen ordered, "otherwise you can face him yourself. I won't help you unless you return the car as well as the ring."

"But I need the car," Brett wailed. "How am I going to get to the airport?"

"That's your problem. Take a cab like the rest of us peasants do."

Brett shot her a murderous look but rummaged in her purse and withdrew the keys. "Here," she said and threw them into Colleen's hand. "I can't take it with me anyway, and it would be a hassle to get someone to sell it for me."

She walked over to the closet, retrieved her fur coat and put it on, then headed for the door. "Oh, by the way," she said as she turned the knob, "you're the only one who knows about any of this. I'm afraid it will be up to you to notify the family and friends and call off the wedding.''

She pulled open the door and rushed outside, slamming it behind her.

Colleen stared for a moment at the offending door, then uttered a most unladylike oath and banged her fist on the table.

For a few minutes she just stood there, too stricken to move. Damn Brett. She'd whirled into town like a tornado, left a trail of destruction behind her and then walked away scot-free. In catechism Colleen had been taught that the meek would inherit the earth. That was a laugh. All the meek ever inherited was the mess left by those strong enough and selfish enough to grab what they wanted and to hell with the consequences.

The sharp ring of the telephone shattered the silence and made her jump, a sure sign of the beating her nervous system had taken. She walked into the bedroom and sank down on the side of the bed as she picked up the insistently jangling instrument. It was April, who had a question about pricing that Colleen answered, and as they talked, a partial solution to her problem of telling Erik about Brett's desertion began to form. "April," she said, "I may not be back at the boutique this afternoon. Can you get along all right without me?"

"Sure, I guess so. We're rather busy, but I'll manage."

Colleen felt a twinge of guilt. "Thanks, I'll make it up to you. One more thing. Do you know if Devin is in his office?"

"No, he's not. In fact, he called just after you left to say he had to go to Lansing, and if he isn't home in time to leave for the wedding rehearsal, then I should go on ahead and he would drive right to the church." April laughed. "I told him not to be late, they can't start without the best man."

Colleen slumped, her hope of getting Devin to go with her and help break the news to Erik smashed. "Oh," she said tonelessly. "Well, look, if he should call back, get a number where I can reach him."

"Colleen, is something wrong? What did Brett want to see you about?"

"Yes, something is definitely wrong, but I can't talk about it now. Just please, try to find out where Devin can be reached." Even if he couldn't be with her when she told Erik, Colleen knew Erik would need the support only a best friend could give, and Devin would want to be around to give it.

She rang off, then hesitated a moment before picking up the phone again and dialing Erik's number at the Ford plant in Dearborn. His secretary answered, and when Colleen asked for Mr. Johansen she said, "I'm sorry, Miss O'Farrell, but Mr. Johansen will be out of the office all day."

Colleen wished she could just breathe a sigh of relief, hang up and forget the whole thing, but unfortunately she couldn't. "This is an urgent personal matter, Trish. I hate to ask, but could you possibly tell me where I can reach him."

"I don't have his itinerary. He's having lunch with some of the engineers and then they're going to be visiting several of the other plants in the area. He said he wouldn't be back this afternoon."

Colleen's frustration threshold was rapidly being reached, and she drummed her fingers on the nightstand as she tried to keep her voice calm. "This is terribly important. If you hear from him this afternoon, please tell him to call me at the boutique immediately."

She decided against driving Brett's car downtown and took a cab back to the Renaissance Center where she confronted a surprised April. "I thought you weren't coming back this afternoon," she said.

"I wasn't," Colleen answered, "but my plans changed. Come in the office and you can listen in on my call to Mom when I tell her what's happened. We can leave the door open in case a customer comes in."

April followed her into the office and sat down while Colleen dialed her parents' home. When Katherine O'Farrell answered, Colleen could visualize her mother's short chubby figure dressed in one of the slacks and blouse sets she always wore around the house. "Mom," she said, "I have something to tell you. Please just listen and don't interrupt until I've finished."

She told her mother, and April, of her encounter with Brett, and both gasped and squealed at intervals with shock, anger and outrage, but neither interrupted until Colleen was finished. " . . . she slammed the door behind her and was gone. I'd hoped to get Devin to go with me when I tell Erik, but he's out of town, and now I can't find Erik, either. I don't know what to do. I have to locate Erik before he shows up for the rehearsal."

Both Katherine and April burst into indignant speech, and Colleen couldn't concentrate on either of them. Finally she held up her hand to April and cut in on her mother's angry sputtering. "Mom, calm down, both you and April are talking at once.... Yes, she's right here with me. Now look, I need you to do something for me. I'm afraid it's going to be up to you to tell Aunt Glenna and Uncle Logan about this."

"You want me to tell Brett's parents?" Katherine gasped.

"I'm sorry, but Aunt Glenna's your sister, and I've got to find Erik. Just don't tell anyone else until I locate him. If I don't catch up with him until it's time for the rehearsal, I'll have to let everyone assemble. At least that way we can tell the wedding party all at once. Just keep Uncle Logan and Aunt Glenna away from there."

Colleen spent the rest of the afternoon telephoning the various Ford Motor Company factories and subsidiaries in and around the Detroit area, but in each case Erik either wasn't expected or had just left. He was well known and liked in the Ford empire. When he'd graduated from college he'd turned down a contract to play professional football in favor of continuing his education, and after he got his master's degree in engineering he went to work for Ford and had been with them ever since. He had a high-salaried position with a lot of responsibilities, and his future with the company was bright.

At five o'clock Colleen started calling Erik's apartment, but by the time she had to leave for the church there was still no answer. Neither had April heard from Devin. The situation had changed from an unpleasant duty into a nightmare. It would have been difficult enough to tell Erik if she'd been able to do it earlier in the day at her apartment or his. Now to have to go to the church where fifty or so relatives and members of the wedding party were assembled for a rehearsal and tell him his bride wasn't going to show up and the wedding was called off was positively sadistic.

She didn't bother to change into the sheer wool and silk dress she'd planned to wear that evening. There'd be no festivities now. Instead she wore the slacks and sweater she'd had on all day as she climbed into Brett's luxury car and drove it to the old brick church from which all the members of her family and Brett's had been baptized, married and buried.

Colleen was early, and the church was lighted and open but empty. She knew Father John and the altar boys were somewhere in the building, but she was glad she didn't have to talk to them right then. The high ceiling and many stained-glass windows made the huge area difficult to heat, and she didn't remove her coat as she slid into one of the pews and closed her eyes.

She was still there a few minutes later when she heard voices and the sound of footsteps as someone came into the vestibule. Colleen stood and turned around, both hoping and dreading to see Erik, but it was two of the bridesmaids and their escorts. Before she had exchanged more than a few words with them three of the ushers and their dates arrived, followed by the organist and her husband. From then on people streamed in, but there was still no sign of Erik, or Devin and April.

Colleen tried to stay out of sight as much as possible, and positioned herself at the back of the church near the door to the vestibule so she could intercept Erik when he finally arrived. Then she almost missed him when he walked in surrounded by his father and mother his two sisters and their husbands and his college-age brother with his date. Colleen groaned and closed her eyes. Why couldn't he have come early and alone? Now she was going to have to make a scene in order to get him away so she could talk to him.

She took a deep breath and started down the aisle after him. She called his name but he didn't hear her and kept walking. She called again, louder this time, and the whole group turned and looked at her. Erik positively radiated happiness. His wide green eyes sparkled, and a grin lit up his whole face. His blond shaggy hair was styled somewhat shorter than usual, and a lock of it tumbled across his broad forehead. The camel's hair overcoat he wore was tailor-made to fit his athletic physique.

His grin grew even broader when he saw her. "Hi, honey," he said and caught her in a brotherly hug. "Where's my beautiful bride? Don't tell me she's even going to be late for her own wedding rehearsal?" He laughed and let go of her.

Several of the group were still standing there listening, and she struggled to keep her voice calm. "Uh— Brett's not here. Please, Erik, could I talk to you for a minute?"

"Sure," he said magnanimously. "What's the problem?" She wasn't getting through to him at all. He was just too happy to notice her desperation.

"I mean I'd like to speak to you alone. Will you follow me, please?" She turned and walked off, hoping he would be curious enough to follow without questions.

She led him through the side door into the office and classroom area and almost bumped into Father John, the tall middle-aged priest who was coming from the opposite direction. "What's the hurry, Colleen?" he said with a chuckle. "Not running off with the bridegroom, are you?" He held out a hand to Erik. "You look happy, Erik. Can't imagine why," he teased, and both men laughed.

Colleen's nerves were almost at the breaking point, and her tone was more brittle than she'd intended. "Please, Father, I must talk to Erik. May we use your office?"

The priest seemed immediately to recognize Colleen's stress and his laughter died. "Of course, my dear. The light's on. Take all the time you want."

Colleen nodded and murmured quietly, "Will you wait here?"

"I'll be here," he said gently, but before Colleen could walk away a hand clutched her shoulder and turned her around.

Erik's expression had changed to one of concern. "Colleen, what's the matter? Is it Brett? Are you trying to tell me she's been in an accident—"

"No! Oh no, nothing like that. Brett's fine, but please, I must talk to you."

His features relaxed, and he nodded and dropped his hand as she walked toward the church office.

Erik closed the door behind him and looked around the austerely furnished room. There were no thick carpets on the floors or heavy drapes at the windows as in his own office, but this one had a warm, homey atmosphere that no business office would ever have.

His gaze settled on Colleen. She was standing in the middle of the room, her face tilted upward to look at him. Her shoulders were hunched, and her fists were clenched.

He smiled. She was such an intense little thing. Always had been, even as a child. Obviously something had happened to upset her, but what? Something to do with Brett he was almost sure. Probably Brett had been held up at the hairdresser's, or spent too much time shopping, and had sent Colleen to make her excuses for being late. He was well acquainted with his fiancée's unfortunate streak of selfishness, but it didn't keep him from burning for her night and day. Still, he wasn't going to let her take advantage of Colleen's compassionate nature. After their honeymoon in the Caribbean, he'd talk to her about that.

He shifted restlessly. Ah yes, the honeymoon. It would definitely have to be after that, because he intended for them to spend the next month in bed with no thinking and little talking. Brett could make a man forget everything but—

"Erik, are you listening to me?"

Erik blinked and grinned sheepishly, and Colleen knew he hadn't heard a word she'd said. Fortunately it had only been a couple of introductory sentences, and they had been awkward.

"Sorry, honey, I guess I wasn't," he said as he took off his overcoat and tossed it onto a chair. "Now, what's the problem? Don't tell me Brett has a case of the pre-wedding jitters." His eyes sparkled with humor.

"I only wish she did." Colleen's mouth was trembling and it was difficult for her to talk. "Erik, I don't know how to tell you this other than to just say it. Brett's gone."

He looked perplexed. "Gone? Gone where? You mean she went out of town and is late getting back?"

Colleen clenched her fists. "No. I mean she's gone to New York, and she's not coming back."

This time she had his full attention. "She's what?" he roared. "What in hell are you talking about, Colleen?"

Colleen plunged ahead before she lost her nerve. "Brett left this afternoon for New York, Erik. She's not going to marry you. She's signing a contract with the Monique St. Amour cosmetic company for a long-term modeling assignment."

The color had drained from Erik's face, but his expression was one of impatience. "Colleen," he barked, "if this is some kind of joke you and the rest of the wedding party have come up with, it's not funny!"

"Joke! Erik, do you honestly think I'd do this to you as a joke? Brett's gone, and I agree, there's nothing funny about it."

Colleen told him of Brett's phone call that morning and repeated everything that her cousin had said and done up to the time she slammed out of Colleen's apartment. Erik just stood there leaning against the door and looking stunned. "I have the ring and the car keys here in my purse," she concluded, and picked up her bag. "The Thunderbird is in the parking lot, and the certificate of ownership is in the glove compartment."

She extracted the items from her purse and held them out to him, but he merely stared at her without responding. "I don't believe you," he said roughly. "Brett wouldn't do such a thing. She loves me. She's looking forward to the wedding as much as I am."

Colleen dropped the ring and keys back in her bag and laid it on the desk next to her. Erik looked as if he'd been poleaxed and didn't quite know how it had happened. When the full force of what she'd told him finally hit, the agony would be nearly unbearable, and she knew she'd have sold her soul in exchange for a way to spare him. In wounding him she'd done violence to herself as well.

She walked toward him and put her hand on his arm. "Of course she loves you," Colleen said, and hoped he'd believe it. At least until he could face the real truth. "That's why she couldn't tell you about this herself, but you know Brett, she's a dedicated career woman. She couldn't turn down this marvelous chance to further her career, and she knew you'd never be happy with a wife who was traveling all over the world.''

"I wouldn't have interfered with her career. I admit I'd have argued against her taking this assignment, but she must have known that I'd agree to anything rather than let her walk out on me." His gaze, which had been slightly unfocused with shock, now zeroed in on her. "Did you say anything to her to make her believe otherwise?"

"Me?" Colleen gasped.

Erik's eyes and voice had turned chilling. "Yes, you. Why didn't you stop her? Why did you let her go?"

"Let her go?" Colleen was stunned by his sudden attack. "Did you ever try to stop Brett when she was determined to do something? I tried every way I could think of to talk some sense into her, but she didn't pay any attention. I was lucky to get the ring and the car keys from her."

"I don't give a damn about the ring and the car," he snarled. "You say you talked to her at noon? Why in hell did you wait so long to tell me? Why didn't you get in touch with me immediately so I could have stopped her?"

Colleen cringed at the fury in his voice. She knew it was unrealistic to be hurt by his accusations. She was the bearer of bad news and had gotten caught in the backlash, but even so it was painful. "I tried," she said, hoping she could make him understand. "I called your office, but Trish said you were out and wouldn't be back. I contacted every Ford plant in the area, but I couldn't catch up with you."

He shook his head, like a fighter who has taken a hard blow. "You're right," he admitted a little less angrily, "I was running around all afternoon, but why didn't you call me at home before you came over here?"

"Oh Erik, I tried, believe me I did. I started calling your apartment at five o'clock. I left countless messages on your answering machine. I did phone just before leaving for the church, but you still didn't answer."

He drew a shuddering breath. "I was probably in the shower. I got home just in time to clean up and come here. I didn't even listen to my phone messages."

He seemed to diminish in size as the rage drained out of him. Colleen ached to go to him, take him in her arms and absorb some of his anguish, but she knew he wouldn't welcome that type of contact from her right now. Instead she said, "Why don't you sit down? This has been a dreadful shock to you. Would you like me to ask Father John to come in?" Maybe the counselor could get through to him where she couldn't.

He moved away from the door, but instead of sitting down he walked to the window and looked out into the night. He was silent for so long that she began to wonder if he'd forgotten she was there, but then he spoke. "I'd like to be alone for a while, Colleen. Please go and make some excuse to the others for the delay."

She hated to leave him but knew she had no choice. There was nothing she could do for him now except run errands. "All right," she said. "Do you want me to explain and send them home?"

He still stood with his back to her. "No. I'll do that in a little while."

She left and pushed the door shut behind her, then leaned against it and closed her eyes. Her knees were shaking, and she felt both physically and emotionally depleted.

Erik saw nothing as he stared sightlessly out the window. His gaze was focused inward, but there was nothing there, either. It was as if there were nobody home in that big rugged body of his. He started to flex his fingers and discovered that his fists were clenched so tightly that his fingernails had left marks on his palms. His whole stance was rigid, and he made a conscious effort to relax.

Why wasn't he feeling something? He'd just been told that the woman he loved with an almost compulsive intensity had walked out on him in favor of a career, and he didn't feel a thing other than cold. He was shivering with the cold. Surely the church could afford to heat the priest's study to a comfortable temperature. When he and Brett got back from their honeymoon he'd make a donation with the provision that it be used to heat the damn office.

But Colleen had said he wasn't going on a honeymoon. She'd said that Brett had already started the honeymoon by herself.

He shook his head roughly, as if the motion would unscramble his thoughts. What was the matter with him anyway? He couldn't feel, and his musing didn't make sense. He suspected that it was an involuntary, protective mechanism that wouldn't last long, and he'd better be prepared for a sojourn in hell when it faded away.

He rubbed his hands over his face. He had one chore to do before this whole thing came tumbling in on him, and that was to face all those relatives and members of the wedding party in the other room, and tell them there would be no wedding, and no rehearsal dinner, and no honeymoon. Oh hell. If he couldn't think straight, how was he going to make a polite little speech and announce that his life had just fallen apart?

He slapped at his arms with his big hands, trying to stimulate the circulation and calm down his shivering. His teeth would chatter when he tried to talk if he couldn't get a little warmth. Funny, he remembered that the room had been warm when he'd entered it. Well, he wouldn't be cold much longer. He'd tell some idiotic lie about the marriage being called off by mutual consent, and then he'd go somewhere and get blind, staggering drunk.

Colleen had just finished telling Father John of her confrontations with both Brett and Erik when the office door opened and Erik appeared. He still looked punchy, as if he had been hit once too many times, and Colleen started to go to him but was held back by the priest's hand on her arm.

It was Father John who spoke. "Is there anything we can do for you, Erik?"

Erik's gaze slowly focused. "No. I have to call off the wedding. Excuse me."

"Erik, wouldn't you like for me to—" Colleen started to say, but he walked right past her.

"Leave him alone, my dear," the priest said. "He needs to do these things himself. When he wants our help he'll ask for it."

She wasn't so sure, but she walked along with him to the sanctuary. She had to find Devin. Surely he would be here by now; it was past time for the rehearsal to start. Someone had to stay with Erik tonight. No one should have to face this kind of anguish alone.

In the sanctuary her gaze swept over the assembly. April was there, but she didn't see Devin anywhere. April spotted her and they walked toward each other. "Where's Devin?" Colleen asked her sister-in-law.

"He's not here." April's tone was sharp with frustration. "He called just before I left the house to say he'd been held up and to tell Erik to go ahead with the rehearsal and he'd practice his part tomorrow before the wedding."

"But Erik needs him," Colleen wailed.

"I know." April ran her hand through her strawberry-blond hair. "I told him what had happened, and he said he'd get here just as soon as he could. Meanwhile we'd better alert somebody else. How about his dad, or maybe one of his brothers-in-law?"

Before Colleen could answer Erik spoke into the public-address system. "May I have your attention please?"

The noisy group quieted and he continued. "I'm deeply sorry to have to tell you that Brett and I have come to the admittedly belated decision that although we love each other, neither of us is prepared to make the total commitment that is required in a marriage."

A gasp rose from the assembly, and Erik paused. Colleen and April were standing a little apart at the back, and Colleen watched him closely. He was pale, but seemed remarkably composed and articulate. She knew it was an act, the result of years of training and practice in the emotional deception of top-level businessmen. *Never let your opponent know what you're thinking.* Erik's pride wouldn't allow him to admit that he was shattered by Brett's desertion. He'd hold his emotions in check until he exploded, and she wasn't going to let him be alone when that happened.

He held up his hand and spoke into the microphone again. "I apologize for the inconvenience that postponing the wedding will cause all of you, but we felt it was better to give ourselves more time and not rush into something that might prove later to be a mistake.''

Colleen studied the faces of the listeners. Their expressions ranged from uncomprehending to stunned. Erik's mother and sisters were crying, and his father just stood there with his mouth open as if he'd been cut off in midsentence. Thank God her mother must have gotten to Brett's parents and kept them away. Aunt Glenna was probably having hysterics, but at least she was having them in the privacy of her house.

Erik was still speaking. ''I'm going to impose on you with one more request. Will all of you please get together and make arrangements to notify the invited guests that the wedding has been canceled. I realize this is a big job, but I'm—I'm just not up to it.''

His voice broke, and Colleen knew his composure wasn't going to hold out much longer. Apparently he knew it too, because he didn't attempt to say anything else but strode quickly down the aisle and out of the church, leaving the shocked wedding party behind watching him.

Without stopping to weigh the consequences, Colleen slid out of the pew and ran after him.

Chapter Three

Colleen reached Erik's prototype Ford Mustang just as he turned the key and brought the powerful engine to life. Without hesitation she opened the door and jumped inside with barely enough time to slam it shut before the auto shot backward out of its parking space in the church lot. It stopped so suddenly that she was thrown off balance and plunged sideways into Erik's solid bulk.

His arm wrapped around her in a protective gesture, but his tone was anything but welcoming. "Go back in the church, Colleen. I don't want company right now."

She didn't move. "I'm not going to leave you alone," she said, and realized he was shivering.

He took his arm from around her and sat her upright. "Yes, you are," he said impatiently. "That's the way I want it. I don't need you."

Colleen winced at the unintentional cruelty of his words. "I know you don't." Her voice was unsteady. "But you need someone, and I seem to be the only one available."

"Colleen, dammit, get out of the car so I can leave before somebody comes looking for us."

She fastened her seat belt. "You might as well get going because I'm staying."

Erik muttered an oath and started the motor. "All right, be stubborn, but don't say I didn't warn you."

They roared out of the parking lot and around several corners before the heavy traffic slowed them down. Erik headed in the direction of downtown Detroit, and neither spoke until about fifteen minutes later when he pulled into the small parking lot beside a rundown frame building with a garish neon sign proclaiming it Willy's Tavern.

Colleen shuddered and huddled further into her coat. It was going to be a long night. However, instead of getting out of the car, Erik turned to her and said, "The keys are in the ignition. Take the car and go home. I'll call a cab when I get ready to leave."

Without giving her a chance to respond, he opened the door and stepped out, slamming it behind him. Momentarily startled, it took Colleen a few seconds to react, then she grabbed the keys, got out of the car and ran to catch up with Erik just before he reached the building.

"Colleen—" he said threateningly.

She didn't wait for him to finish. "Forget it. I'm not going to leave. I won't bother you. I won't even talk if you don't want to, but I'm not going to leave you alone. In a couple of hours when Devin has had time to get home I'll call him and tell him where we are and he can take over, but till then you're stuck with me. Now, can we go inside? I'm freezing.''

Erik uttered an impatient growl, then turned and stalked into the bar, leaving her to follow behind.

The inside lived up to the promise of the outside, shoddy, dismal and packed with blue-jeaned and booted men and women intent on cutting loose after a week of hard work. Erik hesitated for a moment inside the door, then took Colleen's arm and led her toward a table in the corner that was being vacated by a bearded man and a woman with orange hair.

Colleen could feel the appreciative gaze of some of the men as she walked along beside Erik, and she was careful to look straight head and ignore them. In the mood Erik was in, if any of them tried to talk to her or made a suggestive remark, he'd start a fight that would take the riot squad to stop. If he had to drink, why couldn't he have picked a higher-class bar?

When the miniskirted barmaid came, Erik ordered a Jack Daniel's neat and Colleen asked for a plain cola. She could have used a stiff drink, but figured she'd better keep her reflexes sharp. While they waited in silence she looked around the room. It was medium-size with a long bar at the back where noisy Western-clad people congregated three deep and shouted to make themselves heard over the country and western band that seemed bent on breaking eardrums all up and down the block. The wooden tables scattered around the front of the room were scarred and worn, and the chairs were hard and rickety. Smoke as thick as fog, combined with the dim lighting, made it impossible to distinguish features from more than a few feet away.

When the waitress brought their drinks Erik downed his in two gulps and asked for another. Colleen pursed her lips and said nothing. By the time they'd been there for an hour he was nursing his fourth whiskey. Colleen was uncomfortably aware of a need to visit the rest room, but she was afraid he might decide to take off without her if she left him for a few minutes. Finally she said, "Erik, if I go to the powder room will you promise not to run off?"

He looked at her and frowned. "Do you really think I'd leave you alone in this jungle? In fact, I'll escort you. I've seen the way these drunken cowboys have been leering at you."

He stood and reached for her hand to help her up. "But—" she started.

"Come on. You may not be in a hurry, but now that you've brought it to my attention I am."

She grinned and stood. "That's what you get for drinking all that whiskey."

"Yes, Mama," he muttered and swatted her playfully on the derriere. "Now move it."

To Colleen's disgust the rest room was even more crude than the rest of the establishment, and there was no telephone. She'd wanted to call and see if Devin was home yet, but there didn't seem to be a public phone available. It was probably just as well. She wouldn't have been able to hear or be heard above the noise.

Erik was waiting for her outside the rest room doors. "Feel better?" she greeted impishly.

"Sure do," he said as he put his arm around her to guide her through the crowd. "Now we can go back to the table and get started on some serious drinking."

She didn't reply until they were again seated and Erik had polished off what was left of his drink. By then the band was taking a break and they could talk a few decibels below shouting level. "Erik," she said as he

raised his hand to signal the waitress, "if you want to
drink, fine, but not here. Let's go home. Then I'll call
and let April know where we are so she can send Devin
over when he gets back from Lansing."

"I don't need a keeper, Colleen," he muttered. "How
many times do I have to tell you that? Take the car and
leave if you're not enjoying my choice of watering
holes."

She shook her head. "I know you don't need a
keeper," she said, "but you do need someone to care."

Erik's gaze softened as it roamed over her upturned
face, and he put out his big hand and cupped her chin.
"And do you care, little one?"

She'd always hated it when she'd been an adolescent
and he'd called her "little one," but now it was a caress rather than a taunt and the tip of her tongue ran
across her lips in an unconsciously seductive gesture.
"Yes, I care," she said as she looked into the green eyes
that had changed from icy to warm. "I've always
cared."

She swayed toward him as his face lowered to meet
her parted lips. It was a gentle, affectionate kiss, the
kind Erik always gave her. The sort of a kiss a man
would give his best friend's little sister, loving but de-
void of passion. She wondered what he'd do if she
opened her mouth and invited his penetration.

Before she could be tempted to find out he raised his
head and murmured, "Okay, honey, you've made your
point. This is no place for you. We'll go home and
drink."

He helped her into her coat, and the blast of frigid
wind that greeted them when they opened the door
smelled fresh and clean. Colleen breathed deeply to fill
her lungs and drive out the rancid air of the saloon.

They were halfway across the parking lot on their way to the car when Erik stopped. "Damn, I can't find my keys. I must have dropped them back in the bar. We'll have to go look for them."

Colleen reached in her pocket and brought out the leather key case. "I have them. Here they are."

She held them up, but when he reached for them she closed her fist. "No, Erik, let me drive. I haven't been drinking."

His expression darkened. "Don't be silly, I'm in perfect control of my reflexes. It takes more than a few belts of whiskey to make me drunk."

She had to admit that the drinks didn't seem to have affected him at all, but she didn't intend to take any chances.

"You're probably right," she said, being careful not to challenge his macho image, "but your blood alcohol level is bound to be high. If you were stopped by the police they'd arrest you for drunk driving no matter how careful you were."

He opened his mouth as if to argue, but then closed it again and shrugged. "All right, you win, I'll let you chauffeur. Let's go to your apartment."

She was ready for that suggestion. "No way," she said as they climbed into the car. "Once we got there you'd just shove me out and drive away. We're going to your apartment. It'll be harder for you to get rid of me there."

He sighed. "You're an obnoxious little brat. You know that?"

"Sure, but you love me all the same," she teased.

To her surprise he reached for her hand and brought it to his lips. "Ah, that I do, honey," he said and kissed her palm. "That I do." He kissed it again, then held it against his cheek.

Her heart jumped, and her love for him overwhelmed her caution. She turned and put her arms around his neck, and with a gasp he drew her to him and held her close as he buried his face in the fragrant hollow of her neck.

She didn't say anything, afraid of breaking the spell, and he seemed to draw comfort from just holding her and letting her hold him. He'd forgotten his overcoat back at the church so her hands weren't impeded by bulk as they stroked his back and shoulders through his lighter-weight suit jacket. Somehow her quilted coat had come open or been unbuttoned and one of his hands rested on her buttocks while the other one caressed the bare flesh under her sweater.

She rubbed her cheek in his shaggy blond hair, and kissed him on the temple. He squirmed and spoke almost reluctantly. "Don't you know you can get into serious trouble comforting a grown man the way you're doing?"

"Can I?" she murmured and kissed his temple once more.

That seemed to be a sensitive spot because he squirmed again. "You better believe it," he answered and nibbled at her throat.

Now it was her turn to squirm. "What sort of trouble?"

"I can take advantage of you, sweetheart, quickly and thoroughly, and if you don't know what that means I'll spell it out for you." His tone was gruff, but his hand moved up to cup her bra-covered breast.

"I know what it means," she said, and wondered if he could feel her heart pounding, "but you wouldn't do that to me."

"Like hell I wouldn't." His fingers moved under the lacy part of her bra. "I've got all the usual male urges, and tonight I suspect I'll do almost anything to deaden the pain."

She gasped as the tip of his finger circled her suddenly rigid nipple, and her hands dug into his shoulders.

With a swift movement he placed her in a reclining position across his lap and his mouth covered hers, hot and moist and hungry. She was taken by surprise, and for a moment she stiffened. His arms tightened around her, holding her hard against him as his tongue caressed her lips, parting them to allow his tender invasion. If Colleen had been disappointed in his kisses before, this one more than made up for it. Although it was cold in the car, waves of heat coursed through her body, melting it into pliable, boneless flesh that clung to him with unresisting ardor.

Her mouth opened wider to his plundering kiss, and he unfastened her bra and took possession of one full breast while his other hand explored her firm round bottom. Even more exciting was the hard pressure of his urgent desire against her hip. He wanted her, even needed her. In an automatic reflex she wiggled against him and he moaned and clasped her even tighter.

It was a flash of headlights and the raucous honking of a horn that finally brought them to their senses, and they pulled apart as the car that had caught them in its lights sped past and onto the street. Colleen was too disoriented to do more than straighten up as Erik pushed her away. "That does it," he said gruffly, his voice unsteady, "you're going home, right now and no arguing. I'm not yet reduced to seducing the teenage sisters of my friends."

That brought Colleen back to earth with a thud, and a flash of temper. "I'm not a teenager as you well know, Erik Johansen. I'm twenty-four years old, a college graduate and a businesswoman, and I'll make out with whoever I please."

She jammed the key in the ignition and started the motor. "Why I waste my time with you I'll never know," she continued as she backed the car out and headed it toward the exit. "You don't want me. You never have and you never will. To you I'm just Devin's baby sister. Well, open your eyes and look at me some time. I'm not as innocent as you seem to think."

"I have looked at you, and you know what happened," Erik said. "After my performance just now I don't know how you can say I don't want you. As for your innocence, or lack of it, if I ever catch any other guy coming on to you the way I just did I'll break his skull."

"And just what gives you the right to interfere in my love life?" She was almost screeching with rage. "You're not my brother."

"Thank God for small favors," Erik muttered. "Hey, where are you going? You're headed in the wrong direction. I said you were going home."

"And I said, we were going to your apartment, and in case you hadn't noticed I'm the one who's driving the car. You can drink yourself into a stupor, and I'll refill your glass and put you to bed when you pass out."

"That's what I'm afraid of. You'll damn well stay away from me and out of my bedroom or I won't be responsible for what happens. Now do us both a favor and go home.''

Colleen didn't bother to answer but continued in the direction of Dearborn and Erik's apartment. He gave a disgusted grunt and leaned back against the seat with his eyes closed. What was the matter with him? Why was he being so wishy-washy about this? She was just a little thing. He could handle her with one hand tied behind him. All he had to do was get control of the car, take her to her apartment and leave her there. It was simple, so why didn't he do it?

He rubbed his hand over his face and tried not to admit that he wanted her with him. That he couldn't face being alone tonight. Worse, that it wasn't his friend Devin he wanted to keep him company. But soft, warm and cuddly little Colleen—she could keep his mind off Brett for a few hours, and maybe by then he'd be better able to deal with the shock and disappointment of his canceled wedding. Would it be so wrong? After all, he'd tried to send her away and she'd refused to go. As she'd so angrily reminded him, she was a grown woman who had been going out with men for years. Why did he find it necessary to protect her from himself? It wasn't as if he intended to seduce her. All he wanted was her company to help him get through the night.

Like hell it is, you bastard. The voice within him was so strong that he actually jumped as it continued without letup. *You're still throbbing from the ache she aroused in you with her caressing little hands, her soft lips against your skin and her incredibly sexy body snuggled in your arms. If she goes home with you you'll keep after her.*

Erik sat up with a jerk, and the sudden movement had the desired effect of silencing his nagging conscience. He wasn't an adolescent, for God's sake. He had a lot of hard-won control over his basic drives, and the last person he was going to lose that control with was Devin's naive little sister. Just because she had breasts that made his palms itch didn't mean he was going to cradle them in his hands again.

From time to time Colleen glanced at Erik, seemingly asleep in the seat beside her, but she knew he wasn't. There was a restlessness about him that belied his relaxed pose. Was he as disturbed as she by the sudden intrusion into their lovemaking?

Lovemaking! That was a laugh. It might have been love on her part, but for him it had simply been the sudden flare-up of an urgent, basic male need that any willing woman could arouse. She'd made a fool of herself by responding so heatedly. She should have pushed him away gently but firmly and informed him that she wouldn't allow such liberties.

Ha! Who was she trying to kid? She'd allow him any liberties he wanted to take, and they both knew it. Where was her shame? Her pride? Why didn't she take his well-meant advice and go home? Erik had been getting along just fine without her help for thirty-four years, so why was she convinced that he couldn't survive this night without her? Wasn't she just hoping to take advantage of his anguish to make herself indispensable to him?

Maybe. Probably. But was the tug she felt flowing between them really only wishful thinking? It seemed to her that he was sending mixed signals. Vocally telling her to get lost, subconsciously asking her to stay. Whichever, he'd built a fire in her that he hadn't tended and it was damned frustrating.

Erik followed Colleen into the glass-and-steel apartment building, then held the elevator door open while
she entered. The elevator rose noiselessly to the four-
teenth floor, then stopped to let them out. He took her
arm and escorted her down the carpeted hall and
around a corner to the door of his apartment. He unlocked it and reached inside to flick the light switch,
then stepped back to allow her to proceed him.

She did, but he seemed to hesitate as though reluctant to enter. Colleen wondered if it was because he'd
expected to bring Brett back with him this evening.
Maybe he'd even planned on her spending the night.
Although Brett maintained her own quarters it was no
secret that they had been sleeping together, so it seemed
likely that she would have come home with him on the
night of the rehearsal.

Colleen walked through the entryway and into the
black and white living room as Erik closed the door behind them. The stark absence-of-color scheme had been
Brett's idea, and she'd done the decorating. Colleen had
to admit that the room was bold and stunning, but it
suited Brett's personality, not Erik's. The white carpet,
black upholstery and glass-and-chrome tables seemed
cold and unwelcoming, and the large painting of a black
and white Pierrot against a checkerboard background
on the wall directly across from her seemed to swim in
and out of focus and make Colleen dizzy.

Before Brett had "modernized" it, Erik's living room
had been a homey comfortable chamber furnished with
well-used oversize leather chairs and a sofa, and heavy
serviceable tables and a desk. The picture on the wall
then had been a large framed photograph of the Michigan State Spartans taken during the last year Erik had
played quarterback with them.

He took her coat and muttered something about fixing coffee, then headed for the kitchen. She heard the sound of water being run, and moments later the loud clatter of something being dropped. Erik swore lustily as Colleen ran to see what had happened.

She found him looking at an overturned can and a countertop and sink littered with dry coffee. "What happened?" she asked.

"I should think that would be obvious," he growled angrily. "The can slipped out of my hand and spilled its contents." He scooped up some of the grounds in his fist and dumped them into the filter-lined basket.

His anger was all out of proportion to its cause, and Colleen moved cautiously to help. "That shiny metal is slippery and hard to hold. Why don't you let me take care of this? I won't be but a minute."

"Be my guest," he muttered and stalked out of the room.

When she returned to the living room about ten minutes later with the coffee carafe and two mugs on a tray, she found him sitting on the sofa with a drink in his hand. He'd changed out of his dark blue suit and into faded jeans and a maroon velour pullover shirt, and sat hunched forward staring off into space. He looked so shattered. As if his whole life had fallen apart, which it had.

She set the tray on the glass coffee table and reached out tentatively to stroke an unruly lock of hair off his forehead. He jerked back, startled, obviously unaware that she'd come into the room, and the sudden movement caused his whiskey to spill at his feet.

Colleen gasped and stared at the puddle. "Oh Erik, I'm sorry," she moaned, and dropped to her knees to begin scrubbing at it with a napkin. "Your beautiful white carpet. I don't know if the stain will ever come out."

He reached out and grabbed her arm. "Leave it, Colleen."

"But it'll be ruined." She tried to pull her arm loose but his grip tightened.

"I said leave it," he grated. "I always hated this carpet. In fact I'll make sure it's ruined."

He stood, lifted the glass coffeepot off the tray and began walking around the room pouring the hot black liquid in a steady stream on the rug as he went.

Colleen watched in horror as he drained the carafe. "There," he said with satisfaction, "that's more my style. After all, what do I know about taste? I'm just a big, dumb ex-football jock with a degree in intercollegiate sports."

He stood looking around the room until his gaze settled on the portrait of the Pierrot. "Come to think of it I never liked that crazy picture, either." For a moment he hefted the empty coffeepot, then drew back his arm and threw it with all his strength at the painting, splintering the carafe and gouging the picture.

"Erik!" she screamed, but she could see that he didn't even hear her. There was a fanatical gleam in his eyes as he surveyed the damage.

"Now, let's see what we can do about those fragile good-for-nothing tables." He laughed, and there was a chilling note of hysteria in the sound. "Never could understand why Brett insisted I spend money on those things. I can't even put my feet up on the coffee table."

Before Colleen had an inkling of what he intended, he'd grabbed a poker from its stand beside the fireplace and slammed it across the middle of the oblong glass table, totally destroying it. He didn't stop there but swung the poker again and again, shattering tables, lamps, mirrors and anything else that caught his eye including the black designer telephone.

Colleen ran to the far side of the room and cringed against the wall. She wasn't afraid for herself; she knew Erik wouldn't hurt her but the flying glass could. Horrified she watched the rampage that seemed to go on, and on, and on, until finally he simply wore himself out and stood, slumped and panting, in the middle of the room surveying the carnage with sightless eyes.

She huddled where she was a few minutes longer waiting to see what he'd do next. Finally he seemed to snap out of his trance and really see what he was looking at. The poker dropped from his fingers. "Oh my God!" he said wearily and put both hands to his face, covering his eyes.

Colleen went to him then, and he put his arms around her and clasped her so tightly that she could hardly breathe. He was trembling violently and she made no effort to get him to move to a more comfortable place, but just held him and let him hold her.

After a while his hands began making light caressing movements across her back, then gradually moved to her sides where his fingers could stroke the fullness of her breasts. He lowered his head and nipped at the sensitive cord of her neck as he murmured her name. "Colleen, Colleen, my sweet little Colleen."

She shivered as he moved his lips to the cord on the other side of her throat and let one of his hands roam downward to her hip while the other one continued to stroke her tightened breast. Her own hands found their way under his heavy shirt, and she was startled at the hardness of the muscles that ran up the sides of his back and across his shoulders. His skin was warm and damp from the exertion he had just expended, and his breathing was raspy and uneven.

He shifted and braced his legs farther apart, then cupped her well-rounded bottom and lifted her until she fit against him where he wanted her, needed her. "Colleen," he groaned, "why didn't you leave while I could still let you go?"

The question didn't require an answer and she gave none. The fire he'd ignited in her earlier now flamed into a roaring inferno that only he could quench, and she fitted her hands to either side of his face and covered his mouth with her own. She knew what she was inviting and she knew it was wrong. She shouldn't let him use her as a substitute for the woman he really wanted, but she couldn't help herself. She was in an impossible situation. She shouldn't stay and she couldn't leave. She'd loved Erik too long to abandon him when he needed her, and her own need was too insistent to deny.

He responded to her kiss with a frenzy that was contagious, and she opened her mouth to the erotic plunder of his impatient tongue. With a swift movement he swept her into his arms and carried her down the short hall to the spacious bedroom. He put her down beside the king-size bed and pulled off his shirt, then did the same with her sweater.

His hands shook as he unhooked her bra and slipped it off her arms. He gazed hungrily at her ample breasts, then gave in to that hunger and supported each one with his two hands while he bent to fondle first one nipple and then the other with his moist tongue. Colleen's fingers dug into his bare shoulders as her head tipped back and a shuddering moan escaped from deep inside her.

With impatient haste he slid down her zipper and removed her slacks, panties, panty hose and loafers. While she pulled back the bedding he stepped out of his own clothes, then took her in his arms and kissed her again. Without taking his mouth from hers he lowered them to the bed, his body partially covering hers.

His kiss became painful in its intensity, and his hands moved with rough impatience over her slender curves, alerting her to the fact that his tenuous control was about to snap. Much as she wanted him she couldn't allow him to take her only for his own pleasure, even if it was unintentional.

She wriggled beneath him trying to put some distance between them, but it only seemed to inflame him further. His powerful fingers dug into the fleshy part of her hip and she cried out, "Erik, no, you're hurting me."

She could feel the effort it took for him to rein in his runaway passion, but, with difficulty, he managed to lessen his grip and lie quietly against her. He took several deep breaths, then pulled himself up on one elbow and looked down at her with green eyes still glazed with need. "Colleen, sweetheart, I'm sorry," he said, his voice husky and unsteady. "I don't mean to be rough, especially not with you. Do you—do you want to stop?"

He had one leg across her thighs, and she could feel the turgid pressure of his throbbing desire pressing insistently against her. She knew it would be almost unbearable for him to stop at this point, and it wouldn't do her own frustration any good either.

She ran the tip of her tongue over her swollen lips. "No, I want you to continue, but a little more slowly. Give me a chance to catch up."

He managed to relax ever so slightly and kissed her upturned nose. "I'll try," he said and nipped at her lower lip, "but it's not easy to go slow with you. You turn to fire in my arms, and consume what little control I started out with."

She caught his mouth with her own. "I know. It won't take long, I promise."

She kept her promise. It would have been impossible not to, once he started gentling her with his hands, and his mouth and his soft words of endearment. When he gave in to his desire, she knew she couldn't have waited another second, either. It was a moment of violent tenderness that tore asunder the girl she had been and brought forth the woman she was meant to be.

Chapter Four

They slept, Colleen with her back against Erik's chest and her buttocks cradled in the curve of his hips. His arm across her waist held her to him, and a smile of pure contentment tugged at the corners of her mouth.

It was still dark when she became aware that his hand had moved up and was fondling her breast. She lay quietly, afraid to move for fear he would waken and stop. She'd never felt so warm and secure and desirable as she did now, cuddled in his sleeping embrace. How she'd love to wake up like this every morning with Erik holding her, stroking her, wanting her.

After a few minutes his hand moved back to her waist, then inched down until his palm was lying flat against her bare stomach. An indefinable itch started deep inside her, and the muscles beneath his hand twitched. His long fingers began a slow exploration farther downward, and he lowered his head and trailed light kisses along the satin skin of her shoulder. When his roaming fingers tangled in her hidden triangle of ebony hair she caught her breath and drew up her knees. His knees followed hers as he curled around her and continued to probe her pulsating femininity.

Erik knew he should stop before this went any further. He'd already betrayed both Colleen and her brother, his best friend who trusted him. He felt sick with remorse. She was like a narcotic that deadened the pain, but carried the fiery response of an addiction that could destroy his self-esteem.

He wanted her again. He should have known this would happen, and he either should have sent her away or left, himself, after the violent urgency of their lovemaking. But she'd quickly fallen asleep in his arms like a child, trusting and content. He'd told himself he didn't want to wake her and send her out in the cold, but the truth was that he didn't want to be alone. He'd wanted her with him, and he'd drifted off to sleep as easily as she had.

Now his desire was driving him crazy again. It had started while he was still groggy from sleep, and by the time he was awake enough to control himself it was too late. He thrust against her in an effort to appease the insistent ache, and knew that unless she pushed him away he was going to take her once more.

She sucked in her breath sharply and the muscles in her thighs tightened around his exploring hand. "Erik," she gasped. "I want—oh please—"

He removed his hand from her warm moistness and placed it on her hip. Lord knows he was as ready as she and it was agony not to give in to their mutual longing, but he didn't want it to end yet. He wanted to keep her in his arms, in his bed, and make slow, tender, passionate love to her all morning.

He might have managed it if she hadn't rolled over and put her arms around him, pressing her soft nude body full length against his hard, fully aroused one. He gritted his teeth. How in hell could he make it last when they were both being incinerated by the heat from their all-consuming desire?

He couldn't. With a groan he fitted himself within the cradle of her womanhood, and a few seconds later the whole world exploded.

The sun was well up in the sky, bouncing beams off the bright snow and back into the bedroom by the time Colleen woke again. She stretched lazily and rolled over only to find that she was alone in the oversize bed. Where was Erik? Why hadn't she heard him get up?

She looked at her watch. Good heavens, it was almost eleven o'clock! She should have been at work two hours before. Why hadn't Erik called her before he left?

She was startled to hear footsteps in the hall. Did he have a cleaning woman who came on Fridays? She sat up and pulled the sheet around her as the door opened and Erik poked his head in. "It's about time you woke up, sleepyhead," he said as he strolled in, carrying a mug of coffee in each hand.

He was fully dressed in the jeans and shirt he had removed so hastily the night before. Not an outfit he'd wear to the office. He walked to the bed and handed her a cup. "It's instant," he said, referring to the coffee. "I hope you don't mind. My coffeepot seems to have gotten broken last night." His manner was friendly but cool. Maybe "uneasy" was a better description.

"I know." She shuddered as she remembered his destructive tantrum. "Why aren't you at work, and why didn't you call me earlier?"

He walked away from the bed and sat down on a low chest. Apparently Brett hadn't gotten as far as the bedroom with her redecorating, because it was strictly masculine. "I'm not going to the office. My vacation starts Monday so I decided to leave today."

"Leave?" Colleen's hand jerked and her coffee sloshed dangerously close to the top of the mug. "You're going away?"

She set her cup on the bedside table and flexed her knees so that she could clasp her trembling hands around them. If she had thought their night of lovemaking had made him forget Brett in favor of herself, then she'd been a fool. There was pain in his eyes and in the pinched expression on his face. Even though he sat still there was a restlessness about him that told her more than she wanted to know. She'd been a diversion to soften the blow, but that was all.

"Yes," he said, "but not to the Caribbean as planned. I didn't waken you earlier because you were sleeping soundly, and I figured you needed the rest."

A hot flush of embarrassment engulfed her, and she buried her face in her raised knees.

"You can blush at a remark as mild as that." Erik's tone was pained. "Colleen, why didn't you tell me you were—" he seemed to grope for the right word "—innocent."

She didn't lift her head as she spoke. "I think 'inexperienced' describes it better. After all, I'm twenty-four years old. I may not have gone all the way, but neither am I totally innocent."

"Don't quibble over semantics," he said impatiently. "You were a virgin until last night, and still you let me..."

He stood and walked over to the window, then turned to face her. "Honey, I'm sorry. I feel like a first-class heel. You only wanted to comfort me, and I took advantage of your compassionate nature."

Colleen's head shot up. Her embarrassment had been replaced by impatience. "Oh, knock it off, Erik," she fumed, "and stop trying to make a rape out of a mutually enjoyable seduction. So what if it was my first time? It had to happen eventually, and there's nobody I'd rather have had steal my maidenhead."

"Maidenhead?" His eyebrows raised in question.

"Shakespeare. *Romeo and Juliet*. Read it, you'll find it's a perfectly good word, maybe a little archaic."

He laughed, but sobered quickly. "Are you all right? Did I—injure—you in any way?"

His concern brought a lump to her throat. "I'm fine. That maidenhead was getting to be a bother. I'd become an oddity. How many twenty-four-year-old women do you know who are still intact?"

"None, now," he muttered, "but if it makes a difference, you're the only one I ever deflowered."

The corners of her mouth lifted in a tiny smile. "It matters," she said. "I'd have told you if you'd asked, but I didn't think to volunteer the information."

"Asked," he rasped. "I couldn't get at you quick enough as it was. I was in no condition to make polite conversation. Even if you'd told me, I couldn't have stopped. I'm not proud of my actions."

His words made her feel better. He'd wanted her, wanted her badly, and not once had he murmured Brett's name during the night. He'd never lost sight of the fact that she was Colleen, not Brett, and it was Colleen he'd lost all shred of control with. She might have been a substitute, but she wasn't a proxy.

Unfortunately, neither was she second choice, or third. She wasn't even in the running. It would be a long time before Erik would ever again trust a woman enough for anything more than a casual relationship, but when he did it would be another sophisticated, glamour type. Colleen knew that to him she'd always be Devin's sweet little kid sister, and his memories of having taken her to bed would be a guilty torment instead of an erotic pleasure.

The February wind blowing in from the Detroit River was cold. It whistled down the busy streets, swirling loose snow against cars, buildings and thickly padded pedestrians unfortunate enough to be outside. Colleen lowered her chin under her woolen scarf and dug her gloved hands into the pockets of her quilted coat as she hurried down the icy sidewalk. There were times when a car would be worth the expense and frustration of driving in the city, and this was one of them. Her face, the only exposed part of her, was so cold it burned.

Three blocks from the bus stop she entered a sprawling two-story building that covered half a block in its suburban setting. She leaned back against the wall for a moment to catch her breath, then took the elevator to the second floor and the area marked Ob/Gyn on the directory.

An hour later the tall, dark-haired obstetrician who had delivered both of April and Devin's babies stepped into the office where Colleen had been fidgeting nervously for what seemed like hours. He looked down at her upturned, questioning face. His tone was gentle when he spoke. "We have the results of the test and it's positive. You are pregnant, Colleen."

She let her breath out in a rush. Pregnant! Oh dear God, there must be some mistake. The odds against a woman getting pregnant the first time she made love must be astronomical. "Are you sure?" She cleared her throat. "I mean, couldn't it just be a hormonal disturbance or something?"

The doctor chuckled, and walked across the room to sit beside her on the leather couch. "It's a hormonal disturbance all right, and it's going to last eight more months."

He sobered and patted the hands that were twisted together in her lap. "Don't look so stricken. There's a legal alternative, you know. We can—"

"No. No, Doctor, there's no alternative for me. Will you deliver the baby?" She'd never before had need to consult an obstetrician.

"I'll be happy to. Your brother Devin and his wife April are good friends of mine as well as business associate and patient."

Devin had worked in the business department of the medical clinic for the past ten years, first as a trainee then manager.

"You won't tell Devin? Please, Doctor, I—"

"Of course I won't tell Devin or anybody else. Now, since I've never seen you as a patient before, I want to examine you. You look strong and healthy but we have to be sure."

It was noon before Colleen was finally free to leave the doctor's office, still reeling from shock. How could she have been so naive? She'd known she wasn't protected during the night she'd spent with Erik four weeks before, but she'd been too aroused to consider the consequences. Or more likely, she'd subconsciously closed her mind to everything but her burning need to be one with him. Well, they'd been one, and now she was going to be two.

When she walked into the reception area with its wall of windows she could see that the storm had intensified. The barren trees were bent nearly double under the force of the wind. She'd have to call a cab to take her back downtown to work, but not yet. She needed to be alone, to think, to plan. She stepped into the elevator and pushed the Down button. There was a cafeteria in the basement. She'd have lunch and try to come to terms with this astonishing development.

Colleen sipped her homemade vegetable soup and nibbled on a rye cracker. The doctor had told her to eat nourishing meals, but to make sure she didn't start putting on weight for a couple of months. He'd also told her not to drink, smoke or take any form of medication without checking with him first, since anything she took into her system could affect the baby.

The baby. Erik's baby. For the first time she realized the full extent of what had happened to her. She was going to have Erik's baby. She was going to be a mother. Even now there was a tiny human being developing inside her, being nurtured by her body.

She rested her palm against her flat stomach. Was it a boy or a girl? Would it look like Erik—big, blond and Nordic? Or would it be dark-haired and Celtic like her? Maybe it would be a combination of the two of them, with chestnut hair and blue-green eyes, bigger than her but smaller than Erik.

She finished her lunch and took the elevator back upstairs. The storm hadn't let up a bit. She'd have to call for a cab.

She started toward the public phone when she heard her name being called in a familiar voice, one she'd hoped to get out of the building without hearing. "Colleen, wait up. What are you doing here?"

She turned and faced her brother Devin. He was wearing a gray pin-striped suit that had a slenderizing effect on his husky frame. Not that he was fat, but his wide shoulders and barrel chest on a five-feet-ten-inch body gave him a burly look. In college he'd been a wrestler and had no trouble keeping trim, but now, at thirty-four, his sedentary life-style combined with April's rich cooking had resulted in a slight paunch that had been expanding lately. He was still a handsome man with his twinkling blue eyes and the brown hair that resisted all efforts to style it, and Colleen loved him dearly.

"Hello, Devin," she said, and couldn't go on. What was she going to tell him? She wasn't prepared for this confrontation. She hadn't had time to come to terms with the situation herself, let alone make plans for how to handle it.

She tensed, suddenly seized by a sense of panic, and Devin's smile changed to a frown as he grasped her arm. "What's the matter? You're white as a sheet. You've just seen one of the doctors, haven't you? Which one?"

She shook her head as she tried to get hold of herself. "I'm all right, really. I was just going to call a cab to go back to work."

"Forget it," he said grimly as he led her down the hall. "We're going to my office and you're going to tell me what's wrong with you."

She followed along. Colleen knew her brother well. Now that he'd found her here, he wouldn't let her go until she told him why she'd been consulting a physician, and what she'd learned that shook her up so.

As they walked through the outer office Devin told his secretary he didn't want to be disturbed, then ushered Colleen into the next room and shut the door. He seated her in the visitor's chair, then propped himself against the edge of his desk. "Now tell me, are you sick?"

She looked at her hands. "No, I'm not sick. I feel fine."

"Then what's the matter? You certainly don't look fine."

She twisted her hands together. He was going to have to know soon, so it might as well be now, but she wished she'd had time to think things through first. She needed time.

"Devin, I promise you that I'm not sick. The doctor just told me I'm strong and healthy."

"Great." The sarcasm in his tone told her he was having none of it. "So why did you bother to consult him? If you have no symptoms and are in such perfect condition, why spend time and money on a medical examination?"

She took a deep breath. *Might as well get it over with.* She tilted her head up and thrust out her chin. "I'm pregnant."

Devin stiffened and his fists clenched, but when he spoke his voice had a studied calm. "I see. Who's the bastard who did this to you?"

Oh dear. It was going to be just as difficult as she'd feared. "I don't think that's any of your business, Devin."

"Then you're going to be married? Funny, I haven't heard of any engagement announcement. Who's the lucky guy?"

Colleen was well aware of her brother's temper, and she watched it build. "I'm not engaged and I'm not getting married," she snapped, and when the words were spoken she realized for the first time the full implication of them.

Her baby would have no father. No man to love it, to serve as a role model, to teach it the things a boy should know about being a man, or a girl should know about relating to one. No matter how hard she might try to overcome that deficiency, her child's upbringing would be incomplete.

"So he's married." Devin's voice was deadly. "I'll kill the son of a bitch when I get my hands on him."

"No!" Colleen jumped out of the chair and turned away from him. "He's not married, and this is not all his fault. I was there too, you know. I'm a grown woman. I can take care of myself."

"Then why didn't you? If you're so experienced and sophisticated why did you let yourself get pregnant?"

"I didn't. Oh, I don't know . . . I didn't mean for this to happen. Neither of us did, but it happened all the same, and I'm not going to trap him into a marriage he doesn't want." She walked over to the window and looked out at the howling snowstorm.

Devin's tone was heavy with disgust. "Does he know about the baby?"

"No."

"So when do you plan to tell him?"

Colleen shook her head. "I don't know."

This was all happening too fast. He was making her face things she hadn't even thought about yet. She needed time to think, to sort things out in her mind and make plans. She couldn't answer her brother's questions because she just didn't know.

"You do plan to tell him, don't you?"

"I don't know!" She ran her fingers through her hair, and blinked back the tears that burned her eyes. "Stop pushing me, Devin. I just found out about this. I haven't had time to make plans. I'm almost as shocked as you are. Just leave me alone, it's not your problem."

"The hell it's not." He moved away from the desk and began pacing. "You'd better give me the name of the man responsible so I can take care of this. You know what will happen if Dad gets to him first."

Colleen shuddered. Dad. Oh, dear God, she'd forgotten about her father. At age sixty Mick O'Farrell was still a formidable man. Built like his son, but with muscles rock hard from forty years as a welder with one of the automobile companies, he could still arm-wrestle any comer at his favorite saloon and win. He was also first-generation American with a pure Irish heritage and temper. His Old Country ideals included the protection of his women and the avenging of them if necessary. He would consider a bastard grandchild more than enough reason to pulverize Erik, and Erik would let him.

Dammit, she wasn't a sixteen-year-old virgin who'd been seduced by a womanizer, and she wasn't going to be treated like one. "This doesn't need 'taking care of' by either you or Dad, so just back off." They were facing each other now, and she hated the tears that were streaming down her cheeks. "You sound like a character in a bad Victorian novel. I'm not the only woman in the city of Detroit who's pregnant and unmarried. This is my life and I'll live it my way without interference from you, so butt out.''

A tearing sob shook her, and then she was in Devin's arms. His voice was husky with regret. ''Honey, don't cry. I'm sorry, I didn't mean to upset you this way. It's just that you're my little sister and I love you. I don't want you hurt.''

Once started, the sobs continued uncontrollably, while Devin held her and comforted her as he had at times when she was growing up. There was so much difference in their ages that he'd been more like a father than a brother, and although his protective attitude had galled her at times she'd never rebelled against it before. She couldn't blame him for being confused.

Devin drove her home. The storm continued unabated and there was no chance of getting a taxi. He also called April and suggested that she close up shop and go home before traffic came to a standstill. Colleen agreed to talk to him again once she'd had a chance to come to some decisions about her condition and her future, and he assured her that her secret was safe with him until then.

Colleen stood at her living-room window and watched her brother's solid form hunched against the wind as he walked to his car and drove off. He was chauvinistic and possessive at times, but the bond between them was strong and loving. She knew he would always be there when she needed him, but at this point no one could help her. The decisions she made now must be her own.

The baby was a fact. She'd allowed it to be conceived and it was her responsibility.

What about Erik? She hadn't seen or heard from him since that Friday morning four weeks before when they'd locked up his apartment without bothering to clean up the mess he'd made and he'd taken her home. He'd come in with her long enough to make three phone calls—to his office, to his mother and to his automobile club to make arrangements to have Brett's Thunderbird picked up at the church parking lot and stored. He'd offered to let Colleen use the car, but the offer smacked too much of payment for services rendered and made her feel sick to her stomach, although she hadn't told him that when she'd refused it.

He hadn't said where he was going, and his attitude made it plain that he didn't want to discuss it. When he'd left he'd muttered something about thanks for her concern, then chucked her under the chin with his fist as he used to do when she was a child, and fled. Even so, she'd watched the mail diligently hoping he'd write, but he never did. Hardly the promise of a new and fulfilling relationship. He hadn't been able to get rid of her fast enough.

No, she wouldn't tell Erik about the baby. He'd be tormented by guilt and feel that he had to take care of her, support her and the baby. He might even insist on marriage, but she couldn't marry him when she knew he didn't love her. There would be no shotgun wedding, in spite of how her dad and Devin might feel.

There was one person she had to tell, though, and immediately. April. Her sister-in-law would know who the father was. Although Colleen hadn't admitted to April that she'd made love with Erik, April knew that Colleen had spent the night with him and she wasn't stupid. She'd told Colleen later that Devin hadn't returned from Lansing until late the night of the aborted wedding rehearsal, and when he'd called Erik's apartment and no one answered the phone, he'd assumed that Erik was getting smashed in a bar someplace. He hadn't known that Erik had destroyed the telephone along with everything else in his newly decorated living room, and April, bless her, hadn't told him that Colleen was with Erik.

She went into the bedroom and dialed the boutique, hoping that April was still there. She was in luck; her sister-in-law answered the phone. "April, I was hoping I'd catch you before you left. I'm sorry to have to tell you this so abruptly, but I'm pregnant."

A caustic expletive at the other end of the line was followed by a terse question. "When did you find out?"

"This morning. I lied to you about an appointment with the dentist. It was with Dr. Welch. Look, I had the misfortune to run into Devin while I was still reeling from shock and he made me tell him. He's livid and insists on knowing who the father is."

April sounded a little breathless. "Did you tell him?"

"No, and for heaven's sake, don't you tell him either. Just pretend you don't know anything about it."

"I don't suppose Erik knows yet?"

"No." Colleen sat down on the side of the bed. "I don't think he's back in town, but even if he were I wouldn't tell him."

"Why not? He has to know sometime."

"No, he doesn't. I'm not going to tell him. He's got enough pain as it is with what Brett did to him. It's my baby and I'll accept full responsibility for it. No one ever needs to know who fathered it."

"Colleen, honey." April's voice was tinged with exasperation. "I realize you're not thinking straight right now, but there's no way you can keep Erik from knowing this is his baby. He can count just as well as you and I can, and you're not going to convince him that you were sleeping with some other man at the same time. In fact, I'm betting you were a virgin and he knows it."

Colleen groaned. "You're right. But what am I going to do? I've no one to blame but myself, and that includes Erik. He tried to get rid of me that night. He even warned me that he might try to seduce me, but I wouldn't go. I wanted to stay with him. I even wanted to make love with him. I not only didn't resist, I actually encouraged him. I just wasn't experienced enough to tell him that I wasn't protected. I didn't even think of it, and I'm not going to tie him to me now with a baby he didn't ask for and doesn't want."

April sighed. "What makes you so sure he won't want it?"

Colleen stroked her fingers through her rumpled hair. "Why should he? He may have planned to have a family with Brett, but he's in love with her. He was going to marry her. I was just a necessary diversion at a time when he desperately needed someone. A baby was never a part of the deal. Maybe I could go away someplace and have it."

"You mean you'd give it up?"

"No! I mean I could move to another state, California maybe. I have a good education. I could get a job and support us. He'd never have to know."

"Don't be ridiculous," April snapped. "Erik is as much a part of your family as I am. He and Devin are like brothers. Unless you kept the secret from the whole family he'd know about it, and that's impossible now because Devin knows. He'd never let you go away alone. Besides, it wouldn't be fair to deprive Katherine and Mick of their grandchild."

Colleen's shoulders slumped. "I guess you're right, I'm not thinking straight. Please, don't tell Devin about Erik until I've had a chance to decide for sure what I'm going to do."

"I won't, sweetie, and look, call me if you need me, huh?"

"Sure, and thanks. See you." Colleen put the phone in its cradle and stretched out on the bed, trembling with exhaustion and shock.

It was Sunday, February 14. Valentine's Day. The storm that had paralyzed the city for a week had finally moved on, and the sun was a wondrous sight. Colleen had struggled for days with her problem, considering various options and finding none of them satisfactory. Finally she had to face the fact that no matter how she handled the matter her family was going to be disappointed, hurt or humiliated. An illegitimate child was something that had never happened in the O'Farrell family before, at least not to her knowledge, and she was torn with regret for the shame she would bring on her loving parents.

She'd decided that Erik would have to be told about the baby. He was the father and he had a right to know, but not yet. She wouldn't say anything to anybody for a few more months. When she began to expand to the point that she could no longer hide it, she'd tell Erik. Then she'd make the announcement to her family and friends, but nobody but Erik and April would ever know who the father was. She couldn't bear for her family to know. Erik had been like a second son to her parents, a brother to Devin. Their disappointment in her would be hard enough for them to bear, but what they would consider Erik's betrayal of their love and trust would be a crushing blow that she would not, could not, allow.

She'd make no demands on Erik. This was her baby and she'd assume full responsibility. She'd always love him, but she didn't want his guilt, his pity or his money. She could support her child without help from anybody.

She'd slept late on this Sunday morning, and was still wearing her maroon velour robe over her flannel granny nightgown. She was reading the paper and sipping her second cup of coffee when the doorbell rang. With a grimace of annoyance she tossed the paper aside and headed for the front door. She wasn't expecting anyone but was glad she'd taken the time to comb her hair and put on a little lip gloss when she'd brushed her teeth.

She looked through the tiny peephole in the door and blinked, then blinked again. Erik was standing in the hall with a gaily wrapped package in his hand.

She hadn't expected him. Even though she'd assumed he was back in town by now, she hadn't expected him to come to her apartment.

She opened the door, and for a moment they just stood there staring at each other. Finally Erik grinned. "Is there any chance that you might invite me in? I have a Valentine for you."

She stepped back and gestured. "Of course. Please come in. I—I didn't know you were back."

He walked in and shut the door behind him. "I got back from vacation a couple of weeks ago, but then had to leave immediately for the West Coast on a business trip. I just got home again yesterday." He held out the rectangular package. "Here, happy Valentine's day."

She took it and discovered that it was heavier than it looked. "Thank you. May I take your coat?"

"I'll just put it across the chair," he said, and removed the cashmere overcoat as he walked into the living room.

She followed him, tearing the red foil wrapping from the gift as she went. It was a three-pound box of expensive chocolates. Her favorite sin, but one she could no longer indulge and still keep her weight down. "Oh Erik," she said, and smiled with delight at his thoughtfulness, "Thank you. You always remember my favorite candy."

"My pleasure," he acknowledged. "Could you spare a freezing man a cup of coffee?"

"Oh, of course. Sit down and I'll bring it."

She opened the candy and put it on the coffee table, then went to the kitchen and poured two cups of steaming black coffee. "Here," she said and handed one to him, then carried the other to the chair a few steps from the sofa where he was sitting.

She watched him as he selected a chocolate-covered caramel from the box. He was wearing brown slacks and a Harris tweed sport coat with a tan velour shirt open at the throat. He looked much better than he had the last time she'd seen him, but there was still a lingering shadow of pain in his green eyes, and he'd lost weight.

She cleared her throat nervously. "Did you have a nice vacation?"

That wasn't what she wanted to know, but it was the closest she could come to asking how he had survived the past five weeks.

He shrugged. "I just traveled around. Did some skiing in Maine and some surfing in Florida." He looked at her squarely. "How about you?"

She wasn't quite sure what he was asking. "Me? Oh, I'm fine. Been busy with inventory and first of the year sales."

He was still watching her. "That's not what I want to know. Let me rephrase the question."

He paused for a moment, and a cold feeling of apprehension swept over her. Why had he come? It wasn't to bring her a Valentine gift; he used to send her cards when she was a child, but he hadn't done that in years. What did he want of her?

He set his coffee mug on the table and his gaze clung to hers. "Colleen, is there any chance... Would you know yet if..."

He clutched at the back of his neck with his hand. "Oh damn, what I'm trying to ask is—Colleen, are you pregnant?"

Chapter Five

Colleen stared at him, stunned by the impact of his question. "How did you know?"

The words were out before she was aware that she'd spoken, and there was no way she could call them back.

Erik looked sick. "Then you are?"

"I— Who told you?" She set her mug on the lamp table, spilling most of the coffee in the process. "No one knew but Devin. Did Devin tell you?"

The blood had drained from Erik's face and he looked thoroughly shaken. "Nobody told me. I've known all along that this might happen. Neither of us took precautions that night."

He leaned forward with his elbows on his knees and dropped his face in his hands. "Oh God, honey, I'm sorry."

She wanted to go to him and hold him, comfort him. She knew something of what he was feeling. She was still suffering from the aftershocks of having her pregnancy confirmed. It would be heaven to creep into his arms and let him shelter her, assure her that everything would be all right. She knew Erik well enough to know that was exactly what he'd do, but at what price? He already felt guilty enough; she wasn't going to let him accept all the blame and responsibility.

"No, Erik," she said, then swallowed in an effort to steady her voice, "I'm the one who's sorry. You tried to send me away but I wouldn't go. I wanted you as much as you wanted me, and you had no way to know that I wasn't—protected."

"That's no excuse," he said bitterly. "You trusted me. I never should have touched you."

She twisted her fingers together. "The rules of the game changed when I practically threw myself at you." He shook his head but she continued. "We're not going to accomplish anything by arguing over who's sorriest and most responsible. I'm going to have a baby and there's nothing we can do about it now."

His gaze sought hers. "Do you want the child, Colleen?"

She knew what he was asking. "Yes, I do. In fact now that I've had a week to think about it, I want this baby very much. I've always loved children. I made most of my spending money baby-sitting when I was in high school and college so I know how to take care of them. I'll be a good mother."

His expression softened. "Of course you will, but..." He hesitated, as if he had just thought of something. "You asked if I found out about this from Devin. Why did you tell him before you told me?" He didn't sound happy.

"I didn't have any choice. He caught me coming from the doctor's office at the medical clinic and insisted that I tell him why I was there. He knows I'm never sick. I was so shocked and upset that I blurted out everything."

Erik winced. "My God, I'm surprised he hasn't come after me with mayhem in mind."

"Oh no," she said quickly, "he doesn't know it was you."

Erik reared back. "What do you mean? Who in hell does he think it was?"

Colleen was surprised by his reaction. She'd thought he'd be relieved. "He doesn't know who it was. I refused to tell him. I wouldn't do that, he'd never forgive you."

Erik looked confused. "He'll find out soon enough. Why didn't you just level with him?"

Now it was Colleen who was confused. "There's no reason for him to know. I don't intend to tell anyone. I'm a grown woman capable of supporting myself and my child. I don't owe anybody an explanation. It would just cause my parents and Devin even more pain to know that you—that—"

"I don't believe this!" Erik jumped to his feet and stood glaring at her. "Are you telling me that you intend to let my son grow up never knowing who his father is?"

She stared up at him. "I don't understand. I thought that's the way you'd want it."

The anger drained out of him and his shoulders slumped. "Are you truly convinced that I'm so unfeeling and thoughtless that I'd leave you to face this alone? Have I sunk that low in your estimation?"

She scrambled to her feet. "Oh Erik, no, that's not it at all, but nothing will be gained by naming you as the father. This is my baby. There's no need for you to be involved. I won't make any demands on you. I've already started making plans. I can work up to the time the baby's born, then I can collect disability for several weeks. That will give me time to find a sitter or—"

"It's my child too, Colleen." His tone was bleak. "Isn't there any room for me in your plans?"

He looked so beaten, as if she had been railing against him instead of trying to protect him. She couldn't stand to see him looking so miserable, and she stepped closer and put her hands on his shoulders. "There's always room for you in my plans, surely you know that, but only if you want to be in them. I don't want anything from you that you can't give freely and happily."

His arms closed around her and pressed her to him, and he buried his face in her soft black hair. "Oh my little love," he groaned. "I don't deserve you. I'm sure you wouldn't have chosen me to be the father of your children, but if you'll give me a chance I'll try hard to be a good one."

She melted against him, limp with relief. Erik was willing to help her through this, to assume some of the responsibility. More important, he really seemed to want to.

His lips caressed the top of her head. "I'd like for us to get married immediately. I—"

"Married!" Colleen leaned back and looked up at him. "You want us to get married?" She couldn't believe he was serious.

"Of course," he said impatiently. "What did you think I was talking about?"

"But you don't have to marry me. A lot of single women raise children nowadays."

"Not my children, they don't," Erik growled. "I'll not have my son born a bastard. In fact, I hope we can get married quickly enough that it won't be glaringly evident he was conceived before we got to the vows."

She should be ecstatic. She'd loved him for so long and now he wanted to marry her. But it wasn't ecstasy she felt. He'd made it plain that the only reason he wanted marriage was to give his "son" his name and a normal family life.

"It may be a daughter, you know," she murmured as she rubbed her cheek against his tweed jacket.

"Come again?"

"I said the baby may be a girl."

His arms tightened around her. "That it may. I hope if it is she's as beautiful as her mother. Please say you'll marry me, Colleen."

She wanted to. Oh, how she wanted to, but she couldn't let him sacrifice his own chance at happiness. "But you don't love me," she said against his shoulder.

"Of course I love you. I've loved you ever since you were eight years old and wore pigtails and pinafores. You're very special to me, sweetheart."

She sighed, and for a minute was tempted to leave it at that, but her innate honesty wouldn't allow it. "I don't mean that kind of love, Erik. You don't love me the way you should love a wife."

She felt him tense. "If you're talking about so-called 'romantic' love, then you should be glad I don't. I've good reason to know how short-lived that emotion is. Believe me, honey, what I feel for you is much more lasting."

Colleen wondered if he had any idea how much anguish there was still in his voice when he spoke of "romantic love." She didn't want to probe at fresh wounds, but if she were to seriously consider his proposal there were some things she had to know. "What about Brett?" she asked.

His muscles jerked involuntarily. "What about her?" he asked roughly.

"Do you still have...feelings...for her?" She couldn't bring herself to ask if he still loved her cousin.

"Nothing I won't get over," he muttered. "There won't be any problem about her, I promise."

A promise that was easier to make than to keep. Colleen knew all about unrequited love, and it didn't go away because you willed it to. As long as the very thought of Brett had the power to hurt Erik she would be a problem, but unfortunately time was running out. Erik wanted to protect his child from taunting remarks about being born too soon after its parents' wedding. If they were going to be married it would have to be immediately.

She knew he'd be a poor marriage risk. He was in love with another woman, he was marrying Colleen only because she was pregnant with the baby he'd never intended to sire, and his guilt at having seduced his friend's younger sister continually gnawed at his self-respect. Such a union didn't have a chance of surviving, but she wasn't strong enough to refuse.

She moved her head and nuzzled the skin under his square jaw. "All right, darling, if you're sure it's what you want, I'll marry you."

He hugged her close. "It's what I want, and I swear to you, I'll do everything in my power to make you happy, little one."

With his fingers he tipped her face up to his and kissed her. It was a sweet, gentle kiss with none of the passion that had burned her lips that night in his apartment. She closed her eyes and tried not to weep.

Erik and Colleen were married the following Friday evening in a small formal wedding held in the chapel of a church miles from the one where Brett had arranged for her marriage to Erik to take place. When they made the announcement to their parents they explained that they wanted to keep it simple and strictly family. With painful and traumatic memories of the recently aborted wedding plans still fresh, nobody questioned their decision. Colleen's mother and father cried happily, Brett's parents were relieved but more than a little puzzled, and Erik's relatives embraced Colleen with joy and thanksgiving that he had finally seen the light and chosen her instead of her self-centered cousin.

The only dissenter was Devin, but he managed to keep his fury under control during the ceremony, where he served as best man and April was the matron of honor. He'd had four days to cool down, but on Monday evening when Erik and Colleen had gone to his home to tell him they were getting married, he'd exploded with rage.

At first he'd looked as if he didn't understand what he was hearing. Colleen had confided in April that morning when she got to the boutique, so April was prepared to handle the situation, and sat close to her husband on the sofa.

"You're getting married?" asked Devin, unconvinced. "But I thought..."

Colleen could see the exact moment when the truth hit him. The look in his eyes changed from puzzlement to ice, and focused on Erik. "You? You're the bastard who got my sister pregnant!"

The shock and pain in his voice was overshadowed by outrage, and before April could reach out to stop him he jumped up and strode across the room to confront Erik, who was standing by the fireplace. "You were my friend! I trusted you!"

His fist shot out and connected with Erik's firm jaw. It knocked him backward, but he had apparently braced himself for the blow and he stayed on his feet.

Both Colleen and April screamed at Devin and rushed to grab his arms, but he shook them off easily. His muscles flexed as his fists clenched and unclenched, and his face was mottled with rage. The names he called Erik were obscene, and Erik eyed him warily but made no move to stop him, or to defend himself. He just stood there letting Devin vilify him.

It was Colleen who acted. She stepped in front of her brother and struck him with all her strength. He was unprepared for the slap and stumbled backward as his hand shot up to cover his stinging cheek. "Who in hell are you to go around making moral judgments?" she choked, her breath coming in angry gasps.

Erik grabbed her and pulled her back against him, imprisoning her arms at her sides as she continued her tirade. "I'll be the one who decides who I'll sleep with and who I won't. I don't have to ask your permission. I told you before it's none of your business. You hit Erik again and I'll scratch your eyes out." Her fingers flexed as though the idea held great appeal.

Devin stared, flabbergasted at the whirlwind of fury that was his usually placid little sister. Her unexpected violence had tamed down his own, and he rubbed his throbbing cheek. "He's not doing you any favor by marrying you, Colleen. He's in love with Brett."

Erik's arms tightened around her protectively. "Now just a minute—"

Neither Colleen nor Devin were paying any attention. "I know that," she said, as if there had been no interruption, "but it doesn't matter. He wants to acknowledge his child, give it his name, make a proper home for it. What more can you ask of him?"

"Look, dammit," Erik rasped, "I can speak for myself—"

"I can ask that you find a husband who loves you," Devin interrupted, speaking to his sister. "You've got your whole life ahead of you, you shouldn't have to compromise."

"I'm not compromising." Colleen leaned back into Erik's embrace. "I want to marry Erik and have his child. Maybe subconsciously I even planned it this way, I don't know."

"That's nonsense," Devin said, and plowed his fingers through his unruly hair. "You'd never trap a man like that."

"I haven't been trapped!" This time Erik's voice boomed through the room loud and clear. "And will you both stop talking about me as if I weren't even here? Devin, I deserved that blow and I accept it, but don't ever try it again or I'll pulverize you."

He turned Colleen around in his arms and looked at her. "And you, my little wildcat, I don't need you to defend me. I can and will fight my own battles, but this time your hotheaded brother was entitled." He cuddled her closer. "Now that we've gotten that out of our systems, let's sit down and talk rationally. April, I think we could all use a good stiff drink."

He released Colleen, then took her arm and led her to the blue sofa where they sat down together. Devin and April mixed drinks and passed them around, then each took one of the cream-colored chairs on either side of the fireplace.

Erik took a long gulp of his whiskey and soda, then spoke. "First, let's get one thing settled. Colleen didn't 'trap' me. I practically had to beg her to marry me, and it wasn't because I felt it was my 'duty.'" He reached out and took her hand. "I'll be the luckiest man alive to have her for a wife and I'll do my best to make her happy."

Colleen heard the sincerity in his voice and knew he meant what he said. She squeezed his hand, and got an answering squeeze. A glow of happiness engulfed her as he continued. "Second, you're very wrong, Devin. I do love her. I've always loved her. She's precious to me. I know you'll find that difficult to believe under the circumstances, but it's true. I don't blame you for wanting to take me apart. If it had been any other man who did this to her, I'd have helped you dismantle him. I'm not offering either excuses or explanations for what happened that night, but I swear to you that I took her with love and it was—good—for both of us."

He was actually blushing. This giant who could be violent one moment and gentle the next found it embarrassing to talk so intimately about her to her brother, and Colleen found it warmly endearing.

Devin obviously didn't. She could see the anger rising in him once more as his fists clenched on the arm of the chair, but April gave him a quelling look and he said nothing.

Devin and Erik had arrived at an uneasy truce that night, and now Devin was standing at the altar beside Erik while April, in brown lace, preceded Colleen and her father down the aisle of the flower-decorated chapel, which was filled to overflowing with family members. Colleen's café-au-lait gown was fashioned of lace with satin trim and spaghetti straps. Her bare shoulders were covered with a matching jacket whose long sleeves and high-buttoned neckline provided the modesty required of a wedding gown. Since she refused to wear white, a decision that she was unable to explain satisfactorily to her mother, she chose a dress that she could wear as an evening gown later.

The men in the party were wearing tuxedos, and Colleen caught her breath at the sight of Erik. He was all male and looked rugged in anything he wore, but in formal clothes he was absolutely smashing. His blond hair must have been taken in hand by a stylist because it was expertly groomed, and if he had any regrets or doubts, they didn't show.

Erik watched as Colleen walked slowly down the aisle on the arm of her father, and for a minute the bride he saw was tall and willowy with hair the color of sunbeams and brown eyes that flashed almost green in moments of passion. He stifled a groan and closed his eyes to dislodge the image. Goddammit to hell! Would he ever get over Brett? She was a cold-blooded bitch who would have made his life a purgatory and he was lucky that she took off before the wedding, so why did she still haunt his dreams?

He opened his eyes and looked again at Colleen. She was so young, and so loving and so beautiful, and he'd messed up her whole life. She should be marrying a man closer to her own age who would love her with the passionate abandon of a first love. Instead she was being tied by vows that to her were inviolate to a man who in one violent night of anguish had robbed her of her virginity and left a child in its stead. He didn't need Devin to tell him what a bastard he was, but he'd do everything in his power to make it up to her. He'd be a loving husband and a good father, and maybe someday he would even manage to exorcise the ghost of Brett that was like a knife being slowly turned in his gut.

Erik took Colleen's hand and they knelt in front of the priest as the ceremony began. After the vows and the rings had been exchanged he took her in his arms and kissed her. It was a tender kiss of commitment, and Colleen knew that he meant every word of his vow to love, cherish and protect her for the rest of their lives. It was selfish of her to want more, but was it so wrong to wish that there had been just a trace of hunger and impatience in the kiss, too?

The reception was a dinner party held in a private dining room at the luxurious Westin Hotel, the middle one of the three glass towers on the recently renovated waterfront known as the Renaissance Center. It was on the first two connected floors of these magnificent structures that April and Colleen's lingerie boutique, Sweet Dreams, was located in a new and rapidly growing mall of specialty shops. Since Erik couldn't take time off from work again so soon and on such short notice, he had reserved a suite on the seventieth floor of the hotel, where they would spend their weekend honeymoon. On Monday they would move into Colleen's apartment until they could find a suitable one for the two of them. Erik had given up the place where he'd expected to live with Brett before he left town on vacation, and had spent the past week with a bachelor friend.

The dinner seemed to go on forever while Colleen merely toyed with her food. When finally the dishes were cleared away and the combo switched to dance music, Erik led her onto the floor to begin the first waltz. In spite of his size he was graceful and light on his feet as they moved together in time to the lilting melody.

After a few minutes other couples joined them, and Erik's arm tightened around Colleen as he murmured, "How much longer before we can sneak out of here and go upstairs?"

Her heart pounded and her blue eyes sparkled as she teased. "You have something better to do upstairs?"

He nibbled at her earlobe. "Much better, and in another minute everyone who looks at me is going to know it."

She felt the warm blush that turned her face rosy. "My goodness, I didn't realize you were one of those impatient bridegrooms."

He grinned. "The hell you didn't. Now are you going to come with me willingly, or do I have to sling you over my shoulder and carry you off?"

She snuggled against him. "Who's arguing? I thought you'd never ask."

He groaned. "Now you tell me," he said and danced her toward the door.

On the seventieth floor Erik unlocked their suite, then swept Colleen up in his arms and carried her across the threshold. In the tiny entryway he flicked the light switch, then put her down and lowered his mouth to hers in a much more satisfying kiss than they had been sharing lately. She sighed and cuddled into his embrace, and his voice was husky as he murmured, "Do you know this is the first time I've had you all to myself since you agreed to marry me?"

"I thought this week would never end," she said. "It's been so hectic getting ready for the wedding that we've hardly seen each other."

"We're going to remedy that starting right now. I'm not going to let you out of my sight all weekend. No one knows we're up here, and I left word at the desk that we're not to be disturbed for any reason."

He turned her and with his arm still around her waist walked with her the few steps into the living room. "Come and see where we're going to be spending the next two days."

Colleen gasped with delight. The front wall was glass and the view was breathtaking. The wide Detroit River was immediately below them, and on the other side the lights of Windsor, Ontario, in Canada, lit up the snow-covered countryside. Although she worked in the area, Colleen had seen the view from so high only a couple of times before, and then from the revolving restaurant on the seventy-third floor. She leaned against Erik and put her head on his shoulder as they stood looking out. "You know, darling," she said softly, "I'm glad we weren't able to go away somewhere. There's no place I'd rather spend the first days of our married life than right here in this beautiful hotel."

"And nights?" He nuzzled the top of her head.

She turned and put both arms around his waist. "Oh yes, most especially nights." Her face tilted upward to invite the kiss he seemed most eager to give.

His desire for her was no secret as he pressed her against him, but he seemed in no hurry to satisfy it as he lifted his head and said, "How about some champagne?"

He turned her around and for the first time she noticed the bar that opened off the entry and faced the living room. A silver bucket held crushed ice and a bottle of Dom Perignon. He poured the champagne in crystal glasses and handed her one, then led her to the long curved maroon sofa in the middle of the room facing the glass wall and the spectacular scenery.

He removed his formal coat, vest and tie and tossed them across a nearby chair, then undid the first two buttons of his white shirt and sat down beside her. He put his arm around her and pulled her close, and she slipped off her shoes and curled her legs under the long skirt of her gown as she snuggled against him. She'd never been so happy. This was the night she'd dreamed of ever since her adolescent fantasies, but never expected to happen. She was Mrs. Erik Johansen. Colleen Johansen, Erik's wife. She shivered and his arm tightened around her. "Are you cold?"

She shook her head against his chest. "No, just happy. I love sitting here with you. I love having you hold me. I love—" She hesitated. She'd almost said "I love you," but she didn't think he wanted to hear that. It would just make him uneasy to know that she loved him in the way that he was unable to love her. "I love everything about you," she amended.

He rubbed his cheek against her hair. "And I love everything about you, my sweet and beautiful bride. I love the way your lips quiver under mine when I kiss you." He lowered his head and covered her quivering lips with his own. "I love the way your breast fits into my hand and nestles there." He cupped the firm rise and sent pinpricks down her spine as it seemed to swell and mold itself against his palm. "I love the faint scent of you that always clings to your soft, smooth skin." He trailed kisses down her cheek to the little hollow just below her ear, and the pinpricks multiplied and spread.

After a moment his hand moved to the top button on her lace jacket. "The only thing that keeps you from being perfect is that you wear too many clothes," he grumbled as his big fingers fumbled with the tiny buttons.

She chuckled and put her hand up to cover his. "Better let me do it," she said. "It could take you all night."

"I'll give you five seconds," he said and dropped his hand to her lace- and satin-covered thigh. "After that my patience runs out."

Her fingers flew over the buttons. "Now are you happy?" she asked as the jacket parted.

"Not quite," he answered, and slid the jacket off her shoulders and tossed it in the direction of his coat.

He caressed her bare shoulders with his mouth. "Mmmm, that's better, but not much." He moved lower to nuzzle the swell of her breast above the low neckline of her gown. "How many layers do I have to peel off before I get to the real you?"

She put her hands on either side of his head and ran her fingers through his hair. "Why don't you try it and see?" she murmured dreamily.

He'd already found the zipper at the back and lowered it. "Was the bra really necessary?" he muttered as he struggled with the hooks on her strapless undergarment.

She rubbed her cheek against the top of his head. "I was afraid the dress wouldn't stay up without it. You know, for someone as old and experienced as you claim to be you're awfully clumsy when it comes to getting a woman out of her clothes." She stifled a giggle.

"I've never taken a wedding gown off one before," he said as the offending closure on the garment finally opened.

He slipped the delicate satin straps of her dress over her shoulders, and the bodice and bra fell to her waist. "That's better," Erik said as his hand gently eased over one full breast then on to the other. "You're absolutely exquisite," he continued while his gaze followed his hands. "How come it took me so long to notice all the changes that were taking place in you?"

"Just dense, I guess," she replied tremulously as his finger circled her erect nipple.

"Yes, well now that you've gotten my attention you'd better get used to it because I may not let you out of bed until Monday morning." His head dropped lower and he took one of the ripe nipples in his mouth and caressed it with his tongue.

"Oh, I hope not," she whispered as the tingling increased in the deep recesses of her womanhood.

While his mouth was occupied with her breasts, his hand gathered a portion of her long skirt and pulled carefully upward until it could rest underneath on her thigh. "Panty hose," he rasped in a tone of outrage. "Did you dress with the deliberate intention of driving me wild with frustration?"

"They come off," she reminded him.

"Not when you're sitting, they don't," he muttered, and stroked her leg through the sheer nylon.

"I could stand up," she offered as the tingles became stabs of flame.

His fingers stroked higher. "Not yet. We're going to take it slow and easy this time. I want you to know how really great it can be with a gentle, considerate lover."

Colleen found it increasingly difficult to sit still. "If it's any better than last time I don't think I can stand it. I want you just the way you are, Erik."

With a groan he turned and pressed her full length against him, making her aware of the urgency of his arousal. "You aren't making restraint at all easy," he whispered just before his lips took hers in a searing kiss that kindled the flame that was tormenting her.

When they came up for air he pressed her head against his shoulder, but her hands continued to roam over his back and waist.

He rubbed his cheek against hers. "Ah, Colleen," he said tenderly. "That compassionate nature of yours was bound to get you into trouble sometime. I'm just glad that when it finally did it was with me."

His hand cupped her breast and he leaned down to kiss it. "Oh, honey, I feel so good. I know that soon we'll satisfy each other, so I can wait and enjoy all the sensations caused by your snuggling close, touching me, kissing me."

"You mean like this?" she murmured, and rained tiny kisses down the side of his neck as she unfastened his shirt. "Or this?" Her fingers tangled in the mat of blond hair on his chest until they found his flat nipple, which she covered with her lips and licked with her tongue.

Erik moaned softly and shifted. "Sweetheart, I can stand only so many of those sensations."

"You want me to stop?" she asked sweetly.

His strong fingers clenched into her flesh. "Oh God, no, but we'd better move into the bedroom while I can still walk."

Chapter Six

Erik stood and pulled Colleen up beside him. Her bra and unzipped gown fell in a graceful heap on the floor around her, leaving her standing there in nothing but panty hose. For a moment his gaze roamed slowly over her and even in the dim light she could see the appreciation in his green eyes, then he lifted her in his arms and carried her into the bedroom.

The room was unlit but as in the living room one wall was glass. The lights from the waterfront and the Canadian city across the river, plus the reflection from the brilliant whiteness of the new snow, provided just the right touch of illumination. Erik positioned Colleen crosswise on the king-size bed, and followed her down to lie beside her. He raised himself up on one elbow and looked at her as his other hand cupped her breast, which seemed to swell in his palm. He lowered his head and took the tip of it in his mouth and began a gentle sucking that ignited the flame he had kindled in her earlier, leaving her breathless and aching with the need for more.

He didn't leave her wanting, but slid his hand under her panty hose to caress her flat stomach. "I think it's time to get rid of these," he muttered and sat up to pull the constricting garment off her, then stood and undressed himself.

Colleen watched as he removed his shirt, then his shoes and socks, and finally his tuxedo trousers and briefs. Even in the near-darkness she could see that he had a magnificent body, tall and broad with muscles as firm and rippling as they had been when he was a star college athlete more than ten years earlier. The first time they'd made love it had been with such frenzied haste that she'd hardly been aware that they'd undressed, and the next morning he had been up and dressed before she woke, so she'd never seen him nude before. He reminded her of a Greek or Italian marble statue sculptured to the perfection of manhood.

She rolled off the bed and helped him turn back the sheet and blanket, then they both crawled in and he gathered her to him. His mouth claimed hers and her lips parted to invite his entry. He turned her onto her back with his body partially covering hers, his leg flung across hers, and his hand wending its way with agonizing slowness from her breast, to the indentation of her waist, over the swell of her hip and down to her thigh where his fingers stroked the sensitive underside.

Colleen's breath was coming in short gasps as his seeking fingers drove her to the edge of madness. How much longer was he going to keep her in this blissful state of torment? She dug her fingernails into the taut muscles across his shoulders and arched against his pulsating masculinity. He shivered with need and his thighs tightened around hers in an effort to maintain a semblance of control.

When at last his fingers made contact with her dark, damp femininity she grasped him around the waist and cried out his name. He moved quickly then to plunge deep into the fiery heat that fused them and made them one. They rocked together in a rhythm as old as time, and the melody soared until it reached a crescendo of rolling, pounding drums. The song of ecstasy. The melding of life and love. To Colleen it was a harmony of exhilaration and joy.

True to his prediction, Erik and Colleen spent most of their honeymoon in bed. The first morning they got up long enough to order lunch from room service and eat it at the table in front of the glass wall where they watched helicopters flying below them. A fair portion of their time was spent in the large sunken tub where they soaped each other with great attention to detail, got lost in billowing mounds of bubbles and made love underwater. That evening they dressed and took the express elevator to the restaurant at the top of the tower where they dined on prime rib with baked potato and spinach salad, while admiring the view for miles in all directions as the entire floor slowly revolved.

On Sunday they ordered a newspaper to be brought with their brunch, and took turns reading interesting items to each other as they nibbled on scrambled eggs, bacon, danish, fruit salad and hash brown potatoes washed down with champagne in delicate stemmed glasses and steaming black coffee in thick mugs. Afterward they turned on the television, but made the mistake of cuddling up together on the sofa. Whatever program was on the screen lost its audience after only a few minutes. In the evening Erik offered to take Colleen somewhere for dinner and dancing, but she wasn't yet ready to emerge from her enchanted tower and join the real world once more. Instead they had dinner brought to the suite and talked about the baby.

Erik was the first to mention it. They had finished eating and were again curled up on the sofa, her back against his chest and her head on his shoulder, when his hand moved from her breast to her stomach. "Do you really think it will be a girl?" he asked softly.

She put her hand over his. "It's been known to happen. You'd better be prepared for that possibility."

"Maybe it'll be twins," he mused, "a boy and a girl."

"Erik!" Colleen said, moaning. "Don't be in such a hurry. We've got a lot of years ahead of us. If it's all the same to you I'd just as soon have my babies one at a time."

"Would you really be willing to go through this more than once?"

There was a wistful hopefulness in his tone, and Colleen suspected Brett had made it plain to him that she wouldn't be burdened with childbearing.

She turned her head and kissed the side of his neck. "Of course. I'd like a large family. You and your sisters and brother seem to have so much fun when you all get together. I love Devin madly, but there's such a difference in our ages that we never had much in common except our love for each other. He was more like an uncle, or an older cousin. I'd like to have a baby every two or three years for a while so they can all grow up together. I promise that if the first ones are girls we'll keep at it until we get a son for you."

His hand returned to her breast, and he leaned down to kiss her. "That won't be necessary. If you give me daughters I'll adore every one of them even while I'm fighting with them for the use of the bathroom."

Colleen laughed and turned to hug him. "Oh sweetheart, I promise you your own bathroom. You won't have to go through what you did with your sisters when you were all living at home."

It was still dark early Monday morning when Erik woke suddenly from a deep sleep. He blinked and looked around the faintly illuminated bedroom. Everything was as it should be, and there was no sound. What had wakened him?

He turned over and raised himself on his elbow to look at his sleeping wife. She was lying on her side with her back to him, her black hair in tangled disarray and her hand under her cheek. She looked like a child who had played too hard and was recouping its energy in sleep. A sharp stab of guilt reminded him that was exactly what she was, a child in experience but with the sensual fire of a woman.

He brushed the ebony curls away from her face and felt the familiar stirring in his loins. Damn, would he never get enough of her? He should have let her sleep through the previous night. They both had to get up early this morning and go to work, but in spite of his good intentions he'd taken her twice. Every time he touched her his body responded like a teenager's. Even Brett hadn't—

He jerked his thoughts away from the forbidden subject and slid carefully out of bed. Goddamn Brett! He hoped someday she'd roast in hell the way he was doing. He'd never find peace of mind with Colleen, because every time he let down his guard Brett intruded and his guilt multiplied. Why couldn't he put her out of his mind and forget her? Hadn't the three weeks he'd spent alone after she left been penance enough for a lifetime of sins? He'd thought he'd go out of his mind with grief and loneliness. Every time he'd seen a tall, blond woman from a distance his heart had speeded up and he'd dared hope...but it was never she.

He found his robe and tied it around him, then went out in the living room and stood looking down at the busy thirty-two-mile-long river that connected Lake St. Clair and Lake Erie. It was relatively quiet now because of the cold, but from April until December there was a constant parade of mammoth ore boats, freighters flying flags of many countries and pleasure crafts of every kind from rowboats to yachts.

Against his better financial judgment he'd finally let Brett talk him into agreeing to buy a small yacht the following spring when the weather warmed up. He'd saved a pile of money when she'd walked out. Colleen would never demand that he buy something he felt they couldn't afford. For that matter she'd probably never make demands of him at all. She'd given him her love—or more likely what she thought was love but was really infatuation—her trust and her future, and asked nothing in return but his fidelity. Well, she'd have that, but he could never give her the only thing she really wanted of him, his deep, passionate, all-encompassing love. The kind he'd felt for Brett. He couldn't ever allow himself to love like that again; it was too painful. The knowledge gnawed at his very soul.

The next month flew by, and the March days grew longer, but the weather remained cold and the first day of spring was ushered in by another blizzard with snowdrifts ten feet high and traffic practically at a standstill.

Colleen sat at her desk in the living room of the small apartment and gazed out the nearby window. It was no longer snowing and the wind had slacked off from a steady gale to intermittent gusts, but the temperature was still below zero and the streets and sidewalks were layered with ice under the snow. That was why she was working on her books at home instead of at the boutique. She'd wanted to go to work, but Erik wouldn't hear of it. "You're apt to catch cold, or worse yet, fall. April can handle the few customers by herself. You've got to be careful now, honey. We wouldn't want anything to happen to the baby," he'd said.

Of course she wouldn't, but it would have been nice if his concern had been as much for her as it was for his "son" as he still called it. No, that wasn't fair. He was concerned about her. He was a passionate lover and a considerate husband. That was more than most women had and it was selfish of her to ask for more. It was wrong to be jealous of her own unborn child.

She shook her head to dispel the unwanted thoughts and stared down at the columns of figures before her. The profits from the boutique were down for the month of February but that wasn't alarming; most of the shops in the Renaissance Center had the same problem. It was the weather. It was just too cold and windy and nasty for people to get out to shop for anything they could do without. Even the hotel was hurting for guests. Travel was hazardous at best.

A blast of wind shook the house and once again broke her concentration. Erik had been right to be afraid for the baby. She'd have to take good care of herself now that she was nurturing a new life. It was just that she still had trouble thinking of herself as pregnant. She felt great—no morning sickness or spells of weakness. Her breasts were starting to swell and become tender, but her stomach was still flat and firm. She smiled, remembering Erik's delight with the fullness of her breasts and the gentleness with which he handled them.

No, she had no complaints. He was everything she could have hoped for in a husband, and the joy with which he accepted his approaching fatherhood was something she hadn't expected. Most men would have resented being trapped by a child they'd never intended to father, but not Erik. He was looking forward to the baby with an eagerness that positively glowed from him and made it difficult for him to keep her pregnancy a secret.

They'd agreed to wait until two months after the wedding to make the announcement. Both had parents with conservative moral values, and they saw no need to sadden them with the knowledge that this grandchild had been conceived out of wedlock. Erik and Colleen would say that the baby was due in November, and if it was born a month early it could easily be "premature."

Neither of them ever mentioned Brett, but Colleen's mother told her that Brett was still in New York waiting for the various details to be cleared up before she went overseas to start the actual photographing. Colleen wondered if Erik thought of his ex-fiancée often. If he did he was careful not to let his wife know. He was swamped at work after being gone for three weeks on vacation and two weeks on business, and several times he worked through the dinner hour and on into the night. But when he was home his attention was centered on her.

There was no reason for her to be fearful, but still, she was. He'd loved her cousin totally, without reservation, and Brett's desertion had been a shattering blow. It wasn't reasonable to assume that just two months later he would have gotten over her completely. A few times Colleen's gaze had caught him off guard and she'd seen the anguish in his eyes when he thought he wasn't observed. When that happened she would find an excuse to go to him, hold him, tell him how happy she was even as she struggled to hide her own pain. He always welcomed her, and she knew his welcome was genuine. She told herself that once the baby was born he would forget all about Brett Kendrick.

Three days later Colleen woke feeling as if she had slept too long in the wrong position. She had a vague ache that she couldn't seem to pin down or identify, and she dismissed it as an off day.

The storm had blown itself out and the sun shone brightly on the snow, but the streets were still slippery. Erik drove carefully as he headed toward the Renaissance Center, where he would drop Colleen off before proceeding on to his own office in Dearborn on the outskirts of Detroit. At the end of the day he'd pick her up unless he was going to work late; then she would take the bus home as she had always done before her marriage.

Erik didn't like her to walk to and from bus stops in the cold and said so for the umpteenth time. "I have a meeting late this afternoon that may run overtime, so if I'm not here when you get ready to go home, for heaven's sake take a cab." He turned his head to glance at her. "Are you all right, honey? You look pale."

She flashed him a bright smile. "I'm fine, Erik. Besides, pregnant ladies aren't supposed to feel great every minute."

He frowned. "Then you don't feel well? Maybe I'd better take you back home."

"Darling, I feel fine," she said and meant it. "You know something? You're going to be a nervous wreck before this child of ours is born."

He chuckled. "I may be at that, but don't forget, I'm new at this. I've never been a father before."

She felt a glow of satisfaction. Their marriage would be a good one. She loved this big bruiser of hers with all her being, and most of the time she made him happy. He was an insatiable lover, and when they made love he was all hers. He wanted her, needed her and taught her to please him as he pleased her. If at other times she sensed an emotional distance that she was unable to bridge, it was just something that would take time to work out. It would take him a while to get over the shock of losing Brett, but once he held his child in his arms he'd know that Colleen's love for him was not the shallow thing her cousin had offered but deep and abiding and forever. When she presented him with a son or daughter, he'd love her the way she wanted to be loved, the way she loved him.

It was a busy morning at the shop. The cheerful sunshine drew the people out of their homes and into the brisk fresh air, so what better activity than shopping? Although the displays at Sweet Dreams featured the new spring line of silk, satin and lace undergarments and nightwear, the most frequently asked for items were long-sleeved flannel or brushed nylon nighties and pajamas. April and Colleen sold out the few they had left in stock early in the day, but managed to interest late-comers in the wispy, fragile new items with the promise of spring to come.

As the day progressed Colleen's initial discomfort increased. She felt a heaviness in her abdomen, and the ache she'd been unable to identify earlier settled in her lower back. During her lunch period, instead of eating, she wandered over to the hotel's eight-story atrium lobby with its out-of-the-way seats behind plants and trees. She found a secluded area and stretched out full length on the sofa to rest.

For a while she felt better, but by the time she returned to the boutique her back was bothering her again. She stepped into the bathroom to freshen up, and it was there she realized with a shock that this was a potentially serious situation.

Colleen walked into the small office and with trembling fingers dialed Dr. Welch's number. Her voice quivered as she briefly outlined her problem to the nurse, who immediately put her through to the doctor. "Colleen, what's wrong?" he asked.

She told him everything, and his voice was calm and reassuring as he asked questions. "You say there's some spotting?"

"I'm afraid it's more than spotting, Doctor." She took a deep breath. "There's quite a bit of bleeding."

"It's probably nothing to get excited about, but I think I'd better have a look. Are you at home or at the boutique?"

"At the boutique."

"All right then, take a cab and meet me in the emergency room at St. Mary's Hospital in half an hour. And Colleen, hang in there. This isn't all that unusual."

A worried April offered to go with her, but Colleen vetoed the idea. "You're needed here at the shop, and I can get to the hospital on my own. The doctor didn't seem alarmed, but I don't imagine he'll want me to come back to work. Would you mind calling Erik and ask him to come by the hospital and take me home before he gets tied up in his meeting?"

She didn't like to bother her husband, but in spite of the doctor's assurances she was frightened. She needed Erik with her.

April walked her to the front of the hotel where several cabs were lined up at the curb. Colleen climbed into one, and April reached in to squeeze her hand. "I'll send Erik to you, and be sure to call me as soon as you know something."

Colleen nodded and gave the driver the address, but when she leaned back and tried to relax she realized that she was trembling.

Three hours later it was all over. The baby could not be saved.

Erik glanced at his gold watch and swore as he jabbed the elevator button. Four o'clock and he was an hour late for the meeting with McVey and Shaw. Were they still waiting? Probably not. Their time was valuable too, and he hadn't been able to get to a phone to tell his secretary he'd be late.

There were days when nothing seemed to go right and this was one of them. Three key people had reported in sick that morning, one of the VIP stockholders had called to check on a rumor that had no basis in fact but could cause an uproar if the press got hold of it, and then on his way back to the office from a business lunch he'd gotten caught in the backlash of a five-car pileup on the freeway that delayed him for nearly two hours. That did it. He was going to have a phone installed in the car. It was no longer a luxury but a necessity.

He jabbed the button again just before the doors opened soundlessly at the underground parking level. He pushed the lighted button for the tenth floor and then fumed helplessly as the elevator stopped at every level to take on or let off passengers. When he finally walked into his office he found the outer room filled with people waiting to see him, and his secretary on the phone. "Trish," he snapped, disregarding the fact that one of her ears was already engaged. "Are McVey and Shaw still here? Dammit, get off that phone, I need to talk to you."

She said something into the mouthpiece and put it down. "Where have you been?" she demanded. "This place is a madhouse. Everyone in Detroit wants to talk to you!"

"Tell me about it," he growled and motioned her to follow him into his private office.

She shut the door behind her and sighed. "Well, first you'd better call April O'Farrell. She's been ringing every half hour since one o'clock."

His eyebrows went up. "April? What does she want?"

"She didn't say, other than it was urgent."

He nodded and Trish placed the call, then handed the phone to him. It was picked up at the other end on the first ring. "April?" he said. "What's the problem?"

Her quick gasp sounded almost like a sob. "Oh Erik, where have you been? I've been calling and calling—"

"I know. I just came in. I've been tied up in a traffic accident." A small knot of dread formed in his stomach. "What's the matter?"

"It's Colleen. She was having some cramps and bleeding and the doctor told her to meet him at the hospital...."

Erik's hand gripped the phone. The baby! Was something wrong with the baby? He remembered how pale and wan she'd looked that morning. He should have insisted that she not go to work.

"Which hospital?" His voice was tight with the dread that reached out and clutched him.

"I just told you," said April, who he realized had continued talking after he'd stopped listening. "She's at St. Mary's, and—"

Erik slammed down the phone and headed for the door. "Cancel everything," he barked at Trish. "My wife's in the hospital."

He strode out of the office and down the hall to the elevator.

Colleen felt numb. Everything had happened too quickly; she couldn't assimilate it yet. The previous day she'd felt wonderful and had congratulated herself on not even being queasy in the mornings. Now, twenty-four hours later, the baby had simply slipped away and left her alone in this big efficient hospital. Maybe it had never been. Maybe it was a hormonal disturbance after all.

No, she knew better than that. She'd felt it when she'd miscarried. Her baby, and Erik's. The precious gift Erik had given her without ever intending to. Her hope for the future. Before she'd gotten used to the fact of it, it was gone. She'd never hold it in her arms, or nourish it or give it a name. She didn't even know whether it was a boy or a girl.

A nurse entered the room and took her temperature, pulse and blood pressure. "I understand you're scheduled for a D & C later this evening," she said.

"Yes," Colleen answered.

"Has your husband been contacted yet, Mrs. Johansen?"

Had Erik been contacted? April had promised to call him, but that was hours before and he still hadn't shown up. Maybe his meeting had been too important to chance being late. Or maybe he didn't figure that a trip to the hospital for an examination was important enough to interrupt his busy schedule. He'd told her that morning to take a cab home if she didn't feel well, and he had no reason to think there was any danger to the baby. Neither of them had. She was young and strong and healthy, and they hadn't yet discovered that she was also deficient in the most important function of a woman—the ability to carry a child to term.

"Mrs. Johansen, are you all right?" The nurse's pretty young face showed concern, and Colleen realized that she hadn't answered the last question.

"I'm sorry, my mind was wandering. My sister-in-law was going to let my husband know I'd gone to the hospital, but he doesn't know that I lost the baby."

A sob caught in her throat but she swallowed it. Crying wouldn't help anything, but uttering the words that made the loss a reality was a physical pain that made her ache with regret.

"Would you like us to—" the nurse started to say, but the door opened and both she and Colleen looked up, expecting Erik.

Instead it was Devin. He strode across the room and took her hand. "Colleen, honey, I'm so sorry. Frank Welch stopped in my office when he got back to the clinic and told me what happened. Why didn't you have someone call me?''

She squeezed his hand and he sat on the side of the bed as the nurse slipped quietly out of the room. ''There really wasn't time. I expected to come here for an examination, but once I got here everything started going wrong and . . . well, I didn't think of anything else but what was happening to me. April had said she'd let Erik know I was here, and—''

''You mean April knew about this and didn't tell me?'' His expression was like thunder.

''No, it wasn't like that.'' Colleen didn't want to cause trouble between her brother and his wife. ''She didn't know how serious it was. Neither of us did. There was no advance warning. Please, don't be upset with April. I don't think she knows yet that I lost the baby.''

Again she swallowed back a sob, and Devin hastened to reassure her. ''Okay, sweetie, I'm sorry. Where's Erik?''

''I—I don't know. He's not here yet.''

Colleen could see the anger building in her brother's expressive features. ''You mean he wasn't with you when this happened? You were all alone?''

''Devin, please, calm down. I don't know why Erik hasn't come, but I do know he'll have a very good reason.''

''He'd better have,'' Devin muttered and stood up. He leaned over and kissed her, then headed for the door.

''Where are you going?'' Colleen called after him.

''I'm going to find your husband,'' he said and walked out of the room.

At the same moment outside, tires screeched as Erik swung into one of the five-minute parking spaces in front of the hospital and slammed on the brakes. He jumped out of the car and strode quickly into the lobby and the registration desk. "I'm Erik Johansen," he rasped. "I understand my wife, Colleen, checked in earlier this afternoon."

The lady in the pink uniform punched several keys on the computer and scanned the screen. "Oh yes, Mr. Johansen, she's in room 306. That's on the..."

Erik didn't hear the rest of the sentence as he headed for the elevators.

He swore impatiently under his breath as he watched the lighted numbers, some indicating elevators going up and others stopping at each floor as they slowly descended. Finally one of the doors slid open and he made a dash for it just as Devin stepped out. They nearly collided, and Devin's eyes narrowed with anger as he grabbed Erik by the arm. "Where in hell have you been?" he roared.

"Never mind that," Erik answered. "How's Colleen? What's she doing here? Is she all right?"

"You're a little late with your distraught husband act," Devin sneered.

Something snapped in Erik and he grabbed his brother-in-law by both arms. "Now look, I'll give you just two seconds to give me some straight answers before I start taking you apart. Is Colleen all right?"

Devin pulled out of Erik's hold. "No, she's not all right," he snapped. "She lost the baby."

Devin's words were like a punch in the belly, and Erik hunched over with pain. He could feel the blood drain from his face as he leaned against the wall for support. "Oh my God," he gasped.

"Hey look, I'm sorry." Devin's tone was remorseful. "I shouldn't have blurted it out like that. I've just come from Colleen. She's pretty broken up, but physically she's okay.''

Erik pushed himself away from the wall. "I've got to go to her," he said and, leaving Devin staring after him, he stepped quickly into another elevator that had just opened up.

Chapter Seven

Colleen heard footsteps running down the tiled hall just before the door to her room burst open and Erik, looking harried and distraught, rushed in. He didn't say anything, but sank down on the side of the bed and gathered her in his arms. She didn't care where he'd been or why he hadn't come sooner; he was here now and that was all that mattered. She flung her arms around his neck and sobbed, "Oh Erik, I lost the baby."

It was only then that her composure disintegrated, and the grief that had been tearing at her became a keening wail as sobs convulsed her slender frame. He murmured loving words of endearment and held her as the storm of anguish raged out of control. "Sweetheart, don't cry so. It couldn't be helped, these things happen sometimes. It's heartbreaking but we'll have other children."

"I—I don't wa—want oth—other children, I want th—this one," she stammered as sobs continued to shake her.

"I know." Erik's voice quavered. "So do I, but it wasn't meant to be. Thank God you're all right. I was so scared I ran every red light and stop sign between here and the office when I finally got April's message."

"But you wa—wanted the ba—baby?" she cried.

"Yes, I did," he said and kissed her tearstained cheek. "But I want you more."

His words quieted her somewhat and she snuggled deeper into his embrace. "Oh darling, I love you so," she said.

"I don't know why," he said, and his voice was heavy with remorse. "I've failed you every time you've needed me. I left you to find out about your pregnancy all by yourself, and this afternoon when you lost the baby you were alone again. I've brought you nothing but misery."

Colleen raised her head to look at his grief-stricken face. "That's not true," she said, disturbed that he would feel that way. "You came to me and asked if I was pregnant before I had a chance to tell you, you married me even though you didn't love me, and you had no way of knowing what was happening today. Even the doctor wasn't alarmed when he told me to come for a checkup."

Erik kissed her trembling mouth. "I was out of the office when April called. I'd gone to a business lunch and then got caught in a traffic jam on the freeway and didn't get back to Dearborn until four. I came the minute I found out you were here."

She touched his lips with her fingertips. "I knew it was something like that. You're the sweetest, kindest, most thoughtful man I've ever known. I only wish—"

A sharp knock on the door preceded the entrance of Dr. Welch. He looked at them, then spoke to Erik. "Glad you're here, Erik. God, I'm sorry about the baby. It was so totally unexpected."

Erik nodded. "Thanks, Frank. I'd appreciate it if you'd tell me what happened. I just got here and haven't had time to ask questions."

The doctor told him of the events leading up to and including the miscarriage. "These things happen sometimes, and there's no way of knowing why. It's nobody's fault, and couldn't have been prevented. It's nature's way of correcting an error, a pregnancy that got off to a bad start. Colleen is a strong, healthy young woman and there's no discernible reason why she can't carry a baby to term. If you still want a family, wait about six months and then try again."

Colleen leaned back against the elevated head of the bed. "Are you sure?"

Frank Welch smiled. "As sure as I can ever be about these things." He glanced at his watch. "The nurse will be coming to prep you for the D & C. That's a diagnostic procedure, Erik, to make sure the miscarriage was complete. She'll be groggy afterward, but it's just the anesthetic. By morning she'll be fine and you can take her home." He patted Colleen's shoulder. "See you in about half an hour."

Colleen returned to work the following Monday, fully recovered in body. But her mind hadn't fared as well. She couldn't seem to shake the depression that had plagued her since she'd lost the baby. The doctor had warned her about this. He called it postpartum depression, and said it sometimes happened even to women who delivered full-term healthy babies. She felt empty, and alone and unworthy.

Even Erik's tender concern didn't lessen her disappointment. He'd taken the day off when he brought her home from the hospital, and insisted that she go straight to bed and stay there. He'd brought her hot tea and thick creamy soup that he'd reconstituted from its frozen state, then hovered over her while she forced it down to please him. All weekend he'd treated her like a fragile doll that would surely break if subjected to the slightest strain.

She loved him so much, but instead of easing her burden, his attempts to comfort her only made it heavier. He'd wanted the baby as badly as she had, he'd even married her so that his child could have a normal upbringing with two parents to love and guide it, but instead of giving in to his own grief he was trying to lighten hers. It wasn't fair. He deserved so much more.

Why couldn't she do anything right? She'd only wanted to comfort him after Brett left, but she'd brought him even more anguish. Now he was stuck with a wife he neither wanted or needed. One who couldn't even deliver a healthy son or daughter.

They'd talked with Devin and April and decided to tell their parents, families and friends that Colleen had been in the hospital for a D & C to correct a problem with her monthly cycle. There was no need now to tell anyone else that she had been pregnant. Even in this Erik was protecting her.

During the days she managed to stay busy with the new spring stock that was arriving daily, but in the evenings when she was alone with Erik her melancholia returned to rob her of the contentment she usually felt with him. Maybe if they could have made love she would have felt more secure, but the doctor had advised them to wait two weeks, until after her scheduled checkup, to renew marital relations.

Marital relations. Such a restrained and formal name for the fireworks that exploded within them when they were united in body and soul.

They slept in each other's arms every night as usual, but Erik was restrained, careful that they not become aroused only to suffer the frustration of having to bank the flames that smoldered and would not die. Pleasing him with her lovemaking was the only thing she'd managed to do right, and now even that was denied her.

Colleen's keen mind told her to snap out of it, that she was indulging in self-pity that would only prolong her anguish, but her emotions were so tangled with grief that she couldn't shake off the destructive, self-centered mood.

By the end of the first week back at work Colleen had regained most of her strength, and with it part of her natural vitality. She'd managed to shed some of the debilitating depression that had settled over her like a thick fog and clouded her thinking, but her present thoughts were no happier, only more realistic.

They had started the night Erik came home with news. "Honey," he said as he helped Colleen set the table for dinner, "I got a lead on an apartment today."

"An apartment?" She wasn't quite sure what he meant.

"An apartment for us. We never intended to stay here, and this one sounds just about what we're looking for. C. J. Lawrence, the head of truck marketing, and his wife have bought a house and are giving up their apartment. It has three bedrooms, two baths and an all-electric kitchen.''

Colleen felt a clutch of apprehension. "But Erik, we don't need such a large place."

He found the salt and pepper in the cupboard and set them on the table. "Sure we do. We can make the third bedroom into an office. I had an office in my last apartment and it was invaluable."

For some reason the thought of moving into bigger, more expensive quarters made her nervous. "But why now? Why can't we wait a while, take our time before moving?"

Erik turned and looked at her. "Colleen, I know what you're thinking. You figure that now there won't be a baby in the next few months we don't need a bigger place, but you're wrong. It'll do us both good to get out of here, start over again someplace where there aren't so many sad memories. I've been to parties at the Lawrences'. It's a great place, and an ideal location. Almost exactly halfway between your boutique and my office. We'll get you a car so you won't have to mess with bus schedules."

"I don't know," she said thoughtfully. "It'll be awfully expensive."

"No more than we can afford. We've always planned to move as soon as we could find something we liked." He sounded a little irritated. "At least take a look at it. That won't obligate us."

Colleen knew she was being unreasonable and gave in, but when he obtained the key and took her to inspect it on Sunday the uneasiness returned.

The apartment was in one of the newer buildings, and included electronic security. On the sixteenth floor, it had a spectacular view of the surrounding area, and was spacious, clean and empty.

"We don't have nearly enough furniture," Colleen pointed out.

"We'll buy some," Erik answered. "It comes with carpeting, drapes and all the major kitchen and laundry appliances. We can make do with your furniture and the stuff I have in storage, then add really nice pieces as we find them. Where else are you going to find walk-in closets in two of the bedrooms, and a bathtub that's big enough for two?"

He leered comically and she laughed. "So it's the bathtub you're lusting after."

He drew her close and hugged her. "It's you I'm lusting after, sweetheart." His voice was husky with repressed desire. "But I'll admit that tub does intrigue me. Remember the one on our honeymoon?"

She remembered all too vividly, and arched her body as his hands on her buttocks pushed her against his aching masculinity. She felt the tremor that shook him. "How much longer until that checkup?" he muttered.

"Three more days," she whispered, and slipped off one pump so she could caress his calf with her stockinged foot.

He caught his breath, and his fingers dug into her bottom. "Watch it, sweetheart," he groaned. "I'm not averse to taking you right here on the carpet."

"So why are we still standing up?" Her foot continued its loving message.

He swatted the solid flesh his fingers had been clutching and moved away from her. "Oh no," he said as he struggled to slow down his breathing, "we're not taking any chances, so kindly keep your feet to yourself until after you've seen the doctor."

"Yes, sir," she said demurely. "Then can I have my way with you?"

"I'll think about it," he answered solemnly.

"You do that," she said as her fingers inched under the front band of his slacks.

"Colleen!" he yelped, and took her hands in his. "If you don't stop that I'm going to have to take a cold shower before I can appear in public." He kissed her palms lingeringly. "Just three more days, my eager little bride, and then I promise I'm yours to do with as you please. Now for God's sake let's change the subject. Tell me, how do you like the apartment?"

She sighed. "It's beautiful, but could we wait awhile before making up our minds?"

He shrugged. "Sure, but it won't be available long. If we want it we'll have to give them an answer in the next few days."

She knew he was right, and the knowledge lay heavily on her conscience. Erik wanted the new place and so did she. It would be just right for them, so why was she delaying?

She paced around her tiny kitchen while she was supposed to be fixing their dinner on that bright, cold Sunday afternoon. She knew she had been shying away from the real, gut-level problem ever since she lost the baby, but now it had to be faced.

How long would their marriage last now that its reason for being was no longer viable? She knew Erik had intended it to be permanent, but that was when he thought he would have a child to raise.

A wave of despair swept over her and she sank down on one of the chrome chairs and buried her face in her hands. Oh why hadn't Brett married Erik as planned? It would have been painful but she could have coped with it. That was before she'd had him as husband, lover, father of her unborn child. How could she give him up now that she'd known the strength of his passion, the depth of his compassion?

But how could she not give him up if she loved him enough to put his happiness above her own? He didn't love her. Not the way he'd loved Brett. He'd never have taken her to bed if he hadn't been out of his mind with anguish over another woman. He'd never have married her if he hadn't gotten her pregnant in that moment of uncontrollable passion. The only thing he'd wanted of her, a living, healthy child, she'd been unable to give him.

She heard him moving around in the living room and rose quickly to open the oven and check on the roast and vegetables that were bubbling in their own juices inside a tightly closed cooking bag. She couldn't let him see how upset she was. After a moment she heard the excited voice of a sportscaster and knew Erik had turned on the television to watch a basketball game.

She sat down again at the table and resumed her introspection. If they leased a large apartment and bought another car she'd be binding him even closer with financial commitments he'd have to honor. If she finally succeeded in giving him a child, she knew he'd never leave her, but would he ever be truly happy? What if he eventually found a woman he could love as a man should love a wife?

She shuddered. That possibility was too painful to think about. She'd wrestle with it some more later; right now she had a salad to assemble.

Colleen slept badly that night, and she was preoccupied all day Monday. She had to make a decision because of the apartment. When she made her third mistake in as many tries on the electronic cash register, April took her aside and demanded to know what was wrong.

"It's nothing, really," she said as she cast around in her mind for a plausible excuse. "It's just—uh—Erik has found a larger apartment and wants us to move."

"But that's wonderful," April exclaimed. "That little apartment of yours is much too small, and it's a long way from Erik's office."

"Yes, it is." Colleen's tone was noncommittal.

"So what's the problem?"

"Oh, no problem. I was just daydreaming, I guess. You know, about the new furniture we'll need, and how I'm going to decorate it."

April looked at her dubiously but let it drop, and Colleen was extra careful after that to keep her mind on her customers.

Shortly after lunch Dr. Welch's nurse called to say that the doctor was having to reschedule some of his appointments and would Colleen be able to come in for her checkup the next day, Tuesday, instead of Wednesday. Colleen agreed and they set a time.

Later that afternoon Erik also called. "I'm sorry, honey," he said, "but I have to work late tonight so don't fix dinner for me. I'll have sandwiches sent in."

"Oh darn," she said lightly. "I have something to tell you."

He chuckled. "So tell me now."

"I guess I'll have to," she teased, "but I'd planned to do it with candlelight and champagne."

"Colleen!" he said threateningly.

"Dr. Welch has moved my appointment up to tomorrow," she blurted.

Erik's sigh was definitely one of relief. "Good. I don't think I could have stood two more days of celibacy."

The huskiness of his tone made her shiver. "I'm quite sure I couldn't," she murmured and hung up.

At home alone that evening she fixed herself a roast-beef sandwich and a cup of herbal tea, while giving her painful thoughts free rein. She'd finally come to the conclusion that giving Erik his freedom was the only honorable thing she could do. There would be nothing to gain by waiting several months until the marriage fell apart on its own. By then they'd be deeply entangled in community property that would make a settlement more difficult. If she got out now, maybe the pain would eventually become bearable and she could pick up the pieces of her life and, if not happy, at least she would not be unhappy. But if she stubbornly held on to Erik and had to watch his tenderness turn to indifference and finally scorn, it would destroy her.

Colleen was only twenty-four years old, and she was a survivor. She had too many years ahead of her to let them turn sour because she was a one-man woman and her man didn't share her feelings. She'd had six weeks of Erik's undivided attention, his lovemaking, his protectiveness. That was more than she'd ever expected to have, and she would hold it close. A warm, loving memory to help ease her loneliness and despair.

But first she was going to have one more night of lovemaking. One more night of the shared passion that made them truly one. It had been two weeks since the last time they had aroused each other with their hands, and their mouths and their erotic murmurings, to the soaring, mindless ecstasy that united them and made them whole. Erik was looking forward to the next night, and so was she. She didn't have the strength to deny either of them the exquisite pleasure. She would wait until Wednesday to give her husband the gift of freedom.

The examination the following afternoon revealed that Colleen's body had returned to normal, as if the baby had been only a dream too good to come true. She left the doctor's office with a prescription for birth control pills and a diaphragm to use until the pills could take effect. Although she knew she wouldn't need the pills she hadn't wanted to share this knowledge with Dr. Welch so had allowed him to write the prescription.

She'd had another restless night. Why were the nights always the worst when you were troubled? She'd made her plans and at the time they'd seemed the only alternative, but when Erik finally got home, late and tired, she'd clung to him like a child desperately seeking security.

Erik was used to her depressive moods by now and he comforted her, thinking it was the loss of the baby that had upset her again. They fell asleep in each other's arms, but a short time later Colleen woke when he turned away from her in his sleep. She felt cold and abandoned, and huddled against his broad back for warmth as her whole being cried out in pain. How could she ever sleep again without Erik in the bed beside her?

Why couldn't she just accept what she had and let the future take care of itself? Erik wasn't complaining. He seemed content, so why was she tormented by this compulsion to poke and probe and examine the dark areas that were better off sealed?

Eventually she slept again, but later in the cold light of morning she knew she'd been clutching at wisps of hope that had no substance in reality. She had to let Erik go, and now. That was her well-thought-out decision and she'd abide by it. If she didn't, if she tried to hold on to him, she'd spend her life in purgatory between the hope that he would learn to love her, and the terror that he would find another woman whom he could love.

Erik drummed his fingers impatiently on the steering wheel as he waited for the traffic light to change. He was on his way to pick up Colleen at the boutique and take her to dinner, and he was late. Tonight of all nights he'd wanted to be on time. At intervals all day long his concentration had been broken by the tantalizing thought of her soft, warm, nude body under him in their clean, sweet-smelling bed.

A horn blaring behind him alerted him to the fact that the light had changed to green. He chuckled as the powerful motor of the black Mustang shot the car forward in a smooth gliding motion. If he wasn't careful with his daydreams he'd ravish his sexy little wife on the floor of the dressing room before they left the boutique.

He sobered as the thought of Colleen reminded him of their recent heartbreak. Why did they have to lose the baby? Maybe it was his punishment for the way he'd practically raped the virginal young woman who only wanted to comfort him. God knows he deserved to be punished. He'd behaved like a sex-starved maniac with no thought of anything but releasing his agonizing tension.

But not Colleen. She was innocent of wrongdoing, so why was she made to suffer along with him? She was so sweet and loving and kind. She was everything he could want in a wife, a talented housemaker with an inborn maternal instinct, a bright businesswoman and a passionate bundle of exciting femininity that turned to flame in his arms and kept him both hungry and sated in turn.

He was surprised that the enforced celibacy hadn't been more difficult. She'd lain in his arms every night for two weeks and he should have been on fire with frustrated desire, but by tamping down his natural male inclinations he'd found that he enjoyed lying quietly with her. Sometimes they talked, and other times they communicated with their silence. When she cried for the loss of the child he held her and consoled her, and after a while she was comforted. It gave him a sense of well-being to know that he could ease her pain in ways other than the forgetfulness of sex. It amazed him that she could comfort him in the same peaceful way.

He'd never before known a woman he wanted to lie with all night and just hold hands, or curl up together and sleep. His sexual appetites were strong and if a woman couldn't or wouldn't appease them then he wasn't interested. Even Brett . . .

He deliberately turned off his thoughts and focused his attention on the newscaster whose voice was coming over the car radio.

They ate club steak and spaghetti at a popular old Italian restaurant where a strolling singer entertained them with operatic arias. Ordinarily Colleen loved opera, but tonight she was having a hard time keeping her mind on anything but Erik's hand caressing her thigh under the table. "Erik," she grumbled good-naturedly, "finish your dinner."

"What dinner?" he whispered as he nuzzled her ear.

She gave up and they left without ordering dessert.

On the way home she snuggled against him, and he drove with one arm around her and one on the steering wheel. She retaliated for his indiscretion in the restaurant by running her fingers up and down lightly along his inner thigh. He gripped the steering wheel and braced himself to keep from squirming. Finally, unable to sit still any longer, he captured her hand and groaned. "Have a little mercy, sweetheart, you're clouding my vision. If you keep that up I'm going to run right into the oncoming traffic."

She squeezed his hand and contented herself with sucking on his earlobe, which didn't do a hell of a lot to clear his vision.

At the apartment house Erik parked the car in the garage space assigned to them, then turned and took Colleen in his arms. He pressed her full length against him and their kiss was long, and hot, and steamy. She gasped for breath as she murmured, "Not in the car, darling. What'll the neighbors think?"

"It's your own fault," he teased, but his voice quivered with eagerness. "You should have kept your hands to yourself on the way home."

They walked with their arms around each other up the stairs to their second-floor apartment. When they were inside with the door locked Colleen took his hand and led him toward the bedroom. "Would you like to wash my back?" she asked.

He brought their clasped hands to his lips and kissed the back of hers. "I'd love to wash your back," he said huskily, "and several other areas that demand my exclusive attention."

She went into the bathroom and adjusted the shower, then took off her clothes and stepped under it. Erik joined her, and she walked quickly into his arms as the warm water poured over them. He had the most beautiful body she'd ever imagined, big and brawny and superb in its maleness. He was all muscle and bone and dynamic energy.

And he was shivering with need. "Oh-h-h honey, I don't think I can wait."

She was having the same problem and didn't need to be coaxed. She gently disengaged herself and reached in back of him to shut off the water. "We'll shower later," she said as he picked her up and carried her, still dripping with water, into the bedroom and laid her down on top of the thickly quilted bedspread, then followed to lie alongside her with one of his legs thrown over one of hers.

His mouth fastened on her parted lips and his tongue plundered the depths of her willing mouth as his roaming hand cupped her damp breast, fondled it until it was heavy and aching, then moved down to her flat tummy. She drew in her breath and the muscles beneath his palm quivered.

"Erik," she gasped as he moved his hand lower still, probing to be sure she was ready.

He lifted himself over her and her fingers clutched at his hips, guiding and encouraging him as she writhed with agonizing anticipation and desire. His first thrust was deep, and she wrapped her legs around his buttocks and moved with him in the frantic dance of rapture.

They slept little that night, and by morning Colleen was stiff and sore and happily exhausted. She limped toward the bathroom and a hot fragrant tub of water and bubbles. She hadn't forgotten that this had been their last night together, but she kept her mind resolutely shut and refused to let anything dim the glow of her exhilaration. It would wear off soon enough, and then she'd have the rest of the day to wrestle with her personal demons until it was time to confront Erik.

Colleen kept busy at the boutique cleaning shelves and rearranging merchandise when she wasn't working on the books and waiting on customers. She needed to keep her mind as well as her hands occupied so she wouldn't have time to think. She didn't want to plan what she would say to Erik. She couldn't go through it twice, once in her mind and again in the actual confrontation. No, she'd wait for the right moment and then take it a sentence at a time. Somewhere she'd find the strength to let him go. She had to.

Erik had told her he'd be home on time that evening, and she had dinner waiting when he got there. He kissed her lingeringly, and she lost the battle not to respond with every fiber of her being. Fortunately they were both too tired to be urgently aroused.

After dinner they took their coffee into the living room, and Erik picked up the mail from the desk and stood while sorting through it. Colleen walked over to the window and looked out into the twilight. "Honey," he said as he opened an envelope and extracted a bill from the telephone company, "I don't like to pressure you, but we have to let the realtor know whether or not we want the apartment."

She shivered. He had just given her the perfect opening, almost as if he knew what she was going to do and was helping her. She put her mug on the windowsill and drew in a deep breath.

"Erik," she said carefully, "I don't think we should take the apartment. We only got married because of the baby, and now that there is no child there's also no reason to stay married. I— What I'm saying is that I'm willing to file for divorce if that's what you want.''

Chapter Eight

Colleen put her fist to her mouth to stop its trembling. Damn, that wasn't the way she'd wanted to say it at all. It sounded so cold and objective, as if it were a matter of no real importance.

There was no sound from Erik behind her and she hurried on. "I—I mean—the time we've spent together has been great, but it was a marriage of convenience and—"

"You lying, conniving little cheat!" Each harsh word seemed to explode in the room and Colleen whirled around, startled into silence.

Erik stood stiffly by the desk staring at her, and the look on his white face was one she'd hoped she'd never see again. It was the same stunned anguish that had been stamped on his features when she'd told him that Brett had walked out on their wedding. Dear God, what had she done?

First Class Romance

Delivered to your door by

Silhouette Special Edition®

(See inside for special 4 FREE book offer)

Find romance at your door with 4 FREE novels from Silhouette Special Edition!

Slip away to a world that's only as far away as your mailbox. A world of romance, where the pace of life is as gentle as a kiss, and as fast as the pounding of a lover's heartbeat. Wrap yourself in the special pleasure of having Silhouette Special Edition novels arrive at your home.

By filling out and mailing the attached postage-paid order card you'll receive FREE 4 new Silhouette Special Edition romances and a Cameo Tote Bag (a $16.99 value).

You'll also receive an extra bonus: our monthly Silhouette Books Newsletter. Then approximately every 4 weeks we'll send you six more Silhouette Special Edition romances to examine FREE for 15 days. If you decide to keep them, you'll pay just $11.70 (a $15.00 value) with no extra charge for home delivery and at no risk! You'll have the option to cancel at any time. Just drop us a note. Your first 4 books and the Tote Bag are yours to keep in any case.

Silhouette Special Edition

EXTRA BONUS

A Free Cameo Tote

You'll receive brand-new
novels as they're published!

Mail this card today for your
4 FREE BOOKS
and this Tote Bag (a $16.99 value)!

Silhouette Special Edition®

Silhouette Books, 120 Brighton Rd., P.O. Box 5084, Clifton, NJ 07015-9956

☐ Yes, please send 4 new Silhouette Special Edition novels and Cameo Tote Bag to my home FREE and without obligation. Unless you hear from me after I receive my 4 FREE books, please send me 6 new Silhouette Special Edition novels for a free 15-day examination each month as soon as they are published. I understand that you will bill me a total of just $11.70 (a $15.00 value) with no additional charges of any kind. There is no minimum number of books that I must buy, and I can cancel at any time. No matter what I decide, the first 4 books and Cameo Tote Bag are mine to keep.

NAME

(please print)

ADDRESS

CITY   STATE   ZIP

Terms and prices subject to change.
Your enrollment is subject to acceptance by Silhouette Books.

Silhouette Special Edition is a registered trademark.

CAS825

He'd dropped the mail he'd been holding, and his hands were clenched at his sides. "So Brett isn't the only vicious, self-serving female in your family." His voice blazed with scorn and derision. "Did she give you lessons or do you just come by it naturally?"

"Erik," she gasped. "You don't understand."

"The hell I don't. You needed a father for your baby so you plied me with that sweet, innocent, loving act, and I leaped at the bait like a starving fish."

"No. It was your baby, I swear it." She held her hands out to him, palms upward, in an unconscious attitude of pleading.

"I know it was my child, and I felt so guilty I'd have done anything to atone." He ran his fingers through his unruly hair. "You played on that guilt."

Colleen finally understood what had upset Erik so. Brett had dumped him without a word of regret when something she wanted more came along, and now, just three months later while his wounds were still raw and his memory vivid she, Colleen, seemed to be doing the same thing. The male ego simply couldn't handle two rejections of that enormity.

"Oh darling, no! I never wanted you to feel guilty. Please, let me explain."

"There's no need for you to explain, I get the picture," he rasped. "You want something. What is it? I've already promised you a new car. Brett wanted a cabin cruiser. Is that it? Or how about jewelry? What do you like? Diamonds? Rubies? How about sapphires to match your eyes? Come on, Colleen, speak up. I'll give you anything you want." He swallowed and put his hand to his stomach. "Just don't leave me." The last sentence sounded bleak and strained, and he turned suddenly and dashed for the bathroom.

Colleen was galvanized into action, but she was a few steps too late as the door slammed shut behind him and she heard the lock turn. "Erik, let me in," she cried as she pounded on the unyielding wood.

The only reply was the sound of deep, painful retching.

Colleen sagged against the door, her whole body trembling, until he finally stopped being sick and she heard the sounds of water running in the shower. She was too shocked to move. Dear Lord, how could she have been so clumsy and thoughtless? She should have asked him if he wanted to be free before she announced that she would divorce him. It had just never occurred to her that he might not.

She was light-headed with relief that he'd asked her to stay with him, but how could she ever make him understand that she'd never wanted to end their marriage? That she was only suggesting it because that was what she'd thought he wanted. Would he ever believe her now?

She heard the shower shut off, and then the sounds of him brushing his teeth and rinsing his mouth. She hurried to turn down the bed and take off her clothes.

She'd just slipped a raspberry-colored satin nightgown over her head when Erik stepped out of the bathroom. He was wearing only a wide yellow towel wrapped around his waist as he leaned against the doorjamb and looked at her. "You're staying?" he asked politely.

The tears that had been burning behind her eyes trickled out of the corners and down the sides of her face. "Of course I'm staying. I've never wanted anyone but you."

He walked over and sat down heavily on the side of the bed. He looked ghastly, and she went to him and knelt on the floor between his knees. She put her arms around his waist and her head against the still-wet mat of blond hair on his chest. "Sweetheart," she said in a voice that was muffled with tears, "I'm so dreadfully sorry."

He didn't touch her, but neither did he push her away. "Why are you doing this to me, Colleen?" he asked, his tone flat and tired.

"I didn't mean to," she protested. "I thought I was doing the decent thing by letting you go. I love you, Erik."

"Don't talk to me about love," he grated. "It's just a word that women use to get what they want from a man. I've been through that once, remember?"

Her arms tightened around him and she was shaken by a series of sobs. "Oh, darling, listen to me, please. I don't want a divorce. I thought you did. You only married me because of the baby. I didn't want to hold on to you if you didn't want me."

He said nothing, and after a moment she rose slowly and stood, then put her arms around his shoulders and held his head between her soft breasts. "Erik, talk to me," she pleaded. "Swear at me if you want, call me names, but don't shut me out."

He still didn't touch her of his own accord, but he seemed to relax ever so slightly against her. "I'll agree that your compassion is real. Without even setting out to I've managed to trap you into feeling sorry for me, so you've changed your plans to split and decided to stay on as my wife. You won't regret it, I promise. I make a good salary, and I've recently had an offer to head up the sales division. The pay is fantastic, but it would mean a lot of traveling and I'd intended to turn it down. Now that I know you don't need me I'll accept it. I can buy you almost anything you want.''

Colleen felt like screaming and shaking him to make him listen to her. ''You didn't trap me and I do need you,'' she insisted. ''Sweetheart, please pay attention to what I'm telling you. I don't want anything from you but your love.''

That got his attention, and he brought up his hands to push her away, almost toppling her in the process. ''Forget it,'' he roared. ''Love is the one thing you'll never get from me. I'm not a congenital idiot, just a blind fool.'' He stood up and laughed. A short, bitter sound. ''The funny part of it is that if you'd just been a little more patient, waited another couple of weeks you would have had that, too. In spite of my devastating experience with your kinswoman, Brett, I was actually falling in love with you.'' He walked away from her. ''You'd think I'd learn, wouldn't you? Well, I admit to being slow, but you taught me well tonight. You'll be my wife, Colleen, but you'll never be my love!''

A cry like the wail of a mortally wounded doe was torn from deep within her, and she turned and stumbled into the living room, where she curled up in an abject ball of misery on the sofa and sobbed.

After what seemed like an eternity she finally ran out of tears, and the sobs that nearly tore her apart quieted. How could she have been so blind as to have completely misjudged Erik? He'd never once indicated that he wasn't happy being married to her. He'd been loving, and attentive, and as passionate as any man could be. After she lost the baby he'd been deeply concerned for her. He'd consoled her and cared for her and understood her depressive moods.

He'd behaved exactly like a man who was passionately in love with his wife.

His actions should have told her what he hadn't yet been able to put into words. Good Lord, what more could she have wanted? She'd been so wrapped up in her own insecurities and self-pity that she'd never really tried to understand her husband. He'd been in love with another woman before he married her, but Erik wasn't the type to nurse a rejected love and brood over a woman who had treated him badly. She should have had more confidence in her ability to make him love her.

Was it too late now? Had she killed the budding feelings he'd admitted to? Would he ever trust her enough again to let himself care?

Her rumination was interrupted by the sound of Erik's footsteps hurrying toward the bathroom, and she knew he was being sick again. A dry sob of remorse shook her. He was a man of violent emotions. When Brett left him he'd destroyed the furniture. Now that he thought she had tried the same thing, he'd directed the violence inward and his stomach was turning inside out. How could he ever forgive her when she was responsible for the agony he was suffering?

She knew it would do no good to offer her help, so she walked into the kitchen and found the bottle of pink milky bismuth subsalicylate concoction that her mother always gave her family for an upset stomach. It usually worked. Colleen found a tablespoon and headed for the bedroom.

A few minutes later Erik reappeared wearing his pajama bottoms. He looked at her warily, and she knew that she looked awful, her eyes and face red and swollen from crying. He said nothing but walked past her and got back into bed.

She followed, then sat down beside him and poured the pink liquid into the tablespoon. "Here, take this," she said as her gaze roamed over his grim features.

He was propped up against the headboard, but shook his head. "I won't be able to keep it down."

"I think you will, and you can't go on like this all night." She put the spoon to his mouth and he swallowed the medicine.

"Now one more." She poured another spoonful and he took it.

She put the bottle and the spoon down on the bedside table, then reached over and brushed a lock of corn-colored hair off his pale brow. "Have you slept at all?"

"No."

She knew he'd heard her crying, but didn't flatter herself that it was the reason for his restlessness.

"Do you still feel sick?" She cupped his cheek with her hand and was disturbed that his skin was warm and dry.

Erik wasn't the type of man who would weep no matter how great the torment. He'd probably been taught that "big boys don't cry" when he was a child, and it had carried over into the macho image of the athlete who was too much of a man to shed tears. If he only would, it might take some of the pressure off his stomach.

He nodded in answer to her question, effectively dislodging her hand without actually withdrawing from her.

"Are you coming to bed?" he asked, but it didn't sound like an invitation, merely a question.

Whatever, it indicated that he was willing to sleep with her. "Yes," she said, "just as soon as I take a quick shower and brush my teeth." She leaned over and kissed him lightly on the lips. "I'll leave the bathroom door unlocked so you can come in if necessary."

She'd hoped he might come and join her in the shower, but it was a futile thought. She brushed her teeth, then turned out the bathroom light and crept silently into the bedroom.

He was lying on his side with his back to her when she turned off the lamp and slid into bed. He didn't move as she settled herself, and she knew he had no intention of turning over and taking her in his arms. Even from a distance she could feel the tension in him. He lay rigid beside her, as if the possibility of accidentally touching her was distasteful.

Well, what had she expected? Because of her self-centered absorption with her own uncertainties she'd dealt him a crippling blow, both to his ego and to his emotions. All she could do now was show him how much she loved him and pray that eventually he would let down his guard and give himself permission to love her in return.

Still, if he couldn't relax he'd never get to sleep. Tentatively she reached over and put her hand on his waist, afraid that he would move away from it. He didn't. He didn't react at all. If she hadn't known better she'd have thought he was asleep, except that usually when she touched him in sleep he would automatically snuggle closer.

Carefully she moved her hand up to the hard knotted muscles of his broad shoulders and massaged them lightly. At first he tightened up even more, but then he relaxed a little. She got up on her knees, then sat back on her heels and said, "Roll over on your stomach."

"Go to sleep, Colleen," he muttered, but he did as she asked, and she began a more effective massage on his shoulders and back.

As she worked, her hands caressed as well as massaged, but when she leaned over and nuzzled the nape of his neck he jerked away from her. "Lie down and go to sleep," he rasped.

She gave up and lay down again beside him.

A few minutes later she took a deep breath in the hope of steadying her voice, and tried again. "I can't sleep unless you hold me."

She held her breath for a long time before he responded. "I'd be no good for you tonight. Wait until tomorrow."

Some of her fear vanished. Apparently he wasn't planning on letting his rage interfere with their lovemaking for long.

She put her hand on his back again and stroked his bare flesh. "I wasn't asking you to make love with me, just to hold me so we can both sleep."

"Don't work so hard to seduce me." His tone was harsh. "It's not necessary. I have no intention of giving up my so-called connubial rights, but I'm too damn sick to do anything about it tonight. Now will you leave me alone?"

His angry words cut through her and left her breathless with pain. She removed her hand from his back and curled up on her own side of the bed, miserable and defeated.

She lay tense and quiet with no hope of sleep for what seemed like hours. Erik hadn't moved either, and since he usually shifted around quite a bit in his sleep, she knew he was as wide awake as she. Why did he insist on punishing them both? She felt the beginning stirrings of anger. He didn't have to be so damn stubborn.

Finally she couldn't stand it any longer and got out of bed. If he didn't want to sleep with her she wasn't going to force herself on him. She'd apologized. He could at least try to see her side of the situation.

It was chilly in the apartment, and without turning on the light she reached into the closet and fumbled for her plum velour robe. She put it on and tied it around her as she left the bedroom and walked down the short hall to the living room.

Maybe a mug of hot chocolate would help her relax and sleep. She went into the kitchen, turned on the light and heated some milk, then added a dollop of chocolate syrup. Not exactly a gourmet drink, but she wasn't in a gourmet mood.

She shut off the kitchen light and carried the mug into the darkened living room. There was a full moon, and it illuminated the apartment enough for her to get around without bumping into things. She sat down on the couch and took a sip of the hot drink. It tasted good and she would have offered to make some for Erik, but he'd told her in no uncertain terms not to bother him.

She was appalled at how much his cutting remark had hurt. He'd never said an unkind thing to her before, and he'd always welcomed her advances. In fact he'd seemed delighted the times she'd taken the initiative in their lovemaking. He'd told her once that men liked to be seduced by their women; it took some of the pressure off them in the playful game of loving.

She took a gulp of the cooling chocolate. Why had he so strongly resisted her attempts to make up tonight? He must have known that all she wanted was for them to cuddle together and sleep as they always did. Was he really so upset that he found her touch repulsive?

She drained the rest of the chocolate milk and put the mug on the coffee table, then curled up at the end of the sofa with her head on a decorative pillow. To her surprised relief she started to relax, and she had just gotten to sleep when she felt strong arms under her knees and her shoulders, lifting her.

She clasped her arms around Erik's neck and buried her face against his throat. His voice was low as he murmured, "Come back to bed. I need you. I can't sleep without you." He didn't sound happy about it, just resigned.

He carried her back to the bedroom, then set her down on her feet and took the robe off her. She climbed into bed, and he got in on the other side, then turned toward her and took her in his arms. She pushed herself upward until she could nestle his head against her satin- and lace-covered breast. His arms tightened around her, and she held him and stroked his cheek and hair gently until she felt him relax into a deep, healing sleep.

Erik slowly struggled upward out of the fog of sleep, his mind warning him not to wake up. He'd never been so comfortable in his life as he was right now, sprawled halfway over Colleen's soft yielding body, one of her thighs between both of his and his head cradled between the tantalizing rise of her breasts. If it weren't for the persistent nausea that kept his stomach in turmoil he could have persuaded himself that the events of the previous night were only the tormenting fantasy of a nightmare that had been banished in her loving arms.

He knew he should roll away from her and get up, put as much distance as possible between them until he got his fragmented emotions under control. What was the matter with him, anyway? He'd thought that Brett's desertion had caused him all the pain a human being could endure, but he'd never been incapacitated by it. When Colleen so casually mentioned that she wanted a divorce it was like a whopping kick in the belly that kept him heaving long after there was nothing left to come up. Then he'd demeaned himself by practically begging her to come back to bed because he couldn't make it through the night without her, and now he was clinging to her like a damn baby sucking its mother. The thought of moving out of her arms was intolerable.

Where the hell was his pride? Twice in three months he'd let women make a fool of him, and now he was practically asking for it again. Anyone could make the mistake once, but twice, and by women in the same family, was just plain stupid and it was about time he got the upper hand in this little game.

Oh, he'd give Colleen her divorce all right, but not until he was ready. She'd somehow insinuated herself under his skin when his guard was down, and he couldn't stand the pain of losing her yet, but he'd learn. He'd wean himself away from her in stages until he wouldn't even miss her, and then he'd be the one to walk. Never again would he give a woman the power to hurt him. Never.

Even in sleep Colleen was aware of Erik's body tangled with hers, and when he suddenly turned away she involuntarily clutched at him. But he slipped easily out of her sleepy grasp and sat on the edge of the bed. She opened her eyes and reached out to stroke his bare back. "Darling, are you all right?"

"I'm fine," he said coolly. "It's time to get up."

She struggled to a sitting position. "Do you feel like going to work? You were awfully sick last night, and you got very little sleep. Why don't you stay in bed today?"

He didn't answer but stood and headed toward the bathroom.

Colleen wrapped her arms around her legs and buried her face in her knees. Obviously he was still angry. When he'd carried her back to bed and held her so fiercely she'd hoped . . .

She sighed. She guessed she'd better be content with the fact that he didn't want a divorce. That was more than she'd expected to have this morning. She'd been so sure he'd be grateful for her offer of a way out of the marriage, but instead she'd hurt him even more cruelly than Brett had. Oh why hadn't she kept her mouth shut and just accepted the blessing she'd been given? Why hadn't she remembered that Erik was a grown man who was perfectly capable of asking for his freedom if that was what he'd wanted?

She'd made a wretched mistake, and now she'd have to be patient and work toward regaining his trust. She had to believe that in time she could make him understand how much she loved him. If he did, then maybe he could learn to love her. Her arms tightened around her legs and she rubbed her face against her knees in an effort to dislodge her anguish.

They dressed and went their separate ways that morning with a minimum of conversation. Colleen was aware that her makeup did little to hide the ravages of a night of weeping and worrying that marred her features. Erik looked just as bad.

April took one look at Colleen when she arrived at the boutique, then touched her gently and asked, "Do you want to talk about it?"

Colleen realized that she did. This was a burden she couldn't bear alone, and April was not only her sister-in-law but her dearest friend. "Yes," she said, then hesitated, "but you'll have to promise not to say anything to Devin."

April nodded. "Of course. When Rhoda gets here we'll take a break and you can tell me all about it."

Rhoda was a young housewife who helped out four hours in the middle of each day while her small children were in school.

An hour and a half later Colleen sat in the tiny crowded office and told April the whole upsetting story. She'd run out of tears, but her commentary was punctuated at intervals by shuddering sobs. April listened quietly without interrupting, until at last Colleen was finished. "I couldn't have hurt Erik more if I'd deliberately planned it," she said miserably. "And all I ever wanted was to make him happy."

April reached out and patted Colleen's hand. "I wish you'd discussed this with me before you did anything."

"So do I," admitted Colleen. "You'd have talked some sense into me."

"Well, that's water over the dam now. Would it help if I talked to Erik?"

Colleen shook her head. "No, he'd hate it if he knew I'd discussed this with an outsider, even you, and if Devin ever found out..."

April threw up her hands. "Devin," she snorted. "I adore that brother of yours but he's not the world's most perfect husband, and I don't know where he gets off expecting Erik to be. When he gets disagreeable with me and starts yelling, I holler right back at him. We have some lovely screaming matches, but at least we communicate. When they're over we know exactly where we stand, and the making up is worth all the hassle."

She looked dreamy for a minute, but then returned her attention to Colleen. "I'm afraid you and Erik don't communicate at all, you're each too afraid of revealing your true feelings. If you thought that Erik wanted out of your marriage after you lost the baby, you should have sat down and talked it over calmly with him, asked him how he felt. And he's not blameless, either. When he began to suspect he was in love with you he should have told you. He had no right to expect you to read his mind, although I must say you must have been blind not to have seen it."

"Seen it? Seen what? What are you talking about, April?"

"Seen his love for you shining from his face every time he looked at you," April replied. "It was there the day he married you, and it's been there ever since. He may not have recognized it, or more to the point been willing to admit it, but I don't know how you could have missed it. No one else did."

Colleen was stunned. Was it true? Had she really been so insensitive? If so, then she'd lost even more than she realized.

She left the shop early and had dinner ready when Erik got home. He looked exhausted, and merely called "hello" to her in the kitchen as he hung up his coat. Then he dropped down in the comfortable lounge chair in the living room.

Colleen took off her apron and hurried in to greet him properly. Usually he came to her, took her in his arms and kissed her hungrily when they came together at the end of the day. April was right; she'd been a blind fool not to recognize his feelings as going a lot deeper than "like." Had she killed that tenderness forever?

He looked up as she stopped by the side of his chair. "Oh darling," she said with dismay, "you look so tired."

She sat down on his lap and gently ran her finger over the lines of exhaustion in his face. "Is your stomach still bothering you?"

He was rigid with resistance, and she stifled a groan of disappointment. She'd hoped that he'd gotten over some of this overwhelming rage that kept him away from her.

He reached up and carefully removed her hand from his face. "I'm all right," he said. "How soon before dinner?"

She'd fixed a creamed chicken casserole, knowing that it would be easy to digest, and Erik ate a small portion. Colleen tried to keep the conversation going, but he said little and answered her questions with a short "yes" or "no." By the time the meal was over her nerves were stretched to the screaming point. How was she going to get through the rest of the evening if it was just more of this?

She needn't have worried. As she started to clear the table Erik carried his plate and silverware to the sink and said, "By the way, Colleen, I signed the lease on the Lawrences' apartment today. The manager is going to have it repainted, and he'd like you to get together with him as soon as possible to let him know what colors you want." He turned to leave. "Now, if you'll excuse me I'm going to take a shower and go to bed."

Without waiting for an answer he turned and headed for the bathroom.

Colleen watched, unable to move or speak. He'd gone ahead and signed the lease without even discussing it with her, even after she'd told him she didn't think they should move. Of course, that was when she thought they'd be separating, but still it was totally unlike Erik to bypass her completely when making such an important decision.

Three hours later when she climbed into bed he was again lying on his side with his back to her, but this time he was sound asleep. She sighed and curled herself against him, but if he knew he gave no sign and eventually she, too, slept.

Chapter Nine

The next morning was more of the same. Erik was up and dressed before she woke, and she didn't get a good-morning kiss. Not that she'd expected it; he hadn't kissed her since the quarrel. He looked much better after a good night's sleep; his color was coming back, and he no longer carried himself as if he expected to get sick any minute. When she asked him he said he felt fine, which told her nothing since he'd said the same thing the day before when it was obvious that he didn't. He was polite but not friendly.

Later that afternoon Trish, Erik's secretary, called Colleen at the boutique. "Mr. Johansen asked me to tell you not to fix dinner for him. He's tied up and won't be home until quite late."

Colleen thanked her and put down the phone. Why hadn't Erik called her himself? He'd never before sent her messages through his secretary. Was he really inundated with work or was it only a way to avoid spending the evening with her? She closed her eyes and wondered how much longer he was going to punish her.

That evening she fixed herself an omelet and ate it in front of the television as she watched the news broadcast. Later she tried to settle down with a novel, but she couldn't keep her mind on anything but the sounds of activity outside and in the hallways as tenants came and went. Each time a car drove up or footsteps sounded in the hall she hoped it was Erik. Finally at ten o'clock she took a hot shower and went to bed.

It was a long tension-filled hour later when she heard the key in the lock and the front door open. By that time she was too thoroughly upset, from alternating between fear that something had happened to him and anger that he would treat her this way, to feel welcoming. If he wanted anything from her tonight he could ask for it; she wasn't going to offer.

He didn't turn off the dim light she'd left on in the living room, but walked as softly as a big man can in the bedroom and undressed in the dark. She lay quietly with her eyes closed and said nothing. He left the bedroom and a few minutes later she heard water running in the shower.

When he returned, he got into bed and turned away from her and was soon asleep. Colleen lay dry-eyed and miserable, wondering how much longer she could go on this way.

Much to her surprise and delight, the next morning he apologized. Once again he was out of bed before she woke, but when he came into the bedroom and saw her sitting up he smiled.

"Good morning," he said. "Sorry I was so late last night. I got tied up with the auditors and it seemed wiser to keep at it until we were done. You were asleep when I got in so I tried not to wake you.''

Colleen felt an overwhelming surge of relief. So he hadn't deliberately avoided her. She smiled tremulously up at him. ''I heard you. I wish you'd said something.''

He stood looking at her for a moment, then leaned over and cupped her upturned face with his hands and kissed her on the nose. ''So do I,'' he murmured, but when she reached for him he straightened and backed away. ''Wait for me at the shop. I'll pick you up and take you out to dinner.''

All day long Colleen felt as if a weight had been lifted from her. Admittedly a buss on the nose wasn't exactly a declaration of overwhelming passion, but it was the first time he'd voluntarily touched her. Was it too much to hope that he was thawing a little? Also if he was taking her out to dinner it meant that they would be having the meal together.

She shared her happiness with April as readily as she had shared her anguish, and her sister-in-law hugged her. ''He won't be able to resist you for long,'' she promised. ''Men aren't made that way. When Devin and I quarrel he's even more passionate than usual. In fact, that's the way we got Shana.'' She was referring to her second daughter. ''We'd intended to wait until Mackenzie was a couple of years older before having another baby, but one day we had a blazing fight about something, and afterward in the heat of making up we forgot all about protection.''

Which reminded Colleen that she'd better get her prescription filled. She didn't want to spring any more surprises on her poor beleaguered husband.

Erik took her to a steak house where he ordered a ranch-size T-bone and she had a fillet. They ate hungrily, and Colleen realized that it was the first time since Wednesday that she'd enjoyed her food. They talked about the events of the day, and carefully skirted any mention of the subject uppermost in their minds.

They refused dessert but went into the lounge where Erik ordered a Kahlúa and cream for Colleen and Irish Cream whiskey for himself. They sat on one of the numerous comfortable love seats scattered around the room and relaxed. Erik had just finished telling her about the redecorating that was being done to one of the offices before the new general manager moved in. "That reminds me," he said and looked at her, "they're ready to start painting our new apartment. I told them we'd be over tomorrow evening to pick out the colors we want. Is that all right with you?"

She nodded, surprised that he hadn't consulted her first before making the appointment. "Yes, that's fine. Do you have any favorite colors?"

He shrugged. "Not really. I suppose it will depend on the furniture we choose. Would you prefer to go shopping for it first?"

She blinked. "It?"

"The new furniture. Do you want to buy it before we decide on the paint?"

"But I thought we'd agreed to use what we already have for now, and add to that later."

Erik finished off his cream whiskey. "There's no need to delay. It's foolish to move in furniture we don't intend to keep. Why don't we go shopping tomorrow night and wait until next week to pick out the paint?"

Colleen was still puzzled. "But honey, we can't afford six rooms of new furniture."

He frowned, and his tone was considerably cooler. "I don't know anything about your finances, but I can certainly afford to keep my wife in a style commensurate with my profession. I'll cancel the appointment for tomorrow and we'll go shopping for furniture instead." He signaled the cocktail waitress for another drink.

She bit back further argument, afraid he'd freeze up on her again. Why was he being so insistent about this? They'd discussed the question of furniture at length when they looked at the apartment, and it had been his suggestion to use what they already had and add to it as the opportunity came up. It would cost a fortune to furnish that big an area with new things. She didn't doubt that he could pay for it, but it would be a huge outlay and she would have been happy with what they already had.

It was late before they got home. Although she'd stopped after the small glass of Kahlúa and cream, Erik had had several drinks and they'd stayed on to listen to the balladeer, who accompanied himself on the dulcimer.

They talked little on the way home, but the silence wasn't companionable. Colleen was tense. Was Erik going to ignore her in bed again tonight? He'd seemed relaxed and not unhappy during the evening, but now she sensed the same tension in him that was tying her in knots.

At home Erik switched on the television to the late news, then turned to her and asked, "Do you want to shower first or shall I?"

They usually showered together.

She tried not to let him see the disappointment that was like lead in her stomach. "I will. You can watch the news."

When she finished she called to Erik to let him know the bathroom was free, then brushed her raven shoulder-length hair and crawled into bed. She was appalled to discover that she was trembling. If Erik turned away from her again tonight she didn't think she could stand it. They couldn't go on this way; it was rapidly strangling their marriage.

She huddled under the blanket until he finished his shower and entered the bedroom clad only in a towel around his hips. There was a suspicious bulge in the front of the towel, and she relaxed a little. At least tonight he was aroused.

He turned off the light and got into bed without bothering to put on the pajama bottoms he'd been wearing the past three nights. He lay on his back with his raised arms under his head, and Colleen held her breath. She simply couldn't lie beside him, shut out and rejected, one more night.

Finally he took a breath and spoke. "Are you—protected?"

"What?" She didn't understand what he meant.

"Protected."

She breathed a sigh of relief. "Oh, yes."

He turned toward her then and took her in his arms. She arched against him eagerly, and a shiver ran through him when he pressed into her firm hips. With a groan his mouth devoured hers as his hungry, seeking hands roamed over her roughly. She tried to keep up, but when he lifted himself over her and plunged deeply she winced with discomfort and knew he was too far ahead of her with no hope of slowing down.

It was over almost before it began, and when he shuddered and rolled away from her she felt—used. Had he done that on purpose? Was he telling her without words that her satisfaction was no longer important to him?

Oh no, not Erik! He was too tender and loving to do a despicable thing like that. Still, there had been nothing tender or loving about their lovemaking tonight.

They were both silent for several minutes, then he moved beside her and put his hand at her waist. "Colleen," he said hesitantly, "I'm sorry. I didn't mean for it to be like that."

She put her hand over his. "It's all right, I understand."

He squeezed her hand, then turned away from her onto his stomach without kissing her good-night.

Colleen had lost some of her glow the following day, but April didn't comment. Erik picked her up after work and they went shopping for furniture. He insisted on buying only the fine-quality pieces manufactured in the nearby city of Grand Rapids, and it was expensive. They chose a sofa and matching love seat in champagne-colored jacquard, a massive lounge chair in sunset-brown leather for Erik and assorted tables in cherry wood for the living room. They repeated the rich beautiful cherry wood for the dining-room set.

By then Colleen's brain was reeling with figures that added up to an astronomical sum and it was time for the store to close, so they had no choice but to wait before selecting the rest.

On the way home she began to feel uneasy again. Would tonight be a repeat of last night, or would Erik turn away from her again? Either would break her heart, and further undermine their marriage. She could understand his pain, but she would not allow him to abuse her. There was a fine line between the natural desire to protect one's own emotions and a desire to inflict pain on the person who had threatened those emotions. She loved Erik, but she would leave him if she thought he was taking a pervasive pleasure in tormenting her. She couldn't live like that, it would eventually crush her.

Once again she took her shower first while he watched the news, then got into bed and waited for him. He came out of the bathroom nude and partially aroused, and this time there was no hesitation. He got into bed and took her in his arms. She snuggled against him and his lips sought hers with a gentleness that brought an immediate response. Colleen relaxed. If anything went wrong tonight she knew it wouldn't be deliberate.

He cupped her breast, and she felt it swell and fit itself to his hand as if, with a mind of its own, it had hungered for his touch. He moved down and took the erect nipple in his mouth, and she felt the pull all the way to the core of her womanhood.

She caressed his back and shoulders, then moved her hands down to his firm buttocks. He brought his knee up between her thighs and moved his hand and mouth to the breast he'd been neglecting. She was delighted to discover that he was no longer only partially aroused; she knew that tonight she'd have no trouble keeping up. In fact if he didn't hurry she was going to be ahead of him.

He seemed intent on taking his time as he nibbled his way back up to her mouth. Her lips parted and his tongue made love to hers as his hands journeyed slowly down her sensitized body. She was lost to everything but the overwhelming sensations that kept her on the brink of madness, until she moved her hand between them and stroked him intimately. His whole body shuddered and his fingers clenched her soft flesh as he moved quickly to make her a part of him.

Erik's breath was still coming in gasps and he fought to slow it down as he cuddled Colleen close against him. Damn, what had happened to all his good intentions? He'd known better than to think he could remain celibate with her in the bed beside him, but he'd intended to handle their lovemaking with a cool finesse, a detachment that would give him release but not involve his emotions.

His arms tightened around her. Hell and damnation! Last night all he had had to do was touch her and he'd lost control completely. Tonight by reciting mathematical formulas in his head he'd managed to hang on until he was sure she was ready, and then he'd exploded into her almost immediately. Fortunately her control was no better than his this time. She'd never have forgiven him if he'd frustrated her two nights running.

What was there about this young wife of his that scrambled his efforts at detachment and left him vulnerable to anything she wanted to dish out? She'd told him she wanted a divorce and still he resisted, wanting her even if he had to buy her. It was a constant source of humiliation to him that any woman could have that much power over him. He'd never intended for it to happen, hadn't even known it had until she'd said she wanted out.

He winced. His stomach still turned over every time he thought about her standing there so calm and beautiful, telling him there was no longer any need to prolong their marriage.

As soon as he could he'd put her aside and turn away from her to sleep. He'd never be able to leave her if he slept with her in his arms every night, and he had every intention of leaving her. He'd wait until he was sure he could live without her, and then he'd be the one to ask for his freedom. No woman would ever walk out on him again.

For the next two weeks Colleen told herself everything was fine with her marriage, and outwardly it was. Erik no longer sulked, but his happy smile was rare and fleeting. He treated her with all the respect a wife could want, but theirs wasn't the relaxed loving relationship they'd shared before she'd mentioned divorce. He no longer hugged and kissed her impulsively, or used terms of endearment such as darling, sweetheart or honey. If he was delayed at the office he had his secretary call her instead of doing it himself. They had sex every night, but they never made love.

It took Colleen a couple of nights to discover why she felt dissatisfied with their nightly bouts between the sheets. Erik's technique was flawless. He never failed to take the time to arouse her, and they always reached a shattering climax together, but gradually she realized what was missing. It was the tender loving. The love play before they went to bed, the kissing and caressing that was a prelude to arousal, the whispered endearments and the cuddling together afterward.

Now he never touched her before they got into bed, and as soon as it was over he turned away from her and slept. The only thing that kept her from being too upset was the fact that in the middle of the night, when he was asleep, he would turn back and take her in his arms, exhale a little sigh and hold her close until morning. It was as if his body accepted what his mind would not— that he needed to hold her and let her hold him before he could sleep soundly.

They chose a color scheme for the apartment, and the painters were busy redecorating before they could move in. They went shopping again and chose furniture for the guest bedroom and the office. Colleen suggested that they leave the spare room vacant until they could furnish it as a nursery, but Erik seemed curiously unwilling. Finally, without telling him what she was doing, she selected pieces that would be suitable for a guest room now and a nursery later. She intended to get pregnant again as soon as possible after the six months Dr. Welch had decreed they should wait. Erik had known and agreed, so why was he reluctant now to plan for it?

One night, a good share of the reason for their problem was revealed to her when Erik brought her a gift. It was a beautifully wrapped oblong package, and he put it on her plate when her back was turned as she dished up dinner. "What's that?" she asked when she turned around and saw it.

"It's for you," he said.

"For me?" She picked it up and turned it over as a warm burst of pleasure flooded her. "But it's not my birthday or anything."

He was watching her expectantly, but without the excitement that usually built in him when he gave her a small gift or did something for her that he knew she'd like. "Well, go ahead and open it," he said and smiled.

She grinned happily and tore at the fancy wrappings. She loved surprise gifts.

It was a black velvet jewelry box with the name of one of the most prestigious jewelers in Detroit stamped on it in silver. Her blue eyes widened. She'd expected a pretty bauble or even a piece of costume jewelry, but this shop sold nothing but the real stuff.

Carefully she opened the lid and gasped. There, nestled on black satin, was the most exquisite premier diamond pendant she'd ever seen. There was no doubt of its authenticity. The stone was beautifully cut to allow for maximum scintillation and dispersion of light through it, and the twisted gold chain was heavy and expensive. The diamond was brilliant, almost colorless and as cold and hard as the motivation behind it.

Erik still thought he had to bribe her with expensive gifts to stay with him!

Now his insistence on buying an apartment full of new furniture made sense. It was part of the bribe. His cynical words hurled at her that dreadful day reverberated in her head. *You want something. What is it? How about jewelry?*

She knew the anguish she felt was mirrored in her eyes, and she couldn't look at him. She bowed her head and closed the case. "What's the matter?" he asked, his tone wary. "Don't you like it?"

The lump in her throat blocked any words she might have uttered. Instead she stood, laid the case on the table and made her way to the bathroom, the only room with a lock. She sat on the clothes hamper in the small crowded area and cried soundlessly.

After a few minutes there was a knock on the locked door. "Colleen, what's the matter? Are you all right?"

She didn't answer, just sat there letting the tears stream down her face unchecked.

Another knock, stronger this time. "Colleen, either answer me or come out. Are you all right?"

She shook her head, but made no sound. She just wanted him to go away so she could cry in peace.

This time the knock shook the door. "Goddammit, if you don't open this door I'm going to break it down." There was anxiety rather than anger in his voice. "I'll give you until the count of three. One—"

She turned the lock on the count of two, and he burst in, nearly knocking her down in the process.

He reached out and grabbed her shoulder to steady her. "What in hell has gotten into you?" he grated, then stopped as he got a good look at her. "You're crying," he accused.

"Damn right I am," she said with a sob, "and I'd appreciate a little privacy."

"You don't need privacy," he said tenderly, "you need a shoulder to cry on." He put his arms around her and gathered her close. "Now tell me why you don't like the necklace."

She buried her face in his shoulder. "I think the necklace is beautiful."

"Then what's the problem?"

"I don't want you to buy it for me."

He sighed. "Why not? Don't you care for diamonds? I admit they're not your type of jewel, but I thought all women liked them. What do you want? How about emeralds?"

She shook her head against him. "I don't want you to buy me anything, I just want you to trust me."

"Trust you to what?" he asked suspiciously.

"Trust me to love you," she murmured, and caressed the side of his neck with her lips.

"Oh God, if only I could," he whispered, more to himself than to her, then released her and reached for a tissue, which he handed her. "Here. Now dry your eyes and let's eat before everything is cold."

He took her arm and led her back toward the dining room. "Unless you'd rather have something else I'd prefer that you keep the pendant. You'll find it's much more dependable than love."

Colleen decided to give in gracefully and accept the expensive gift. It would do no good to argue with Erik about it and would merely upset him. The only way she could convince him of her love was by showing him in every way she could over a long period of time. He wouldn't trust her words, but maybe eventually he would trust her actions. Meanwhile she wore the pendant every day and exclusive of any other jewelry, as if it were a gift of love instead of a badge of possession.

Colleen and Erik were notified that they could move into the new apartment the last weekend in April, which gave them just a week to make all the arrangements. One task still undone was choosing the furnishings for their bedroom. Colleen tried again to reason with Erik and get him to agree to use what they had, but he was adamant. Everything had to be new.

They went shopping on Tuesday evening and found a gleaming, solid-brass king-size bed that Colleen coveted on sight. Erik had been unusually quiet during their search, and now he questioned the clerk hesitantly. "Does this same design come in twin size?"

Colleen gaped at him, sure she had misunderstood. *"Twin size?"*

He avoided looking at her directly. "I thought...well, there's plenty of room for two beds. I just thought we might sleep better...."

He plodded on but she'd stopped listening. Erik didn't want to sleep with her anymore! Why did he insist on bribing her with expensive gifts to stay with him when he didn't even want to share a bed with her? Thank God she wasn't feeling anything. She was numb! Oh, why had she ever gotten involved in a marriage of convenience?

She was aware of Erik's hands on her shoulders as he shook her gently. "Colleen, look, I'm sorry, I . . ."

She shook off his hands and finally managed to focus her gaze on him. His face mirrored concern, and he was saying something but the words weren't coming through to her. He didn't really want her. All he wanted was someone to keep his home running smoothly, and serve as a convenience when the urge struck him. He must be satisfied with her services because he was paying a high price in new furniture and jewelry.

Well, damn him to hell! She'd had enough of his sulking, his coldness and his insulting insinuations. If he was too damn lazy to warm up a TV dinner and a partner each time he needed one or the other, then he could do without. She wasn't going to be any man's convenience.

Erik had his hands on her again and was trying to pull her against him. This time she struck out and gave him a rough shove that took him by surprise and caused him to release her. She straightened to her full five feet six inches and glared at him. "You can take your twin beds and go to hell," she grated, then stalked past him and out of the store.

There was a city-transit bus at the curb loading passengers, and Colleen plunged into the group of people boarding it and got on just before the doors shut. She glanced out the window on her way down the aisle and saw Erik standing on the sidewalk looking up and down the street. He hadn't seen her. Good, let him worry for a change, although she wasn't at all sure he would.

She sank into the first empty seat, and only then realized that her heart was pounding and her breathing was labored. She must have run out of that store and onto the bus. She'd intended to exit coolly and gracefully, but she never seemed to do anything right.

Well, this time she would. She'd wait until she was sure Erik was asleep, then she'd go home and spend the night on the couch. In the morning, when she'd had a chance to calm down and act with a little dignity, she'd pack his things and tell him to leave. After all, it was her apartment. He could move into the big fancy one and sleep by himself to his heart's content. She'd learn to live without him. She was damned if she was going to stay with a man who didn't even want her in his bed except occasionally when his baser urges demanded fulfillment.

The bus run ended at one of Detroit's large suburban shopping centers, and Colleen got off and went into the enclosed mall. She wandered around for a while until she came to a movie theater. A double bill was advertised outside, and the last showing wasn't over until after midnight. It was the ideal place for her to spend the time until she was ready to go home.

She bought a ticket and started inside, then hesitated. She couldn't remember the last time she'd gone to a movie by herself. Was it safe? On the other hand it was probably safer than riding after dark on the city-transit system. She glanced around and saw a couple of uniformed security guards and a public telephone booth. If anybody bothered her the guard was close by, and she could call a cab when she was ready to leave.

She handed her ticket to the girl at the door and walked inside.

By the time she'd sat through both shows she was feeling much calmer. According to her wristwatch it was twenty minutes past midnight, and it would take her at least half an hour to get home. Surely Erik would be asleep by then. She really didn't want to confront him tonight.

It was almost one o'clock when the cab pulled up in front of the big white Victorian house that she called home. There were no lights on in her second-floor apartment. The driver waited until she'd unlocked the front door and had gone inside before he drove on. The foyer was dimly lit as always at night, and she made her way up the stairs.

She inserted her key quietly and pushed open the door, then closed it behind her. She'd noticed from the outside that the front drapes were pulled, and the living room was in total darkness. She reached for the light switch, but before she could flip it the lamp by the lounge chair came on, and she saw Erik sitting there looking up at her.

She'd hoped he might worry about her, but he looked as if he'd spent the time she'd been gone stretched on the rack. In spite of herself she winced when he rose slowly as though with difficulty from the chair. "Wh— why are you sitting here in the dark?" she asked, unable to either rail at him or apologize for upsetting him so.

He walked wearily toward her. "I was afraid you wouldn't come home if you knew I was here."

He stopped in front of her and touched her face with his fingertips, as though assuring himself she was real.

"Are you all right?" She recognized the look in his green eyes as a mixture of pain and fear.

"Yes," she said, "I went to a movie. It was a double feature."

His tenuous composure disintegrated then, and he clasped her in his arms so tightly that she could hardly breathe. "Oh, dear Lord," he murmured brokenly, "I've been alternately going crazy and dying by inches. You looked at me like I'd slapped you and then just disappeared off the face of the earth. I walked up and down the street calling for you, but it was as if you'd evaporated into thin air."

He was shivering, and she couldn't resist the urge to put her arms around his neck and hold him. She'd never dreamed he'd be so distraught. "I got on a bus that was just leaving the curb in front of the store. It took me to a shopping mall, so I went to a movie until I'd calmed down enough to come home."

He rubbed his cheek in her hair. "Sweetheart, I'm so sorry. I don't know why I even asked about those damn twin beds."

She cringed and he held her even closer. "Yes, I do," he continued. "I thought if we slept in separate beds I couldn't reach for you in my sleep, and maybe I could eventually learn to live without you."

She felt a stab of anguish. "You want to learn to live without me?"

"No!" It was a cry that seemed to have been torn from deep inside him. "Oh no. It's not possible anyway, but I thought you wanted to leave me and I was determined to learn to live without you so I could let you go."

So that was why he'd seemed reluctant to let her get close to him either physically or emotionally. Why, he'd been acting more like a brother than a husband except when they crawled into bed together at night. Then he'd been her reluctant lover.

That was what had been bothering her. He'd been making love to her as if it were strictly forbidden but he couldn't help himself!

She stroked her fingers through his disheveled hair. "Erik, I told you I only offered you your freedom because I thought it was what you wanted. I love you, my darling. I've loved you ever since I was eight years old and Devin brought you home to me. There's never been anyone else, you have to believe that. I know you don't love me but—"

"You're the dearest person in the world to me," he murmured as he nipped at the underside of her jaw. "Do you think I'd suffer such torment when you casually mention leaving me if you weren't?"

She knew that what he said was true. She was dear to him, and though it wasn't the same as the overpowering love he'd felt for Brett it was enough for now. Eventually she'd teach him to love her the way she loved him.

She stood on tiptoe and whispered in his ear, "It's awfully late. Do you suppose you could conquer your modesty long enough to shower with me tonight, Mr. Johansen?"

He outlined the creases of her ear with his tongue before he whispered back, "It will be my pleasure, Mrs. Johansen."

He kissed her then with a passion so filled with relief and need that the shower was forgotten until early the next morning.

For almost two weeks Colleen existed in a glow of happiness. It radiated from her, and from Erik, and was commented on with envy by family and friends. They curled up with their arms around each other for hours and talked, sharing the doubts and uncertainties they should have discussed from the start. At night they were truly lovers, with nothing to mar the glory of their coming together in the most intimate form of communication.

They moved into the new larger apartment, and Colleen was glad Erik had insisted they lease it. He was right, it was perfect for them. He also bought her a new car, a blue Ford Tempo that suited her perfectly. She could accept this gift from her generous husband with delight because she knew it wasn't given as a bribe, but as a convenience and a pleasure.

Then one Friday in mid-May when the last of the snow had melted and colorful daffodils and tulips were just beginning to bloom, Colleen was ringing up a sale at the boutique when a startlingly familiar voice spoke from directly in front of her. "Hello, Colleen. I just stopped by to let you know I'm back, and this time I'm going to stay. Count on it."

Colleen dropped the package she was holding and looked up into the exquisitely beautiful face of her cousin, Brett Kendrick, the woman Erik loved.

Chapter Ten

Colleen felt the shock all the way to her toes. Brett! But it couldn't be. She was halfway around the world from Detroit.

She knew her dismay was written on her face, and Brett's lips curled into a nasty little smile. "I trusted you and you moved in on my man." Her voice was deadly. "That wasn't very nice, little cousin. You kept telling me how heartbroken he'd be when I left, but he must have recovered in a hell of a hurry. What did you do, take him to bed to console him and then make him feel so guilty that he did the 'proper' thing and married you?"

Her tone was cool and controlled, but Colleen was familiar with the icy rage it concealed.

She continued to stare, unable to think or put words together in a coherent form. What Brett had said was too close to the truth.

It was April who saved her as she walked over. "Why Brett, what on earth are you doing here?" She picked up the package Colleen had dropped on the counter and handed it to the interested customer, who then reluctantly walked away.

Brett's gaze released Colleen as she turned to the intruder. "Detroit's my home, April, I have as much right to be here as any of you."

April glanced quickly at Colleen, then turned her attention to the other woman. "Of course you do, but I understood you were in Europe gracing some of the historic shrines for posterity and Monique St. Amour cosmetics."

"Then your understanding was in error," Brett snapped. "That project's been scrapped so I decided to come home. I must say neither of you seem especially glad to see me."

Her green-flecked brown eyes widened as they focused again on Colleen. "Not feeling a little conscience-stricken are you, dear?"

The shock was finally wearing off, and anger replaced it. "Don't hold your breath," Colleen said shortly. "When did you get here? I talked to your mother a couple of days ago and she didn't say anything about you coming home."

Brett shrugged. "She didn't know, I didn't make up my mind for sure until yesterday. My flight just got in and I rented a car at the airport. I'm on my way home now to surprise her and Dad."

"Oh, Aunt Glenna and Uncle Logan will be surprised, all right. I'm sure they'll welcome you with all the warmth you feel is missing in April and me."

April spoke up. "How long did you say you intend to stay?"

One of Brett's perfectly shaped eyebrows raised inquiringly. "I thought I made that clear, but I don't mind repeating it. I plan to make my home here now."

"If I remember correctly that's what you said last time," April reminded her sweetly.

"True," Brett agreed, "but this time I mean it. I even have a job. I'll be doing fashion modeling for one of the agencies here in Detroit."

Colleen gripped the cash register and closed her eyes. Oh, dear God! Why did Brett have to come back? What had gone wrong with her fabulous offer from Monique St. Amour? How would Erik react to seeing her again?

Thank heaven April was carrying on the conversation while Colleen tried to pull herself together. April was saying, "Will you be staying with your parents again?"

"Only until I can find an apartment," Brett replied. "I'll also need a car." Her gaze returned to Colleen. "What happened to my Thunderbird, Colleen? Did Erik give it to you?"

Colleen gritted her teeth and hoped she wouldn't scream. "He sold it," she said, and was pleased that her voice was cool and steady. "You were very definite about never coming back."

"Ah yes." Brett sighed. "That was a mistake, but I'm hoping to reclaim everything I gave up so hastily." She looked directly at Colleen and her brown eyes were icy. "Everything."

Erik put down the phone and looked at his watch. Twelve-thirty. He might as well go to lunch now, he didn't have any more appointments scheduled until two.

He stood and started to walk away from his desk when the light on his intercom blinked. He flipped the switch. "Yes, Trish?"

"Ms. Kendrick is here to see you, sir. She doesn't have an appointment."

"Glenna?" He was surprised. Brett's mother never called on him at work.

"No sir." Trish sounded strained. "It's Brett Kendrick."

"Brett!" He rocked backward, as off balance as if he'd been hit by a giant fist. Good God, what was Brett doing here?

"Give me a few minutes, then send her in," he said raggedly as he sank back down in his chair.

What in hell did Brett want with him? Hadn't she done enough damage? Did she have to come back and wreak more havoc? He rubbed his hands over his face. Damn her, why wasn't she in Europe, or wherever she was supposed to be? Or if she had to come back why didn't she stay the hell away from him?

Automatically he checked his tie and brushed a lock of hair away from his forehead, then stood as the door opened.

Brett walked in looking every bit as beautiful as he'd remembered. She wore a brown suit and a silky blouse the same honey color as the soft vibrant hair that swung unrestrained, like a cloud, around her face and shoulders. Her smile was hesitant, little more than a gentle relaxing of her full apricot-tinted lips, and her almond-shaped eyes shimmered with uncertainty.

For a moment they just stood there looking at each other. Finally Brett was the first to speak. "Aren't you even going to say hello?" Her voice was husky.

Erik forced his clenched jaws to relax. Damned if he was going to let her know how shaken he was. "Why should I? You didn't say goodbye," he said, and was relieved that his own voice was cool and controlled. "Sit down, Brett." He motioned to the chair in front of his desk. "What are you doing back in town?"

She walked over and lowered herself gracefully into the chair. No matter what or how Brett moved she was graceful, and sexy. He continued to watch her with an assumed mask of indifference.

Slowly she crossed her long slender legs and leaned back in her chair. "I've come home to live," she said carefully. "I'm going to be doing fashion modeling for one of the agencies here in Detroit."

Damn it to hell. Erik flexed his fingers slightly so he wouldn't clench them into fists. "What happened to the assignment for the cosmetic company? I understood that would be a long-term deal." His casual tone cost him plenty.

Brett lowered her eyes. "It was supposed to be, but I'm afraid I didn't measure up to their expectations. In plain words, they fired me."

He frowned, interested in spite of his resolution not to be. "What do you mean, fired you? Didn't you have a contract?"

She nodded, but still refused to meet his gaze. "Yes, but there was a clause in it that if, in the company's sole estimation, the pictures did not meet their 'high standards' then I could be 'released' with no obligation on their part."

"That's got to be illegal." Erik was appalled that any legal document could have such a loophole.

"No," said Brett, "it's not. Not when it's worded properly, and this contract was drawn up by Monique

St. Amour's high-powered legal department. Apparently it's fairly standard."

Now Erik was totally involved in the discussion. "But surely there was nothing wrong with your pictures. You've been a successful photographers' model for years."

Brett finally raised her eyes and looked at him through their pain-filled depths. "But that's just the problem, love," she murmured. "They decided I was too old."

She bowed her head again, and Erik swore. "Too old! You're only twenty-eight, for God's sake."

"I just turned twenty-nine," she said bitterly, "and the most successful photographers' models are in their late teens and early twenties. The test pictures they took of me in the studio were great, but the first ones we shot on location at the Lincoln Memorial in Washington, D.C., had to be scrapped. The people in charge claimed that outside in the natural sunlight the camera picked up and photographed the extra years. In their words, I simply didn't come across as 'the dewy-eyed, innocent young girl-next-door type' they were looking for. They pointed to that damned clause in my contract and sent me packing."

Erik sat sprawled in his chair, tapping his fingers on the arm. "But why come back here? Surely there are other advertising accounts in New York that focus on the more sophisticated type of woman. You're not going to do your career any good in Detroit."

Her short laugh was more of a jeer. "Erik, darling, you're too kind. Even in the sophisticated ads the models are seldom over twenty-five. No, I was right the first time I came home. My career as a photographers' model is definitely over. I'll do okay as a fashion model.

I've got the figure and the flair for it, and on the ramp it doesn't matter if your face no longer looks eighteen."

"Sounds reasonable, but surely New York has more opportunities for fashion models than Detroit."

"And more competition." Brett's expression pleaded with him to understand. "Every pretty girl in America with dreams of being a model or an actress goes to New York City. For every opening in those professions there are hundreds of desperate women to fill it. I can earn a great deal more in Detroit than I could ever hope to in the Big Apple."

She uncrossed her legs and leaned forward, her hands turned upward in supplication. "Oh Erik, the biggest mistake I ever made was choosing that offer from Monique St. Amour over you and our marriage. You can't know how deeply I've regretted it."

He felt a sharp thrill of satisfaction and shifted uncomfortably. Mustn't let this conversation get personal. "Yes, well, that's all in the past. I don't flatter myself that you'd have regretted the decision if your pictures had been exactly what the company wanted."

Brett tensed, and her expressive eyes narrowed. "I notice you didn't lose any time grieving over our canceled wedding. You just substituted my cousin for me and went right ahead with it."

Not grieved? Erik's hands gripped the arms of his chair. How one fragile-looking, self-centered woman could have unleashed such torment in a grown man who'd been around as much as he had was a mystery he wasn't prepared to delve into. He forced himself to relax before he spoke. "I'd say it all worked out for the best, Brett. We'd never have been happy together. Actually, you did me a favor. Colleen is everything I could ever want in a wife."

He enjoyed watching that jab hit home even as he chided himself for his cruelty. This couldn't be easy for Brett. She'd given up everything for that job, and now she'd had to crawl back home with her pride in tatters.

Brett winced at Erik's words, but her expression remained calm. "I'm sure she is, now, but eventually you'll get tired of all that sweet submissiveness. You're too much like me, love. You need the more rough-and-tumble relationship, both in and out of bed."

She stood and so did he. "I must run," she said as she hooked the long straps of her leather purse over her slender shoulder. "I just got in this morning and haven't even been home yet."

She walked across the room and Erik followed. At the door she turned to face him. "Do me a favor? Don't tell anyone I was fired. I'd rather the family thought I quit."

She held her hand out to him, and he looked quickly away. No way was he going to touch her. This woman was dynamite and he wasn't lighting any fuses. "Of course, Brett," he said and opened the door for her. "I hope everything will work out all right for you."

She dropped her ignored hand and smiled. "Oh, it will, Erik. I guarantee you, it will."

Colleen got home before Erik. She usually did now that she had her own car and didn't have to rely on bus schedules. She'd always been convinced that a car would be more of a problem than a convenience in a city the size of Detroit, but she'd been wrong. She loved her Tempo.

She also loved her husband, and her head throbbed with the pain of wondering how she was going to keep him now that Brett was back and ready to take up where they'd left off. Not that she was afraid he'd walk out on her. Quite the contrary. Erik was an honorable man, and he'd never leave his wife for another woman. But could he control his feelings as well as he controlled his actions?

How did he feel about Brett? How would he feel about her once he saw her again, knew that she was living within arm's length? He'd loved her deeply only a few months ago. Had Brett killed that love when she'd deserted him practically at the altar for her career? Or was it still there, capable of being fanned into flame again at her touch, her smile, her nearness?

Colleen shivered. Oh, why did Brett have to come back? And just when things were going so well with their marriage. Erik had told Colleen he cared for her and she believed him, but was that caring strong enough to survive the constant awareness of the passion he'd felt for her cousin? She didn't believe for a moment that Brett would fade into the background and leave them alone. She was a part of Colleen's close-knit family, and she'd made it plain this morning that she considered Erik hers for the taking.

Colleen had dinner ready by the time she heard Erik at the door. Usually he walked hurriedly, with a jaunty swing, but now his steps seemed to drag with a reluctance that told her more than she wanted to know.

Erik knew that Brett was back.

Colleen met him at the door, and as usual he took her in his arms and kissed her, but it was a chaste kiss, more like that of a dutiful brother than a passionate husband. They looked at each other and she saw the harried, uncertain expression he was unable to hide. "You know that Brett's home, don't you," she said quietly, and it was a statement not a question.

His arms tightened around her and he rested his chin on the top of her head. "Yes, I do, but how did you know?"

"Brett stopped at the boutique on her way home from the airport."

"It didn't occur to me that she'd seek you out. Damn her, did she upset you?"

"We didn't have a screaming hair-pulling match if that's what you mean, but yes, she upset me. She wants you back."

Colleen hadn't meant to add that last remark, and she bit her lower lip in remorse as he let go of her. "Did she tell you that?"

Now that she'd raised the subject she had no choice but to answer him. "Yes, more or less."

His expression was bland, unreadable. "And you let it bother you?"

She nodded.

He sighed. "Ah, Colleen, I'm sorry you find it so difficult to trust me." He put his arms around her again and held her. "Don't you know how deeply I care for you? Haven't I shown you often enough? Don't you understand that you're the most important person in my world?"

She clutched him around the waist and pressed herself against him. "Erik, my darling, I'd trust you with my life, and yes, you do show me how much I mean to you. It's just that I was so shocked to see her. I had no idea she wasn't happily trailing around Europe." She pushed herself back so she could look up at him. "By the way, how did you know she was here?"

He looked a little unsettled. "She came to see me, too. It must have been right after she left the boutique. I was just getting ready to go to lunch."

The fear Colleen had successfully banished minutes before came pounding back. "Oh. Did you take her with you?" She couldn't bear the thought of him taking Brett to lunch.

He dipped his head and kissed her on the nose. "No, I didn't take her with me. I got rid of her as quickly as I could. I don't need that kind of gossip going around the office. I'm sure the place is buzzing with speculation as it is. Brett is the most insensitive person I've ever known, and I've no intention of letting her upset you."

Colleen let out her breath with relief. "What did she say to you?"

"Not much. Just that the promotion deal with St. Amour had fallen through and she'd come back to Detroit to do some fashion modeling."

Colleen suspected there must have been more, but she wasn't going to grill him. She knew he wouldn't welcome Brett back with open arms at noon and still be so sweet with her only a few hours later. No, whatever had happened in Erik's office, it hadn't been physical.

The following Sunday Brett's parents held an open house in honor of their daughter, and all of Colleen and Brett's large family were expected to attend. When Colleen told Erik of the invitation he brushed it aside. "Tell them we can't come."

"I did," she said, "but Aunt Glenna won't take no for an answer."

"Then tell her we're going out of town for the weekend."

Colleen looked at him. "Are we?"

He hesitated. "No, I can't. I have to work Saturday. Can't we just say we're going?"

She sighed. "You know how the grapevine in my family works. Aunt Glenna and Uncle Logan would know before the day was over that we were in town and had deliberately stayed away. Aunt Glenna would berate my mother and Mom would come down on me. I'm afraid it would look like we couldn't face Brett."

Erik muttered an oath. "I suspect you're right. We'll have to accept the fact that there's no way of avoiding her. We might as well get that first public confrontation over with. Tell Glenna we'll come. We can just drop in, say hello, have a drink and leave."

It didn't quite work out that way. The hours were set from noon to seven with a continuous buffet of sandwiches, salads, soup and desserts, plus a bar. The guests could come at their convenience and stay as long as they pleased. Colleen and Erik planned to arrive a little after three, assuming that the middle hours would be the most popular and they could come and go quickly without anyone noticing.

Colleen's mother was watching for them when they walked into the crowded house. "Colleen, I thought you'd never get here," Katherine complained. "We need help in the kitchen. One of your Aunt Jeanette's children got sick and Jeanette had to take her home. You won't mind filling in for her, will you?"

Aunt Jeanette was the youngest of her mother's three sisters and two brothers.

Colleen's hopes of an early departure plummeted. "Well I— Gosh, Mom, we'd planned on leaving—"

Katherine wasn't one to allow a child of hers to shirk her family duty. "Nonsense, you just got here. The crowd will thin out after a while and then you can circulate. Erik won't mind, will you, dear?'' She looked at him with full confidence of his agreement.

His smile was a little forced, but he didn't disappoint his mother-in-law. ''Of course not. I'll help too.''

''There's no need for that,'' Katherine insisted. ''There's nothing more useless than a man in the kitchen. Mick and Devin are around here somewhere, you go talk to them.''

She took Colleen's arm and headed toward the kitchen without giving her daughter a chance to protest further.

Colleen grimly tied an apron over her scarlet silk dress and reminded herself that neither her parents nor any of her other relatives except Devin and April knew the circumstances of Erik and Colleen's wedding. They all assumed that Colleen and Erik had discovered they loved each other after Brett left town, and shortly thereafter were married. They didn't know that Erik had only married her because she was pregnant, or that she later lost the baby. They didn't know that Erik was probably still in love with Brett no matter how vehemently he protested otherwise. She knew her mother would never have separated Erik and Colleen this afternoon if she'd known the truth, and the truth was something Colleen couldn't tell her.

As Colleen went between the kitchen and the dining room replenishing food for the buffet she watched for Erik. First she saw him with her father, Mick O'Farrell, and she smiled and waved at both of them. The second time he was talking to Brett. He had his back to Colleen, but she had a full view of Brett smiling and hanging on his every word. She looked away quickly, unwilling to let Brett think she was watching them.

After that she didn't see either Erik or Brett, and her imagination ran wild. Were they together? If so, where? What were they doing? Why was she stuck in the kitchen while Brett was making a play for her husband? To hell with the food. She'd been hidden away for over an hour, let someone else take over. She pulled off the apron and went in search of Erik.

She found him in the den sitting on the sofa with Brett. Several of Erik and Brett's friends who had been scheduled to take part in their suddenly canceled wedding were grouped around, and their hearty laughter was what had attracted Colleen to the den. It sounded as if they were having a great time, a happy reunion to which Colleen hadn't been invited.

The merriment faded as they gradually became aware of her standing in the doorway. Erik didn't see her immediately, and when he did she couldn't mistake the initial look of guilt that flashed across his features before he brought it under control.

He jumped up more quickly than was really necessary. "Hi, honey," he said, "are you finished with KP? I was just about to come looking for you."

"So I see." The sarcastic words were out before she could discipline her tongue, and she saw the smug look on Brett's face.

Something inside Colleen snapped. She wasn't going to be made a fool of. "I'm ready to leave, Erik," she said, and tossed her head impatiently. "I'll wait for you in the car." She turned and walked away.

Erik caught up with her in two long strides. His hand fastened roughly around her arm and slowed her down to walk beside him. "Smile, dammit," he commanded as he took his own advice and nodded pleasantly to a woman who waved to him.

They proceeded at his leisurely pace, stopping at times to say goodbye as they headed for the front door. Once inside the car he turned and glared at her. "Now what was that all about?"

Colleen's temper simmered. "I don't know what you mean."

"Oh, knock it off." Erik jammed the key in the ignition and started the engine. "If you're going to behave like a shrew, at least be honest enough to tell me what brought it on." He let the motor run while he sat waiting for her answer.

"A shrew!" She was incensed. "Just how was I supposed to act when I walk in and find my husband being chummy with the woman he wishes he'd married?"

"Oh for..." He slammed the gear shift into Drive and maneuvered the high-powered car out of the tight parking space before he continued. "I'm not going to dignify that remark with an answer. If you hadn't been hiding in the kitchen you'd have been with me, and there wouldn't have been a problem."

"Oh no, you're not going to place the blame on me." Even as she spoke she knew she was overreacting, but she couldn't help it. She felt so inadequate around Brett. "You know I had no choice. Mom needed help."

"You had a choice, Colleen," he grated. "That wasn't your party, or your mother's either for that matter. All you had to do was refuse. There wasn't one of those guests who would have starved if the food had been a little slow in appearing. Your place was with me, not running around like a good little girl doing your mother's bidding."

She knew he was right, and the knowledge fueled her irrational anger. "Are you telling me that you can't be trusted out of my sight, so from now on I'm going to have to follow you around like a shadow to keep you away from Brett?'' She hated the way she sounded. He was right, she was a shrew.

Erik muttered a coarse expletive and his hands tightened around the steering wheel. He pushed down on the gas pedal and broke all speed limits as he drove the rest of the way home in silence.

At the apartment Colleen changed into jeans and busied herself with housecleaning, while Erik turned on a baseball game and buried his attention in the television. They spoke only when necessary.

Colleen hated the silent tension, and the fact that it was mostly her fault didn't make it any easier. Erik was right, she should have stayed with him. Her first duty was to her husband, and she'd been an idiot not to have realized that.

Or had she? Had she agreed to help so she could hide in the kitchen, as Erik had put it? Had she subconsciously not wanted to be present when he and Brett met for the first time in public since the aborted wedding? But that wasn't subconscious. She'd known it would be painful, but it was also inevitable. Had she panicked as the time drew nearer and jumped at the first excuse to shove her head in the sand and hope the unpleasantness would go away?

She had to admit that it was entirely possible. She was terrified that Brett was going to take Erik away from her again. Not that she'd really had him before Brett came into the picture the first time, but they'd been going together and she'd hoped that eventually he would fall in love with her. She was still hoping, but she was afraid the chances were slim with Brett in the picture again.

Colleen pushed the vacuum cleaner across the deep pile of the carpet with all her pent-up frustration. She hated the jealousy that was eating at her. Why couldn't she believe Erik when he said she was precious to him and he wanted to be married to her? He'd always been loving, and seemed content. But would he be content now that Brett was home and available? Brett was his first choice, the woman he'd fallen in love with even though he'd been dating Colleen at the time, and Colleen had given him plenty of reason to fall in love with her if he were ever going to. She'd shown him in every way she could that she loved him. Every way except sleeping with him, and the only reason she hadn't done that was because he'd never suggested it.

No, Erik hadn't been in love with her when he married her, and he wasn't in love with her now. She knew she was special to him, that he was grateful to her for making his life bearable after Brett walked out, and that he'd come to depend on her as a wife. That would have been a foundation on which they could build a lasting marriage if Brett had stayed away, but now she was back. Could the passion Colleen aroused in him transcend the deep love he'd felt for Brett such a short time before?

That night when they went to bed they'd reached the stage of being polite but uncommunicative. Each kept to his and her own side of the wide bed, and Colleen was miserable. Since she'd been the one to start the quarrel she should make the first move toward ending it, but the memory of their last row was still too vivid in her mind. She didn't think she could stand to open herself up to the cold rejection she knew he was capable of.

While she was lying there trying to think of a way to approach him he finally broke the silence. "I think I have a problem." His voice was suspiciously gentle.

"You have?" She was surprised, and a little uneasy. "What?"

He reached over and took her hand and directed her to him. "I think I need you," he stated simply.

All the wary tension drained out of her, and was replaced with a tremor that started deep within her most erogenous zones and spread outward. "Yes, you do," she whispered sympathetically.

He turned to her then, dislodging her hand, and took her in his arms. "I don't want to quarrel with you, sweetheart." He kissed her closed eyelids and the tip of her nose. "I'm sorry I upset you by talking to Brett, but there wasn't any way I could avoid it without being obvious and causing a lot of speculation."

She captured his elusive lips with her own and snuggled against him. "I know, darling, and I'm the one who should apologize. I knew I was overreacting but I couldn't stop myself. I was..."

She'd started to say *I was so afraid*, but she didn't want to appear to beg for his fidelity. If he couldn't give it voluntarily it would bring her nothing but pain. "I was jealous," she substituted. Jealousy was an emotion she could more easily admit. "Brett's so beautiful and sophisticated."

He was nibbling his way down the side of her throat. "A lot of women are beautiful and sophisticated." His mouth reached the rise of her breast. "But not many are beautiful, and pliant in bed the way you are."

Pliant? She wasn't sure what he meant, but his tongue was circling her nipple and she was rapidly losing her train of thought.

"Yielding. Adaptable. Loving. Willing to give as well as receive," he murmured as he trailed kisses where his tongue had led. "For one who started out so innocent four months ago you've learned with amazing speed."

He took the nipple in his mouth and sucked gently.

She gathered two fistfuls of his shaggy blond hair, and shifted so that she could accommodate his impatient thrusts. "Do you think I could have another lesson to refresh my memory?" She spoke in soft little gasps as her eager body sought fulfillment.

He positioned himself above her. "Happy to oblige," he groaned as he slid into her ready softness, and ravaged her mouth with his own.

Chapter Eleven

Erik hurried into the lobby of the Dearborn Hyatt Regency Hotel and took the elevator to the revolving rooftop restaurant. He was five minutes late for his lunch date with Paul Forbes, and he didn't like to keep the senator waiting.

Erik gave his name to the hostess and explained that he was meeting Senator Forbes. On learning that Paul hadn't yet arrived he told her he'd wait in the bar. The room was crowded, and he ordered a whiskey on the rocks from the bartender. He was standing there nursing his drink along when a familiar, husky feminine voice spoke from behind him. "Hello, Erik, what a surprise running into you here."

He turned and looked squarely into Brett's beautiful, expressive brown eyes. A warm rush of feeling swept over him and he almost reached out for her before he caught himself and stopped. Damn! When was his body going to get the message his mind was frantically sending it, that she was off limits and not worth the trouble it cost him to be polite to her?

"Brett," he said. "Are you doing a show here this noon?"

Her low laugh was sexy as hell. "No, I'm meeting a realtor for lunch, and afterward we're going to look at some apartments. I got here before him so I decided to have a drink while I wait. I've a table, come share it with me."

So she was meeting a man. He glanced around the room. "I'd better stay here, I'm expecting a business acquaintance."

She put her arm through his and tugged. "You can wait at the table just as well. I'll let you have the chair facing the door. Come on, I don't like to sit alone in a bar."

He knew he should refuse, but he didn't want to give her the advantage of knowing she made him uneasy.

She led him to a small round table, and he seated her and then himself. Brett led off the conversation. "Do you come here often for lunch?"

He nodded. "It's close to the office, and they take reservations so I can get right in." He glanced at his watch. "That is, I can when the person I'm lunching with is also on time."

Her smile could only be described as dazzling. "Don't be so impatient. We have a lot to catch up on."

Her hair was the color of warm honey as it swirled around her shoulders, and he remembered how soft it had been when he'd stroked it away from her face, how deliciously tousled it looked in the early morning. He clamped a lid on his thoughts and quickly changed the subject. "I gather you're looking for an apartment to lease."

"Right," she agreed. "I love my parents dearly, but living with them is something else again. They treat me like a teenager, and I'm not used to having my comings and goings monitored."

He couldn't suppress a grin. How true. Brett had never been answerable to anyone, not even him. She'd made it plain that when they married she wouldn't give up so much as a shred of her independence. He was jolted to realize that for all her beauty and desirability she'd be a bitch to live with.

"Decent apartments aren't easy to come by," he said. "Do you have anything special in mind?"

She shrugged. "It'll have to be within my price range. I won't make as much money doing fashion shows as I did as a photographers' model." She dipped her head, then looked up at him through thick sable lashes, and there was a catch in her voice as she asked, "Erik, why did you give up our apartment?"

Her words had the thrust of a knife. His hand clenched around his glass, and he tore his gaze from hers just in time to see Paul Forbes walk through the door. He'd never been so happy to see anyone in his life, and he lifted his arm and waved to catch Paul's eye.

It worked, and the senator walked toward them. Erik stood and greeted him, then introduced him to Brett. Paul was a Michigan state senator. He was in his early forties, tall and slender, with blue eyes and dark hair with a touch of white at the temples. He looked down at Brett, making no attempt to hide his admiration, and smiled. "Oh yes, I received an invitation to your wedding, but I was out of the country at the time so wasn't able to attend." His gaze swung back to Erik. "You're both looking great. Married life seems to agree with you."

Erik was momentarily dumbfounded. What in hell could he say in a situation like this? Paul was more of a business acquaintance than a personal friend, and although they'd talked on the phone briefly from time to time they hadn't seen each other in months. He realized now that the subject of his marriage had never come up.

Brett came to his rescue. "Erik and I aren't married, Senator." Her tone was properly regretful. "We—we realized in time that neither of us was ready for that deep a commitment so we called off the wedding." She lowered her head and didn't look at either of the two men.

Paul patted the hand that lay conveniently within reach. "Call me Paul, Brett." He kept his hand over hers. "I'm really sorry, but maybe things will still work out given time."

Oh damn! Erik could feel the hot flush that stained his face. How did he ever get himself into this? How was he going to explain the situation without coming out of it looking like a heel? "You don't understand, Paul," he muttered. "I'm married to someone else."

The look Paul Forbes turned on him was one of utter astonishment, and Erik could read his mind as clearly as if his thoughts were coming across on ticker tape. *How could any man in his right mind call off a wedding to a stunner like Brett? And, hey buddy, what are you doing having drinks with her in the middle of the day if you've got a wife waiting for you at home?*

Erik lifted his whiskey and gulped the rest of it. "I'll go tell the hostess we're ready for our table," he said and started to rise.

"No need," replied Paul, "I told her when I came in, but since I was late they gave ours to someone else, so we'll have to wait."

Erik groaned silently and sat back down as Paul turned to Brett. "Do you work for Ford too?" he asked.

She favored him with her sweetest smile. "No, I'm a model."

"I should have known." His hand tightened on hers. "A woman as beautiful as you must be swamped with offers to model."

Brett's smile warmed. "How very nice of you to think so." Her voice had lowered a notch. "I don't exactly have to fight them off, but I do all right."

Paul's eyes slid over her breasts and lingered on her parted lips. "I'm sure you do."

Erik fought the unbidden anger that rose steadily in him as Paul and Brett flirted with each other. He had no right to feel possessive about her, but when Paul made a slightly off-color remark and they both laughed, Erik cut in. "How's your family, Paul?" His tone was cool. "I imagine your wife's run ragged now that your sons are teenagers."

Brett's eyes widened, but Paul shot Erik a look that read, *Thanks, pal, I'll remember that,* and said, "Susan and I are separated, and the boys are living with her for the time being. I expect one or the other of us will file for divorce soon."

Erik felt like a fool. "Sorry, I didn't know," he muttered, but he wasn't surprised. Apparently Susan Forbes had finally learned that her handsome husband couldn't resist a beautiful and willing woman.

They were all saved from further embarrassment by the timely intervention of the hostess, who came to tell

Paul that he had a telephone call. He excused himself, and returned a few minutes later looking annoyed. "Sorry, Erik," he said, "but there's a problem at my office in Detroit and I'm going to have to go down and straighten it out. I won't be able to stay for lunch. Can we set up another appointment?"

"No problem," said Erik, relieved that he wouldn't have to spend any more time trying to keep his temper under control. "Just call my office and Trish will take care of it."

He stood and shook hands with Paul, and Brett rose also. Paul took her hand in both of his and pulled her closer. "It's been a pleasure meeting you, Brett," he murmured huskily. "Is there any chance we could have dinner sometime soon?"

"Of course," she replied, as Erik stood by fuming. She opened her purse and took out a small pad of paper and a pen. "I'll write down my address and phone number for you. I'm temporarily living with my parents, but if I'm not there Mom can relay a message."

Paul took the slip of paper. "I have to return to Lansing tonight, but I'll be back early next week. I'll call you then, I promise." He squeezed her hand and walked away.

"He's married, Brett," Erik grated as they sat back down.

Before she could answer they were interrupted by a handsome, upwardly mobile young man whom Brett introduced as her realtor friend, and Erik excused himself and stalked out of the bar toward the elevator. He'd lost all appetite for lunch.

Erik behaved like a bear with a sore paw all afternoon. He was aware of it but couldn't seem to help it. When he left the office at the end of the day he made an effort to calm down and get in a better frame of mind before he got home to Colleen, but when he arrived at the apartment she wasn't there yet and that set him off all over again.

When she finally walked in he snapped at her, then sulked all through dinner while she sat there looking puzzled and unhappy. He knew he had no right to take his frustrations over Brett out on Colleen, but again he couldn't help it. He felt guilty, and he hated feeling guilty. He hadn't done anything wrong. It wasn't as if he'd made a date to meet Brett, it had been totally unplanned. If he still had a residue of feeling for her it wasn't something he encouraged. He'd been wildly in love with her, and it wasn't easy to shrug off emotions like that.

It didn't mean that he cared any less for Colleen, but he knew she'd never see it that way. Lord knows he didn't want Brett back, but it would take a little time to work her completely out of his system. Meanwhile he hoped there wouldn't be any more accidental meetings.

When bedtime came he kissed Colleen good-night and held her close. He needed her in his bed, in his arms, but he wasn't in the mood to make love and she didn't press the issue.

Erik's meetings with Brett continued, but after the first one they weren't accidental. She called him the next day at the office, and he was furious. "I don't want you calling me here, Brett," he barked. "You know how office gossip works."

"Sorry," she said, "but I didn't think you'd want me to call you at home, either."

"There's no need to call me at all. We haven't anything to say to each other."

"But we have, darling." The endearment stirred forbidden feelings. "I want you to tell me about Paul Forbes."

Damn the woman! She knew just what buttons to push to stir him up. "I'm sure he'll be happy to tell you about himself," Erik snapped.

She chuckled. "I'm sure he will, but will it be the truth? I'm certain he's going to call me, and I want to know what I'll be getting into if I go out with him."

Her argument was effective. He should warn her about Paul. The senator's public image was a great deal different from his private one. He sighed and looked at his watch. "There's a bar called The Unicorn." He gave her the address and directions for finding it. "I'll meet you there at five-thirty and buy you a drink."

"Why such an out-of-the-way place? Anyone would think you didn't want to be seen with me."

"I don't. It's that or nothing, and if you're not on time I won't wait around."

"Okay, okay," Brett said. "You needn't be such a grouch. I'll be there."

She was, and she looked radiant. More like she was meeting a lover instead of a cast-off fiancé. Her navy-blue suit couldn't have been more circumspect, but it was cut to mold to her slender body and remind him of what was underneath.

She'd waited for him in her car, and when they walked into the small, dimly lit bar heads turned to look at them. They'd been told they were a spectacular-looking couple, and Erik supposed it was true. They attracted attention everywhere they went.

He led her to a booth on the darkest side of the room, and hated the furtive feeling he had. This wasn't a lovers' tryst, but still he had no business being with Brett at all. If they were seen and recognized it would get back to Colleen, and then there'd be all hell to pay. Besides, he didn't want to hurt Colleen. He had no intention of ever falling in love again the way he'd loved Brett, but Colleen was his wife, his responsibility, and she was dear to him. When she turned away from him in anger he bled.

Brett's voice cut off his thoughts. "Talk about clandestine meetings," she purred, "this is the ideal place for it. So romantic. Right out of an old movie, like Charles Boyer and Hedy Lamarr, or Bogart and Bergman."

"Romantic, hell," Erik snorted. "There's nothing romantic about it. It's a place to talk where we won't be recognized."

She reached over and put her hand on his. "Are you ashamed to be seen with me, Erik?"

He pulled his hand away. "Not ashamed, guilty. Colleen wouldn't understand, and I won't have her hurt."

"Then why are you here with me?" Brett's voice was sharp.

"Good question," he ground out and started to rise.

Brett caught him by the wrist. "Erik, no, I'm sorry. Please sit back down."

Just then the cocktail waitress arrived, and he settled back as they gave their orders.

Someone put money in the jukebox and Willie Nelson's voice blared across the small area with a good ol' boys' footstompin' number. Brett and Erik didn't speak again until the waitress returned with their drinks. By then the song had ended and Brett broke the silence. "I do appreciate this, Erik. I know your time is limited, but

I'd like you to tell me what you know about Paul Forbes.''

Erik took a gulp of his whiskey. "Paul's bad news for you, Brett. He's married, has been for a long time and has two sons, but it's never kept him out of the bed of any woman who captures his fancy.''

She ran her long slender finger around the rim of her cocktail glass. "Is that why his wife left him?''

Erik shrugged. "I don't know. He's not that close a friend, but I'd bet money on one thing, he'll never divorce her or let her divorce him. It would damage his political image.''

"But how could a divorce be more damaging than sleeping around?''

"He keeps his sexy playmates reasonably secret. Those close to him know about them, but it's never been hinted at publicly. A divorce would hit all the newspapers and his constituents would find that their charismatic senator isn't the happy family man they've been led to believe he is.''

Brett frowned. "But divorce is a common occurrence nowadays. Surely it wouldn't make that much difference.''

"His religion forbids it," Erik said, "and he's always run on the promise that he would uphold the high moral values of his church. Can't you just imagine what would happen if his wife divorced him on grounds of adultery?''

Brett cringed. "Yeah, I see what you mean. You think I should steer clear of him?''

"I know you should. You don't need the kind of anguish he'd set you up for. I'll tell you exactly what'll happen when he calls you. He'll suggest dinner at his apartment, and if you object he'll take you to some out-

of-the-way restaurant where it's unlikely he'll be recognized.''

"You mean the way you do?" Brett asked bitterly.

Erik didn't flinch. "Exactly. Running around with
married men is a losing game. You should know that.''

Her face flushed an unbecoming red. "Thanks a lot,''
she said sarcastically and slid out of the booth. "Sorry
I took up your precious time.''

He also stood up and followed her out of the building and to her car in the tiny parking lot in back. "Take
my advice, Brett,'' he said as she unlocked her door
with an angry twist of the key. "When Paul calls tell
him to get lost.''

"You know what, Erik," she said. "I think you're
jealous.''

She got in, slammed the door shut and spun her
wheels in the gravel as she took off.

Erik swore lustily as he walked to his car. Her accusation didn't bear thinking about.

For the second evening in a row he sulked through
dinner, and that night, after he'd kissed Colleen good-
night, they each slept on their own side of the bed.

Colleen applied the finishing strokes of brown mas-
cara to her long thick eyelashes and studied herself in
the dressing-table mirror. Through the miracle of mod-
ern makeup she'd managed almost to hide the dark circles under her eyes and the lack of color in her cheeks.
But she knew she wasn't fooling herself or anyone else,
except possibly Erik. The sparkle that resulted from the
sheer joy of living, which had always been a vital part
of her, had dimmed, and it had left a mark that couldn't
be covered with foundation cream and blusher.

The month since Brett had returned to Detroit had been a slowly lengthening nightmare that was eroding her marriage and driving her to the depths of despair. What made it so unbearable was that she honestly didn't know if there was a problem, or if it was all just a product of her suspicious imagination.

The trouble had started with the quarrel at the open house for Brett shortly after she had returned. It had been unpleasant, but the making up had been almost worth it, and Erik had convinced her that her jealousy had been unfounded. But later in the week he'd come home two days in a row surly, uncommunicative and too tired or upset to make love. She'd told herself he was just overworked, and tried to be understanding, but the cold tentacles of fear were again robbing her of self-confidence. Was he seeing Brett?

Then on the third day he'd picked her up early at the boutique, kissed her breathless and taken her out to dinner where he'd apologized for his churlishness. They'd made love all night long, and again she was lulled into a sense of security.

It hadn't lasted, though, and in the three weeks since then Erik had worked late several times, and had gone out of town one weekend. She'd offered to go along, but he'd told her briskly that he'd be too busy to entertain her. He hadn't even bothered to call. She'd been determined not to think of him and Brett together, but of course she did and she could neither eat nor sleep. When he came home he claimed he'd missed her, and proved it with passion, but lately even that had seemed a little forced. Sometimes several nights went by when they didn't make love.

She suspected he was seeing Brett, but she had absolutely no grounds to accuse him and her anguish was tearing her apart.

Colleen wanted to be a supportive wife, and she'd tried to keep her temper under control. If things were going badly at work, as she well knew they sometimes did, then she didn't want to add to Erik's burden by quarreling with him. He had a highly responsible position with a lot of pressure, and it was understandable if he sometimes took his frustrations out on those close to him.

On the other hand there was Brett. Colleen felt demeaned by the jealous suspicion that haunted her, but she couldn't banish it. Did Erik want the woman he'd first intended to marry? Was he still in love with her? If so, what was she, Colleen, going to do about it?

She picked up her brush and listlessly stroked it through her long black hair. Last night Erik had been late coming home, and when he finally arrived he'd been in a foul mood. Colleen's tightly controlled anger had snapped and they'd had a blazing quarrel. It occurred to her later, as they lay like strangers in the same bed, that it was almost as if he had deliberately provoked her anger. That morning he'd left for work early with only a curt goodbye.

She put the brush down and covered her face with her hands. Did Erik want out of their marriage? If so, why didn't he ask for his freedom? Or was she overreacting to a natural moodiness in him brought on by the strain of problems at work?

She stood and slipped into the peach linen dress she'd selected earlier. There was one thing she was sure of. She couldn't go on like this any longer. She had to see Erik and talk to him, and it wouldn't wait until tonight.

They were busy at the boutique until almost noon, and when things slacked off Colleen decided to go to Erik's office and catch him before he went to lunch.

Unfortunately it didn't work out that way. When she got there both Erik and his secretary, Trish, were gone and the office was locked.

Colleen muttered an indelicate oath and leaned against the door, wondering what to do now. She should have called and told Erik she was coming. She'd thought about it, but hadn't wanted to give him a chance to tell her he was too busy to see her. Not that he would have. She was getting positively paranoid.

She was still standing in the hall when a middle-aged woman approached carrying a white paper sack. "Good afternoon," she said, "may I help you?"

Colleen nodded. "I'm looking for Erik Johansen."

The woman clucked sympathetically. "Oh, I'm sorry, he's already gone to lunch. I don't expect him back until about two."

"You?" Colleen didn't remember ever having seen the lady before.

She rummaged in her purse with her free hand and came up with a key, which she inserted in the lock. "Yes, I'm filling in today for Mr. Johansen's secretary who's sick. I just stepped out to pick up a sandwich at the deli down the street." She swung open the door and led the way into the outer office. "Did you have an appointment?"

"No," Colleen said. "I'm Colleen, Mr. Johansen's wife, and I'd hoped to catch him before he left. Do you know where he's having lunch?"

"As a matter of fact I do." She seemed pleased to be able to relay information to her temporary boss's wife.

"He asked me to make a reservation for him at the Rusty Duck."

Colleen hesitated. She knew the place, but with so many restaurants in this area why would he choose to drive all the way to the waterfront? "Was he meeting someone? Or taking a guest?" she asked.

"I don't know. He just asked me to reserve a small table and I did. He didn't mention a guest."

Colleen thanked the woman and left. It wasn't off the beaten track for her to stop at the Rusty Duck on her way back to the Renaissance Center. She'd psyched herself up to discuss this matter with her husband, and she didn't want to put it off.

The popular waterfront restaurant was crowded as usual, but a car was just backing out as she entered the lot and she slid easily into the empty space. Inside there were people waiting to be seated, but she explained to the waitress that she was meeting her husband, and she was allowed to go into the dining room.

She stood in the entryway and looked around the room. At first she didn't see Erik, but then she caught a glimpse of him at a table partially hidden behind an oversize plant in the far corner. She skirted between the closely set tables and concentrated on not bumping into anything, so that she had her head down until she was within a few inches of the potted bush. She smiled and walked around it. "Erik, I hope you don't mind, but—"

It was then that she realized he wasn't alone. Across from him in the secluded area was Brett, and they were holding hands on top of the table!

Colleen rocked with the shock that tore through her. Even though she had suspected that Erik was seeing Brett she wasn't prepared when confronted with the inescapable proof. She stood there with her mouth open, but nothing issued from it.

The look on Erik's face left no room for doubt. His first expression of blank surprise quickly turned to one of sickening guilt as she watched the blood drain from his features, and his eyes cloud with anguish.

It was Brett who acted first. She stood and put a hand on her cousin's arm. "Colleen, it's not what you think."

The words made no impression on Colleen's stunned mind as she shook away the hand. The touch and her reaction snapped her attention back to her surroundings, but the searing pain that accompanied it rendered thought and speech impossible.

A strangled cry that she didn't recognize as her own caused voices to still and heads to turn as she whirled and plunged back across the crowded room, bumping into tables and people, and upsetting an occasional empty chair.

Once she finally cleared the dining room she ran out of the restaurant. She'd almost reached her car when Erik caught up with her. She'd been vaguely aware of a voice calling her name as she made her hasty exit, and her only thought was to get away. She couldn't face Erik yet. Right now she never wanted to see him again.

She wasn't given a choice. Erik caught her by the arm and stopped her headlong flight. She struggled but his grip tightened. "You might as well stop fighting," he said, "you're not going to get away from me. Now come quietly before we attract even more attention."

"Go to hell!" she snapped as she tried to pull away.

"I already have," he replied, and with an arm around her waist half carried her across the lot to his own car.

"Put me down, I'm not going anywhere with you," she yelled as he opened the door and pushed her into the driver's seat.

"Scoot over," he commanded, and she did, then grasped the handle on the passenger side. But Erik pushed the button of the experimental security system that made it impossible to open the locked doors.

He started the engine and backed up while she struggled to get out. It was a maddening waste of time, and she finally gave up and sank back as the car swung out into the line of traffic.

"I want you to let me out of this car," she demanded, and it wasn't until she heard the quiver in her voice that she realized she was trembling.

Damn him! Oh damn him to hell! Why hadn't he agreed to a divorce when she'd offered it to him instead of putting on that big act about being callously rejected? At least then it would have been amiable. They could have remained friends without the ugliness of recriminations and name-calling, the agony of betrayal.

"Sweetheart, I'm sorry." Erik's voice was unsteady too. "I know what you're thinking, but it's just not true."

She bristled with rage. What kind of an idiot did he think she was? "Stop it, Erik. There's nothing wrong with my eyesight. I know what I saw."

He was trying to maneuver the Mustang through the noonday Detroit traffic and had to keep his eyes on the road. "I'm not denying what you saw, only the interpretation you're putting on it."

She was getting her voice and her thoughts under control now. "Are you telling me this is the only time you've been out with Brett since she got back?"

He hesitated, and his hesitation told her everything she didn't want to know. "Not exactly," he said, "but—"

She winced. "How often, then? Twice? Three times?" Why couldn't she just shut up? She didn't want to know.

Again he hesitated, and she wished she could die. "We've had drinks together a few times, and lunch twice," he said reluctantly.

"And did you hold hands each time?" The question was out before she knew she was going to ask it.

He turned to look at her then in spite of the traffic, and she saw the red splotches of guilt on his cheeks. "No!" he said emphatically, then braked suddenly as the car ahead stopped, throwing them both forward.

He reached over and pulled the ends of her seat belt together and fastened them across her, then fastened his own. "Look, honey, let's wait till we get home to discuss this. I've got to keep my mind on my driving."

Home. She didn't have a home anymore. She had an apartment that she'd been sharing with a man who was in love with another woman. And she'd felt guilty for suspecting that he was seeing Brett. She'd flagellated herself for being so disloyal as to mistrust her husband!

"I'm not going home," she grated. "I'm going back to work."

The car was moving again. "You're going home with me, and we're going to stay there for as long as it takes to get this mess straightened out."

His tone brooked no arguing, and she knew they had to talk sometime. She closed her eyes and bided her time until they reached the apartment. Now that the shock was wearing off she saw no reason to rush the discussion that would shatter her life and leave her rejected and alone.

At the apartment building they parked the car in the underground parking area and took the elevator to their floor. Neither spoke until Erik locked the apartment door behind them. He walked over to the bar and poured himself a glass of whiskey. "What'll you have?" he asked.

She shook her head. "Nothing." Her senses were fuzzy enough; she didn't want to cloud them more with alcohol.

"Please, sit down." He motioned her to the couch, but she ignored him and walked over to look out the picture window.

They were high enough up that she could see for miles. She wondered if she could get her old apartment back. No, of course not. She'd moved from it nearly two months before. It would be rented again by now.

Erik spoke from directly behind her. "Turn around and look at me, darling. I can't talk to your back."

He put his hands on her shoulders and she stiffened. "Don't touch me," she said quietly, but there was ice in her tone.

"All right." He dropped his hands to his sides. "I can't blame you. I know how I'd feel if I found you lunching with a man under the same circumstances."

"Do you? I doubt it." Even in her wildest thoughts she hadn't come close to imagining the strength of the pain.

"I'd kill him," Erik said simply.

"I find that hard to believe. Besides, I don't think that killing Brett is one of my options, she's bigger than I, and much more ruthless." She drew a deep breath. "What is it you want, Erik? A divorce?"

"No." His voice was harsh. "I told you before, you're my wife and I'll never let you go."

"Oh yes, so you did." She uttered a brittle, mirthless laugh. "But that was before Brett came back. The scenario has changed now. What did you have in mind, keeping me as a wife and taking Brett as a mistress?" She watched the tiny people scurrying around on the streets below, and tried not to picture in her mind what she was saying.

"You know better than that," he gritted, and she heard him walk a few steps away.

She reached out and clutched the sheer panel curtain that covered the window. "I don't, but you should," she said. "I'm not sophisticated enough for a ménage à trois. Have you made love to her since she came back?" The last sentence seemed to come out of nowhere. It didn't even sound like Colleen's voice.

Erik's patience snapped. He was beside her in two steps and spun her around to look at him. "That's enough. Now come over here and sit down with me so we can discuss this rationally."

He gripped her arm and led her over to the sofa, but for all his bluster she noticed that he didn't answer her question.

Chapter Twelve

Erik seated Colleen on the couch, then dropped down beside her. "Now listen to me, sweetheart," he said more calmly, "and try to understand. After that quarrel we had over the open house I had no intention of seeing Brett again unless you were present, but I bumped into her totally by accident a few days later."

He told her of seeing Brett in the bar of the Hyatt Regency while he was waiting for Paul Forbes, and of the meeting with her the following day to discuss the senator's intentions.

Erik sat forward with his arms on his thighs and twirled his glass between his palms. "I told her she was a fool to get involved with married men. She took exception and we quarreled. I didn't see her again until late the following week when she showed up at the office and asked me to have lunch with her."

Colleen didn't doubt that Brett had been the aggressor, but couldn't Erik have tried harder to resist her?

"I was furious," he continued. "I'd told her straight out that I didn't want to see her, but she was anxious to tell me about her date with Paul and I was curious. I wanted to know what he was up to. I didn't want her taken in by his so-called charm."

"It was none of your business," Colleen grated.

"You're right, it wasn't," he answered, "but I guess I still felt protective of her." Colleen grimaced and he continued. "I finally agreed to go to lunch, and she told me that I was right about him taking her to a secluded place where he wasn't likely to be recognized, but that he was a gentleman and didn't even suggest taking her to bed. I figured she'd been warned so from then on she could take care of herself."

"Then why did you see her again?" Colleen wasn't buying this watered-down explanation.

Erik put his empty glass down. "I didn't for about ten days, and then it was another accidental meeting."

"Oh, come on, Erik." Colleen jumped up and strode across the room. "Do you expect me to believe that in a city of a million and a half people you and Brett just happen to bump into each other every few days?"

Erik stood and walked to the fireplace. "I don't know if it was deliberate on her part, but it sure as hell wasn't on mine. I have lunch several times a week at the Hyatt Regency, and she was there that day when I walked in. I bought her a drink and she said she'd seen Paul Forbes again and they were just friends. I wasn't with her more than fifteen minutes before my table was ready and I went into the dining room to have lunch—alone."

She found this difficult to believe. "You weren't lunching alone today." Her voice cracked and she took a deep breath. "And don't try to tell me that you met accidentally clear over at the Rusty Duck."

His shoulders drooped and he thrust his hands in his pockets. "No," he said regretfully, "this noon wasn't accidental. Brett called and wanted to see me. I won't even attempt to explain why I agreed. She sounded desperate and begged me to have lunch with her and, idiot that I am, I finally gave in. I asked my temporary secretary to make a reservation at the Rusty Duck because it was so far away that it wasn't likely we'd be seen."

Colleen couldn't hold back a little cry of anguish, and Erik reached out and pulled her into his embrace. "Oh, sweetheart, don't," he murmured as his arms tightened around her. "I was only trying to protect you. I realized you'd be hurt if you knew I was seeing her, no matter how innocently."

His words rained down on her like blows, and she pushed herself away from him and put several steps between them. "Then why did you see her?" she cried, and her voice was tight with pain.

Her pain was mirrored in Erik's eyes. "I don't know," he said simply. "I honestly don't know. I suppose I felt a lingering sense of responsibility for her. I loved her very much at one time."

Colleen cringed, but he plodded on. "It's not easy to shrug off such strong feelings overnight. There seems to be a residue of caring even though it's not love. I didn't want to see her get involved in the kind of mess that dating a married politician can become if I could prevent it. As I'd suspected she told me Paul had asked her to go to Mexico with him for a few days. Furtively, of course. I told her she'd be a fool to go, and she had just put her hand over mine and started to thank me for listening when you came. We were not holding hands."

"Not then, maybe, but what about last weekend?"

He blinked. "Last weekend?"

"When you went to Chicago and wouldn't take me with you," she said impatiently.

His eyes widened. "You think I took Brett with me?"

He looked so astonished that she began to doubt it. "Why not? I'm sure if she asked to go you couldn't have refused her." She knew she sounded waspish, but then it wasn't every day that her husband told her he still cared for the woman who'd been his first choice for a wife.

A flash of agitation crossed his face but was quickly banished. "I was booked up every minute of the time I was gone. I'll give you a copy of my schedule and you can check with the people listed if that's what it takes to convince you. I'll plead guilty to terminal stupidity, but not adultery."

"Don't bother," she snapped. "You may not mind carrying on in public with another woman, but I'm not willing to bring others into our personal problems."

"Now you're being childish," he growled. "I haven't been 'carrying on' as you put it, and I think you know it."

"Childish!" She'd almost been ready to believe him but he'd just pushed the wrong button. "You consider it childish for me to be upset because my husband has admitted that he's been seeing another woman behind my back? You think I'm overreacting because I'm upset that you still care about Brett even after what she did to you? Are you suggesting that I just look the other way when she crooks her finger and you come running?"

She could feel the hysteria rising in her, but couldn't control it. Tears burned behind her eyes, and she blinked to keep them from falling. "If that's the kind of wife you want then you'd better go back and pick up where you left off with Brett, because I can't live that way!"

The tears broke through and she ran to the bedroom and slammed the door, then threw herself face down on the bed and sobbed.

The mattress beside her sagged and Erik's big hand caressed her back. "Colleen, I'm sorry. Please don't cry. What can I say to make you believe me?"

He stretched out beside her and nuzzled the back of her neck. "I don't need another woman," he murmured as his hand moved to cup her breast. "I have all I can handle right here at home."

Colleen closed her eyes and felt her tense muscles relax. It would be so easy to give in and let him seduce her. When he touched her like this all her reason fled, leaving her a captive of her passionate nature. She loved Erik. Apparently nothing he could say or do would change that. But they'd had variations of this argument before and this time, in the interest of her own sanity, it had to be resolved.

He pushed aside her hair and his lips brushed across her nape sending shivers down her back, while his hand stroked her throbbing breast. His body was pressed close to hers, and she could feel him against her hip. If she didn't stop this now she'd be lost, and nothing would have been resolved.

It took all the willpower she could marshal to roll away from him and sit up. "No, Erik," she said when he reached for her again. "We both know that you can get around me that way, but when we get out of bed the problem's still there. I want you to leave me alone. I can't think when you're near.''

Erik rolled over and sat beside her. "Neither can I, honey." His voice was husky. "When I'm this close to you all I can do is feel. You know what you do to me."

"Yes," she agreed sadly. "If we could stay in bed all the time life would be simple, but unfortunately that's not possible. We do erotic and exciting things to each other and it's wonderful, but passion is only a part of marriage. It won't hold two people together if they have nothing else going for them. Especially if one of them is still attracted to someone else."

"Dammit, Colleen—"

She stood up. "Don't deny it, Erik. We wouldn't be having this argument if it weren't true. Just go back to work and give me some space. I need time to think."

Erik stood also and ran his fingers distractedly through his shaggy hair. "All right, if that's what you want, I'll leave, but you've got to promise that you won't do anything rash until I get back."

"Don't worry, I'm not going to run away again. I couldn't get very far without a car, and mine's still parked in the Rusty Duck's parking lot."

He looked relieved. "So it is. I'll have someone pick it up and bring it to you later."

After he left, Colleen called April to tell her she wouldn't be back to work that afternoon. She didn't offer an explanation, and April didn't ask for one. Was it possible she knew Erik had been seeing Brett?

No. If she'd known, then Devin would have known, too, and with Colleen's brother's explosive temper the furtive meetings wouldn't have remained a secret for long.

The picture of Brett and Erik sitting at the secluded table smiling at each other, their hands entwined, brought a fresh wave of pain that rocked Colleen and left her knees trembling. She lowered herself into the depths of the cavernous leather chair that Erik had chosen for himself, and huddled there with her knees drawn up and her arms wrapped around her shins.

Would she ever understand this enigmatic husband of hers? What on earth did he want, and just how far was she prepared to go to give it to him? He'd acted insulted when she'd accused him of wanting her as a wife and Brett as a mistress, but he didn't seem inclined to let either of them go. Why? If he wanted Brett then why did he put up such a fuss when Colleen suggested divorce? Or if he wanted to stay married to her, then why did he continue to let Brett manipulate him?

Could she share him with her cousin if it was the only way to keep her marriage intact?

No! Never. Not only was it contrary to the code of morality that had been instilled in her with her mother's milk, but it would make a mockery of the very marriage vows she was trying to protect. She couldn't bring children into an arrangement like that, and both she and Erik wanted a family.

Was that it? Was Erik confronted with a choice between the woman he loved, and the family he wanted? Brett had made no secret of the fact that she didn't like children, and had no intention of ruining her model's figure by having babies. On the other hand he had good reason to know how badly Colleen wanted a child, how deeply she'd love it.

Impatiently she uncurled herself from the chair and stood up. That kind of thinking would have her going around in circles. She was a married woman and she had every right to expect her husband to be faithful to her, not only physically but emotionally. If he couldn't, then she had no choice but to leave him. She simply wasn't equipped by temperament or training for an open marriage. It would destroy her. She'd have to make Erik understand that it wasn't a matter of pride, it was a matter of survival.

He called later that afternoon and sounded genuinely regretful. "Honey, I'm sorry as hell, but I'll be late getting home." When she didn't respond he continued. "We have a tax man here from the IRS and he wants to finish up tonight so he can catch a flight back to D.C., first thing in the morning. I tried my damnedest to get out of it but there's no way. I have to be here."

Colleen gripped the telephone and sat down. Could she believe him, or was he seeing Brett again?

"Colleen, are you there?" His tone was anxious.

"Yes, Erik," she said. "I heard you."

He hesitated, but when she said nothing more he spoke. "We're having a meal sent in so go ahead and eat your dinner, but please wait up for me. I want to talk to you."

She was almost sure he was telling the truth, but how could she trust him? She fought to keep her voice steady as she said, "I'll see, Erik. It depends on what time you get in. I have to be at work early in the morning."

She went to bed at ten o'clock, after pacing the floor for hours trying to decide what she should do. Would she ever be able to trust Erik again? Would she have visions of him making love to Brett every time he was late coming home? If he was innocent how long would he put up with her suspicions before he lost patience and walked out on her?

She finally came to the conclusion that she couldn't possibly make a decision tonight. This wasn't just a jealous quarrel that could be settled when one or the other party said they were sorry. It was a rip in the very fabric of their marriage and she wasn't sure it could be mended. The problem was too fundamental for a quick solution. It could be summed up in two basic questions. Was Erik still in love with Brett? And if so why wouldn't he let Colleen divorce him?

Until she had the answers all she could do was compromise. She wouldn't move out of the apartment, but neither would she sleep with him. She was too inclined to forgive him anything the minute they climbed into bed together. All he had to do was touch her and she caught fire. She'd never be able to make a rational decision if they continued to make love.

She made up the double bed in the guest room and crawled into it with a feeling of dread. Was she a fool not to accept what Erik was willing to give her and make the best of it?

It was midnight before she heard her husband's key in the lock. She'd barely closed her eyes in the two hours since she'd gone to bed. Her mind was like an out-of-control movie projector that kept playing the day's events over and over. Now she listened.

Erik closed the door and bolted it, then walked across the living room and down the length of the hall to the master bedroom. She held her breath. Would he accept her nonverbal message?

No way. Within seconds the hallway was illuminated and she jumped as her name was shouted into the silence. She reached up and turned on the headboard lamp, afraid he'd wake everyone in the building. "For heaven's sake, Erik," she called, "lower your voice."

He appeared immediately in the doorway, and glared down at her. "What are you doing in here?" His tone was harsh.

She felt too vulnerable lying down, and pulled herself to a sitting position. "I'm trying to sleep," she said quietly.

His glance traveled over the rumpled bed, which was considerably smaller than the king-size one they shared. "I see." This time his voice was barely above a murmur. He started unbuttoning his jacket and vest. "All right, have it your way." He turned and walked back to the master bedroom.

Colleen stared at the empty space. He wasn't even going to argue!

She lay back down, curled up in a ball with her arms across her stomach and felt sick. He didn't care whether she slept with him or not. She'd expected him at least to protest. Was he angry or just indifferent?

She closed her eyes tightly and pressed her fist to her mouth to stifle the sob that fought for release. A soft noise in the hall caused her to open her eyes, but the light in the other bedroom had been turned off and the apartment was in darkness except for the moonlight that filtered through the sheer curtains.

She heard the noise again, and realized that it was footsteps just before she saw the bulky outline of Erik's large frame approaching. He pulled back the sheet and blanket on the empty side of the bed and slid in beside her.

"What do you think you're doing?" she hissed, but there was more relief than anger in her tone.

"I'm coming to bed, what else would I be doing this time of night?" He pulled the sheet over him, and she felt his nude body against hers as he settled down.

"Erik, dammit, you're supposed to sleep in the other room." She tried to sit up, but he had his arm across her waist and she couldn't move.

"I sleep wherever you sleep," he explained while his fingers moved up to stroke her breast through her satin nightgown. "If you want to sleep in here I'll go along with it, but this bed was never built for a man my size. My feet hang out." He brought up his knee and wedged it between her legs.

The banked fire of her womanhood heated up, and she tried desperately to ignore it. "I won't make love with you," she said through clenched jaws.

His fingers moved to her other breast and stroked it as his moist lips made little nipping forays across her bare shoulder. "All right," he whispered into her ear as his teeth caught at her lobe. "If you don't want to."

He started to move his knee, and she clasped it between both her thighs as his lips and fingers turned her heat to flame. He chuckled softly. "You like that, don't you?" he said, and raised his knee so that it was cradled against her most intimate femininity.

She sucked in her breath and turned on her side to clasp her arms around his waist. He held her close and gently moved his knee back and forth, sending fingers of fire spiraling through her until she was oblivious to everything but the driving need that threatened to consume her. "Erik, Erik, Erik," she moaned in a ragged litany that was stilled only when his mouth covered hers, and he moved over her to plunge deep into the inferno he had created.

For Erik it had been far more than just a sexual release, although Lord knows he'd needed that badly enough once he'd crawled into bed with his irresistible little wife. She never failed to stimulate him to a pure erotic agony that drove him wild until it was finally sated. He smiled as he cuddled her damp nude body to him. If he ever tried to tell another man about it he'd be accused of fantasizing.

This had been one hell of a day, starting with the moment he'd looked up to see Colleen staring down with wide-eyed horror at Brett and him sitting in the restaurant. He'd never been so terrified in his life as when she'd turned and run away from him. He deserved every hurtful word she'd flung at him, every nasty accusation she'd made, except one. He'd never broken his marriage vows. The idea of taking Brett to bed hadn't crossed his mind since she'd come back to Detroit. Why should it when he had such a sweet, responsive, and eager wife?

How could he have been such a damn fool as to take a chance of losing her just because he felt a certain fascination for the woman who'd gotten away? He suspected it was strictly an ego problem. He enjoyed watching Brett trying to seduce him; it was balm for the pride she'd wounded so badly a few short months before. He'd told himself that since she no longer turned him on, seeing her now and then could do no harm, but he'd deliberately shut out of his mind the damage it would do to Colleen if she ever found out about it.

Now he was paying the price for his thoughtlessness. It was bad enough that Colleen had insisted he go back to work and leave her alone before they'd settled anything, but then when that accountant had gone over those pages of figures with maddening deliberation until all hours of the night he'd nearly lost his mind. He'd raced home only to find the apartment dark and Colleen gone from their bed. It was then that he'd nearly come unstrung.

He rubbed his cheek in her soft fragrant hair. It was time he stopped letting one bad experience distort his relationship with his wife. Time to let go of his wounded pride and self-pity and admit both to himself and to Colleen how he really felt about her. He'd been taking so greedily, but giving nothing in return.

Colleen lay snuggled in Erik's arms, warm and sleepy and marvelously fulfilled. Even her nagging conscience couldn't dispel the magic of their short, violent lovemaking. She smiled. In novels she'd read long drawn-out scenes of foreplay where it seemed to take the hero and heroine hours to get from the first murmur of agreement to the final consummation. She and Erik were lucky if they got their clothes off before they exploded in the searing conflagration. All they had to do was touch each other and the inferno raged out of control. Surely that much wanting must mean something.

She flicked her tongue and licked the salty sheen of his bare shoulder. Of course the wanting meant something. It meant that she was one of those few fortunate individuals who'd found a soulmate. She and Erik shared a relationship that was very special. If it wasn't perfect, if the romantic love she yearned for from Erik was missing, well . . . nobody'd promised her perfection.

She suspected that what she had was as close as mere mortals ever came. It was certainly worth fighting for, and that was what she intended to do.

She licked his shoulder again, more slowly this time, and he kissed her on the temple and moved his hand to her breast. She'd given him a second chance with Brett. She'd offered him his freedom and he'd refused to consider it. He was hers now, by his own choice with no strings attached, and she wasn't going to let Brett walk off with him by default. If she ever again caught her scheming cousin coming on to her husband she was going to punch her out, in front of the whole world if necessary.

She reached down for him. He bit her ear. "I assume you know what you're doing," he said, and blew into the ear he'd been nibbling on.

She shivered, but managed to keep her voice steady. "I just wanted to get your attention." She stroked him gently and he twitched.

"You got it," he assured her, "and if you keep that up you're going to get a lot more. Did I ever tell you that you're insatiable, Mrs. Johansen?"

She hid her mischievous grin against his muscled chest. "I haven't heard you complain, Mr. Johansen."

"Fat chance." He groaned, as his arms tightened around her. "Look, honey, do you have a particular fetish for this bed, or can we move into the big one in the other room? Every time I turn I'm afraid I'll crush you."

She tilted her head and caught his lips with hers in a kiss that he quickly claimed. He coaxed her mouth open and invaded it with his darting tongue, drawing a gasp of excitement from deep inside her. Her fingers involuntarily tightened around the exquisitely responsive part of him that she was holding, and his body arched as he thrust against her hand. "Sweetheart!" It was a cry of torment. "Have mercy. I can only stand so much of that."

She unclenched her fist and released him. "I'm sorry," she said, "I didn't mean to hurt you."

He took her hand and brought it to his lips. "It didn't hurt, it felt good. Too good." He was trembling as he kissed her palm.

She caressed his cheek with her fingers. He hadn't taken the time to shave before coming to bed and the rough texture was arousing. "I didn't answer your question," she said as she pushed him onto his back and climbed on top of him.

"What question?" he murmured huskily while positioning her so she lay full length on him.

She trailed tiny kisses from one side of his throat to the other before answering. "You asked if we could go into the other bedroom."

"Later," he moaned, as her bare feet slid sensuously up and down his twitching legs.

His hands were kneading her firm, rounded buttocks and making her squirm against him. "If we go now it may slow us down a little," she murmured against his collarbone. "I want you to teach me foreplay."

His hips moved in rhythm with her squirming lower body. "Foreplay?" He sounded as if he thought he'd heard wrong as he accelerated the pace of their movements.

She clutched at his shoulders and shuddered with need as she forced herself to speak. "Yes, foreplay. We never seem to have time for it."

With minimal effort he flipped her over on her back and straddled her. "I hate to tell you this, love," he murmured as he arched her to him and closed the gap, "but we don't have time for it now, either."

With every ounce of restraint he could muster Erik thrust slowly into the warm, moist, throbbing darkness of her, and just before his control shattered she heard him speak clearly. "I love you, Colleen. Oh God, how I love you."

The world around her fragmented into billions of brightly colored slivers of ecstasy as their two bodies fused and became one.

Colleen woke just minutes before the alarm would wake them. She looked around her in confusion. This wasn't her room. Then she remembered. She was in the bed in the guest room, and Erik's big body was jammed into the space beside her.

She propped herself up on her elbow and looked down at her sleeping husband. His mouth was turned up at the corners in a tiny smile, and he looked so—so content. Had she put that expression on his face? She knew she had, and she stroked his tousled blond hair away from his broad forehead, then leaned down and kissed his closed eyelids.

His smile broadened as her lips nibbled their way down his cheek and finally reached his mouth. He opened his eyes then, and she looked directly into them from a distance of not more than two inches. She marveled at how incredibly green they were, so clear, and direct, and magnetic.

His arms went around her and she buried her face against the side of his neck. "Tell me again," she whispered shyly.

He made no pretense of not understanding. "I love you," he murmured. "I wasted a lot of time fighting it, but it was a losing battle. I didn't have the proverbial snowball's chance in hell of holding out against the sweet, loving warmth of you." His arms tightened. "Now all I can do is trust you to love me too."

She snuggled against him, and ran her hand over the thick mat of hair on his chest. "I do. You know I do. I've loved you all my life."

"Yes, I know, and that's what scares me," he said bluntly. "You've never given yourself a chance to get to know other men, men your own age who share your interests. You love opera and I'm a sports nut; you read an average of two books a week and I haven't read anything but technical material since I graduated from college; when we go to a movie you choose the latest version of *Hamlet* and I opt for *Rocky II*. We're totally incompatible, sweetheart, except in bed."

Some of Colleen's joy dimmed. She didn't doubt Erik's declaration of love, but he didn't sound happy about it. Would he grow tired of her when their passion cooled? She was sensible enough to know that even the smoldering heat that consumed them so readily now would have to simmer down eventually, and then what would they have? Would they grow apart while he went to ball games with the guys and she attended concerts with fellow music lovers?

Erik interrupted her musing by kissing her thoroughly. He patted her lovingly on the bottom, rolled reluctantly out of bed and headed for the shower.

It was still early, and Colleen curled up under the sheets and resumed her disturbing thoughts. Erik was right, their interests were very different, but although his love for her was new and frightening to him, she'd loved him deeply ever since she could remember. He was as much a part of her as her arms and legs and she'd do anything to hold him.

Fortunately there was a way she could assure herself of a permanent place in his life. She could give him the family he wanted. If she had a baby every few years for a while it would be a long time before she'd have to worry about his attention lagging. They'd be too busy raising children to worry because she loved the misty romantic ballet paintings of Degas, and he preferred the vivid action-filled westerns of Frederic Remington.

When it was her turn in the bathroom she reached into the medicine cabinet for her compact of birth-control pills. The doctor had said to wait six months before trying for another pregnancy, but she felt strong and healthy. Besides, it might take her a while to get pregnant the second time.

She opened the compact and emptied the remaining pills into her hand, then hesitated. Maybe she should talk it over with Erik. He'd had the first pregnancy sprung on him with an unwelcome jolt, would he welcome a second surprise? Still, if she asked him she was sure he'd insist that they wait four more months until they could get the doctor's blessing.

She couldn't afford to wait. Brett wasn't going to go away, and Colleen wasn't taking any chances. She trusted Erik, but he'd admitted that he still harbored vagrant feelings for his former fiancée and she sure as hell didn't trust Brett. No, she wanted a hold on him that couldn't be broken. She'd present him with the accomplished fact of an expected son or daughter.

She flushed the commode and watched the pills disappear down the drain as fast as they spilled out of her overturned hand.

Chapter Thirteen

Six weeks later Colleen was jubilant. She was two weeks past due, and since her rhythmic cycle had always been twenty-eight days on the dot it could only mean one thing. She was pregnant again!

She wiggled with excitement as she once more sat in the doctor's office waiting for the results of her tests. She glanced down at her flat stomach. If she hadn't lost her first baby she'd be wearing maternity clothes by now. She'd be extra careful this time, maybe work shorter hours for a while so she could relax more.

The door opened and Dr. Welch entered wearing a big grin. "You were right, Fertile Myrtle, the test's positive."

Colleen was sure she must glow with happiness. "I knew it. Oh Frank, I want this baby so badly."

Frank Welch sat down in the chair behind his desk. "I should scold you, you know, for not waiting a few more months. We don't want to take chances with your health. You'll need a lot of energy to care for this little one when it starts waking you every three hours to eat. Do you plan to breast feed?''

''Of course, I wouldn't miss the experience. I want natural childbirth, too. No drugs or anesthetic. When can I enroll in a Lamaze class?'' She was positively bouncing with exuberance.

Dr. Welch laughed and held up his hand. ''Slow down there, girl. All in good time. Shouldn't you go home and tell your husband the good news first?''

A tiny prick of conscience dimmed the brilliance of her smile. He was right. The time for procrastination had come to a screeching halt. She had to tell Erik, and she was certain it would come as a surprise to him this time.

Since it was late in the day Colleen didn't return to work but drove straight home. She wanted to dress in something long and slinky, and prepare Erik's favorite meal. If she clouded his thinking with food and sex maybe he wouldn't be too upset because she'd tricked him into getting her pregnant.

She shook her head impatiently. No, ''tricked'' wasn't the word to describe what she'd done. She'd meant to tell him she was no longer taking precautions, but the time had just never seemed right. Besides, he wanted a baby as much as she did.

She let herself into the apartment and headed straight for the shower. The spray of warm water was like gentle fingers massaging her tired muscles, and the shadow that had dulled her jubilation disappeared. She'd never been so happy and content as she had these past six weeks since Erik had admitted that he loved her. Those three words, ''I love you,'' had banished all her doubts and insecurities, and for the first time since he'd proposed to her she'd been able to relax and accept their marriage as a real and lasting one.

Well, maybe it hadn't been quite all that idyllic, she admitted to herself as she turned off the water and reached for the towel. She wouldn't have been so relieved today when her pregnancy had been confirmed if she hadn't had lingering doubts about her ability to hold Erik's love without the added inducement of a family of little Johansens. Even so it had been a minor flaw in her joy. She was no longer plagued with the suspicion that he might be with Brett on the nights he worked late, or the days he was out of town on business. This had happened several times since that night he'd declared his love for her, but now she could trust him completely.

She dressed in a mauve hostess gown that hung straight from the shoulders to her ankles, barely touching her breasts and hips. It had a demure, virginal look until she moved. Then the slit on the left side from the hem to the top of her thigh revealed one long slender bare leg. It was incredibly sexy and, not surprisingly, a favorite of Erik's. She wore nothing underneath but satin and lace bikini panties, a fact he'd discover the minute he took her in his arms. She wrinkled her nose at her image in the mirror. Better wait to start dinner until he arrived. If she knew her impatient husband he'd keep her busy for quite some time before they got around to eating.

An hour later she looked at the clock and frowned. Erik should have been home half an hour before unless he'd had to work late, but he always let her know when that happened.

She waited another half hour, then called his office. She let the phone ring eight times, and was ready to hang up when a breathless Trish answered. Colleen identified herself and asked for Erik. "He's not here, Mrs. Johansen," the secretary said. "Everyone's gone. I worked late finishing up some letters and was on my way out when I heard the phone ringing, that's why I was so slow in answering."

Colleen frowned. "How long ago did my husband leave?"

It seemed to her that Trish hesitated longer than necessary before she answered. "Well, he actually wasn't in the office today except for first thing this morning. He left about ten o'clock and told me to cancel all his appointments."

Colleen felt a chill of apprehension. Erik hadn't said anything to her about plans to be out of his office all day. Apparently he hadn't expected to be if he'd canceled his appointments at the last minute. "Could you tell me where he went?" she asked. "I'm a little concerned because he didn't tell me he'd be late, and I'm waiting dinner."

"I—I really don't know." Trish sounded hesitant again. "He just said he was leaving and might not be back to the office today. Uh—look, Mrs. Johansen, I have to run or I'll miss my bus. There really isn't anything more I can tell you. I'm sure he'll be home soon. Bye." The connection was broken.

Colleen stood holding the phone for several seconds before she put it down. Where had Erik been all day, and why hadn't he told his secretary where he was going? If he knew he'd be late why hadn't he called her?

She felt uneasy. It wasn't like Erik to go off and not let anyone know where he was. He always kept his secretary informed of his schedule. She thought about the events of the past week. There hadn't been any problems at all. Erik had worked late a couple of times, but he'd called and told her not to expect him. He hadn't seemed upset about anything, and they'd made love every night. Surely he'd be home any minute now, and have a perfectly logical explanation for his lateness.

She decided to keep busy by setting the table and preparing the salad. Fortunately Erik was a meat and potatoes man, so she'd bought T-bone steaks and baking-size potatoes for their special dinner. If she'd fixed a fancy casserole it would have been ruined by now.

When she'd finished all the advance preparations, she went into the living room and turned on the television. It held her interest for a while, but by nine o'clock she was too jumpy to sit still. Where on earth was Erik? Could he have tried to call her at the boutique while she was at the doctor's?

She went to the phone and dialed her brother's number. April answered, and Colleen questioned her. April assured Colleen that there had been no phone calls for her, and Colleen thanked her and rang off. She hadn't told anybody, not even April, of her suspected pregnancy. She'd wanted Erik to be the first to know. She knew she should go ahead and eat, but although she'd been hungry earlier, now the thought of food made her nauseous.

Damn Erik anyway! Where was he, and who was he with?

Colleen cringed as that last thought broke through, unbidden and unwelcome. Had she gone back to distrusting him again? Surely she wasn't going to suspect him of being with Brett every time he was late getting home. She had no reason to think he was seeing Brett or any other woman, and she wasn't going to degrade herself by checking up on him.

An hour later, frantic with worry, she reluctantly telephoned Brett's apartment. There was no answer.

Colleen continued to dial Brett's number at fifteen-minute intervals. Finally at one o'clock she gave up. The rest of the night was a blur. She sat huddled in a corner of the sofa, numb with shock and despair. The only part of her that functioned was her mind, and it seemed to go around in circles. Were Erik and Brett together?

The suspicion was repugnant. Not once in the past six weeks had he given her any reason to doubt him. He'd sworn he no longer loved nor wanted Brett. He'd insisted that he loved her, Colleen, and all of his actions since then had proved that he'd spoken the truth. He'd been loving, attentive, concerned for her welfare, anxious to please. Why would he have gone to all that trouble if he'd been lusting after Brett?

As the minutes became hours and the hours moved into the first pale fingers of dawn, Colleen's thoughts continued to go around and around until she was too bruised and battered by their pounding to attempt to make sense of them. Her only salvation was her absolute certainty that Erik, the man she'd known and loved for sixteen years, would never cheat on his wife. He was too honest. There had to be some other explanation.

She had just looked at her watch when the phone rang. It was 5:36, and the raucous screech of the bell was like an explosion in the lonely silence of the apartment.

Colleen jumped up and raced for the wall phone in the kitchen. The voice on the other end was cool and professional. "Colleen Johansen, please."

"This is Colleen speaking." Her voice sounded raspy, and she cleared her throat.

"Mrs. Johansen, this is Mrs. Howard at Memorial Hospital. A male patient has been brought here whose identification lists him as Erik Johansen, and a Colleen Johansen as his wife."

Colleen gasped as the woman continued. "He's a tall, husky man with blond hair and green eyes. Could this be your husband?"

Colleen wanted to scream, but the air seemed to be knocked out of her. "Yes," she breathed barely above a whisper. "What's wrong with him? Why can't he tell you who he is?"

"He's been burned, and he's unconscious."

Colleen's knuckles whitened as they tightened on the phone, and a wave of dizziness caused her to sway. Erik burned! Oh, dear God, no!

"Mrs. Johansen, are you all right?" The taut voice steadied her.

"How badly is he burned? When was he brought in? My God, what happened?" Her voice rose with each question until it was almost a shriek.

"Please, try to stay calm," the placating voice said. "His hands and arms have second- and third-degree burns, and there's been some smoke inhalation. He's still unconscious, but it's not a life-threatening situation at the present. They were brought in by helicopter about two hours ago, and the doctors have been attending them."

"Them?" The one word burned in Colleen's brain. "Is there someone with him?"

The voice hesitated. "Yes, a woman. Her identification gives her name as Brett Kendrick and an address in New York City, but the phone number has been disconnected."

Brett! So Erik was with Brett. She closed her eyes and leaned heavily against the wall. Whatever had happened had happened to them when they were together. Colleen realized that she was shaking all over.

"Mrs. Johansen, are you still there?" The voice sounded concerned.

Colleen fought against the dizziness that engulfed her. "Yes, I'm sorry. What were you saying?"

"I asked if you could give us any information about Brett Kendrick? Is there someone we should notify?"

Colleen licked her dry lips. Why was she wasting time talking on the telephone? She had to go to Erik. "Yes," she answered, impatient to hang up. "Ms. Kendrick is my cousin. I'll notify her family, and I'll leave immediately for the hospital. I'll answer any more questions after I've seen my husband."

Colleen's spike-heeled sandals tapped out a steady rhythm on the bare hospital floor as she hurried toward the nursing station. She hadn't stopped to change her clothes, but had flung a lightweight coat over her sexy dress to protect her from the early-morning chill. Downstairs at the reception desk they'd directed her to the area known as the burn unit, but had been unable to give her any other information about Erik.

She stopped at the counter and identified herself to the motherly looking nurse. "Please, can you tell me about my husband?" she pleaded. "May I see him?"

The nurse pulled a chart from the rack and opened it. "He's doing very well considering the extent of his burns," she said in a reassuring tone, "but he's in a lot of pain and has been sedated. You can go in and sit with him if you'd like."

"Oh yes," she said, then remembered. "I'm also concerned about Brett Kendrick, who was brought in with my husband. She's my cousin. Was she badly burned?"

The nurse pulled another chart and scanned it. "Yes, hers were more extensive, and she's been put in intensive care as a precautionary measure. There's a notation here that we need some information about her."

"I know," Colleen said, unable to contain her need to see Erik any longer. "I'll notify her family and tell you anything you want to know, but first I must see my husband."

The nurse escorted Colleen to a private room a few doors down the hall. Erik lay flat on his back in the hospital bed, his hands and arms swathed in bandages and his face and hair streaked with dirt. His eyes were closed, and he looked so—so vulnerable. Colleen reached out and gently caressed a bruise on his jaw.

The nurse spoke. "They cleaned him up as best they could under the circumstances. I understand he and Ms. Kendrick had rolled in the muddy ground covering to put out the fire."

Colleen blinked. "Mud? Where on earth were they?"

"I don't have that information. You'll have to talk to the charge nurse who was on duty in the emergency room when they were brought in." She pulled a chair to the bedside. "Here, why don't you sit down? You look badly shaken."

Colleen thanked her but continued to stand as she watched Erik's still form. "Is he unconscious?" she asked.

"Not really. He was lucid before we sedated him, but he'll be out for quite a while. You can use the telephone here on the table to notify Ms. Kendrick's family.''

The nurse left, and Colleen leaned down and kissed Erik. His lips were hot and dry, and she wondered if he was running a temperature. She stroked his bristly cheeks, and brushed an unruly shock of hair away from his forehead. "Oh Erik," she murmured brokenly, "what happened? Where had you taken Brett, and why?"

She continued to caress his face, throat and shoulders with her hands and her lips until she realized that her knees were shaking. Then she sat down and reached for the telephone.

After pondering for a moment she dialed her brother's number. Fortunately it was Saturday and he didn't have to go to work. She told him in detail what had happened, and for once he didn't lose his temper but listened quietly. "I think it would be best if you'd go over and tell Aunt Glenna and Uncle Logan in person," she said. "You know how excitable they are, and maybe you can calm them down before they start for the hospital."

"I'll go get them and drive them to the hospital," he said. "Hang in there, honey, I'll be with you just as soon as I can."

Her lips trembled. "Thanks, Devin. I can always count on you."

"Damn right," he said harshly. "Which is more than you can say for that son of a bitch you married." He broke the connection.

Colleen sighed, then dialed Erik's parents' home.

In less than an hour the burn-care unit looked like an O'Farrell/Johansen family reunion. Colleen's parents, Brett's parents, Erik's parents with two of his sisters, and Devin all arrived at approximately the same time. Colleen learned that Brett's extensive burns were concentrated on her left side, from the shoulder down her leg. Colleen's emotional Irish relatives were in various stages of hysteria, and Erik's Scandinavian family was coolly stoic, but all felt the same deep pain and anxiety.

When Colleen explained that she didn't yet know where Erik and Brett had been or how they had gotten injured, Devin volunteered to find out. It was nearly an hour later when he sought Colleen in Erik's room. His face had that tight look that meant he was trying to control a raging anger.

Instinctively Colleen rose from the chair and motioned Devin to a corner away from the bed. "What did you learn?" she asked, keeping her voice low.

"The fire was in a cabin in the wooded area north of Bay City," he said, keeping his voice down with an effort.

Colleen's eyes widened. "But that's over one hundred miles from Detroit."

He looked grim. "I know. Smoke was sighted by the rangers at shortly before eight last night. By the time they located the fire the cabin was totally involved and Erik and Brett were found barely conscious and incoherent on the pine-needle-covered ground several yards away. They were given first aid there, then transported to the hospital by helicopter."

Colleen slumped, and Devin put his arm around her. "I don't suppose I have to ask what they were doing in a secluded cabin so far away," she said tonelessly.

"No, I don't suppose you do," Devin answered. "Come on, Sis, let me take you home."

She straightened and pulled away. "No. I have to be here when Erik wakes up. I've misjudged him badly before. I won't make that mistake again. I'll give him a chance to tell me what happened."

Devin shook his head, but there was a look of reluctant admiration in his eyes. He left the room without arguing.

Erik's family moved silently in and out of his room during the morning. Their manner toward Colleen was loving but constrained, as though they wanted to apologize to their son and brother's wife for his indiscretion but didn't know how to go about it. She tried to put them at ease, and finally they went home after promising to return that evening.

It was nearly noon before Erik began to stir. Colleen couldn't touch his bandaged hands, but she stood at the side of the bed and spoke softly to him as she caressed his face, shoulders and chest. He didn't open his eyes, but moaned and moved restlessly as though trying to escape the pain.

Colleen called to the nurse on the intercom, and by the time she got to the room he was thrashing around on the bed and groaning. The nurse put her hands on his shoulders and spoke briskly. "Mr. Johansen, open your eyes and look at me."

He stopped moving and opened his eyes. "Brett?" His voice had a strangled sound, but the name he called was unmistakable. "Brett. My God, Brett!"

He tried to sit up, but the nurse wrestled him back down. "Brett, where are you?" His head rolled from one side to the other as his gaze searched the room.

Colleen was momentarily stunned into silence, but when he began fighting the nurse again, she rushed to the other side of the bed and tried to calm him. "Erik, it's Colleen. Brett's all right. She's here in the hospital."

He looked directly at her, and said with agonizing clarity, "Brett. I want Brett. Please, I've got to see her."

Colleen watched numbly while the nurse gave him a shot, then she gathered up her purse and coat and walked out of the room. She was several steps down the hall before she could no longer hear Erik's desperate calls for Brett.

She'd always heard that people died of a broken heart, but now she knew that wasn't true. She could walk, and talk, and maybe someday she would even smile again, but would she ever learn to live with the silent scream that tore her soul asunder?

Chapter Fourteen

By the time she went back to work on Monday morning, Colleen could recall little of the nightmarish weekend. She'd left the hospital immediately after Erik had made it plain he wanted Brett and not her, and from then on her impressions were of moving about in a fog of anguish and despair. She hadn't left the apartment, but a steady stream of relatives had come and gone. They all offered sympathy and support, but she'd been unable to respond and had been relieved when they finally left her alone.

She'd called the hospital several times to check on Erik's condition, and each time she'd been told that he was asking for her. He probably was. He'd no doubt feel he owed her an explanation, but she didn't want to hear it. She'd reached the limit of her capacity for suffering, and this time she would not, could not, forgive.

Her natural compassion also compelled her to ask about Brett, and she learned that her cousin would be undergoing skin grafts and later plastic surgery, but there would be no lasting disfigurement.

When Colleen walked into the boutique April took one look at her and frowned. "Colleen, what are you doing here? I told you not to come to work today."

Colleen shook her head. "I've got to have something to do. I'll go mad if I spend any more time in that apartment."

April sighed. "All right, but you really don't look well. Maybe you should see the doctor again. How'd your checkup go? Is everything okay?"

"Checkup?" Colleen said. "What checkup?"

April looked worried. "You took time off Friday to go see Dr. Frank Welch. You said it was a checkup. Was everything all right?"

The jolt of total recall brought on by April's words made Colleen's head swim. The baby! Dear Lord, she'd forgotten about the baby! At some time on Friday night her concern for Erik had eclipsed her joy over her impending motherhood, and the call from the hospital had erased everything else from her mind. Even the child she'd wanted so badly.

She felt April's arm around her waist, and allowed herself to be led to a chair and lowered into it. She was pushed forward from the waist and April commanded, "Bend over and put your head on your knees."

Slowly the room stopped spinning, and Colleen straightened and looked into April's worry-clouded eyes. "You're in no shape to work," her sister-in-law informed her. "Did you have breakfast?"

Colleen shook her head.

"Dinner last night?"

Again a negative shake.

"Did you eat at all yesterday?"

The past two days were a blur to Colleen. "I don't think so."

"Damn," April muttered. "You probably haven't eaten all weekend. There's a restaurant just down the corridor. As soon as you feel strong enough I'm going to take you down there and force-feed you if necessary."

Force-feeding wasn't required. Now that Colleen had remembered the child she carried she made a determined effort to eat, and once she'd started on her pancakes, eggs, bacon and orange juice she discovered that she was hungry. Afterward she felt better, more alert and able to cope.

April finished her coffee and looked at Colleen across the table. "You little nut," she scolded, "you know better than to stop eating altogether."

Colleen swallowed the last of her pancakes. "I didn't do it intentionally. I guess I just forgot to eat. It won't happen again, I promise."

"It better not or I'll insist that you move in with us for a while," April threatened. "Now, let's talk about your appointment with the doctor. What did he have to say?"

All the joy Colleen had felt on Friday shriveled and died. If things had gone as planned, by now everyone in the families would have known about her pregnancy, and she and Erik would have been deliriously happy and proud. She wondered how she'd managed to reach the age of twenty-four still believing in fairy tales. Well, that oversight had been brutally corrected, but not before she'd made the mistake of deliberately bringing an innocent child into her fantasies. A mistake there was no way to rectify.

Her jaw tightened with the effort to keep her voice steady. "Oh, he said everything was fine," she told April. "I'm fully recovered from my miscarriage."

It was true as far as it went, but now she couldn't tell anybody about the baby she was carrying. That was her secret, and she had a lot to think about before she came to any decisions.

Colleen went back to work, over April's objections, and put in a full day. When she got home her phone was ringing. It was Erik's father, an older version of Erik in looks, who considered a woman's place to be in the kitchen, the bedroom and the nursery. He got right to the point. "My son has been asking for you. He's suffering and he needs his wife. Can't you forget your differences until he gets out of the hospital?"

Colleen resented her father-in-law's interference, although she could understand it, and she tried to be kind but firm. "I'm sorry," she said, "but Erik doesn't really want to see me."

"Good Lord, woman." Lars Johansen's voice practically exploded across the wires. "He wouldn't be insisting that we bring you to him if he didn't want to see you."

She knew her choice of words had been unfortunate. Of course he wanted to see her. He probably wanted to apologize for hurting her so publicly, and to ask for a divorce so he could marry Brett.

She tried to explain, but Lars cut in rudely. "Colleen, your place is with your husband. The doctor tells me that Erik is so upset by your refusal to visit him that he's not responding to treatment as well as they'd like.

Surely you can put aside your grievance long enough to come and find out what's bothering him."

"My grievance!" She almost shouted into the phone. Damn the man. How dare he accuse her of indifference to his son's well-being. He acted as if she were mad because Erik had forgotten to pick up his socks.

She made a supreme effort to lower her voice and speak with decorum. "You're well aware of the situation between Erik, Brett and me. I will not look the other way while my husband has an affair with another woman, and you have no right to expect me to. You can tell Erik for me that I'll talk to a lawyer before the end of the week." She hung up before the sob she'd been holding back broke through.

It was a long evening that started with Colleen forcing herself to broil and eat one of the steaks she'd planned for Erik's special dinner Friday night. There was no sense in letting it spoil, and she needed the nourishment for the baby. If she couldn't provide the poor child with a father, the least she could do was take care of herself so it would be healthy.

A wave of self-disgust enveloped her. How could she have been so selfish and foolish as to have deliberately gotten pregnant without Erik's knowledge when she'd suspected that their marriage was shaky? She'd known it was wrong. Her conscience had sent all sorts of warnings, but she'd ignored them. Now her son or daughter would pay the price.

This time there was no question of telling Erik. She wouldn't hook him with the same trick twice. She'd leave Detroit, and the sooner the better. She'd sell her share of the boutique to April at a price and terms her sister-in-law could afford, and then go as far away as she could get.

She would not share this baby with Erik. There would be no child-support payments or joint custody. He'd had no choice in its conception, and he would have no part in its upbringing.

It would probably mean a complete break with her parents and brother. If Erik married her cousin, Brett, he would still be a part of her family, so she couldn't let any of them know about her child. Maybe she could get a job in one of the overseas branches of American industry. She had a degree in business administration, with a minor in accounting, and she remembered that some of the big corporations had been recruiting on campus for overseas assignments at the time she graduated.

Colleen put her head down on the upholstered arm of the sofa and closed her eyes. She felt sick to her stomach, and her head ached. She devoutly wished that she'd never met Erik Johansen, but at the same time it took all her strength not to heed his father's plea and rush to his bedside. Why did he insist on tormenting her?

Because she was exhausted she slept well that night, and woke feeling rested and better able to face the day, if not the future. She'd read someplace that the journey of a thousand miles starts with the first step, and she supposed that was the best way to survive the next fifty years, a day at a time.

At the boutique she found April tired and irritable. When questioned April admitted what Colleen had suspected, that the whole O'Farrell/Johansen/Kendrick clan was in a state of turmoil. Colleen's family blamed Erik, Erik's family blamed Brett, and Brett's family staunchly defended her and blamed Colleen for marrying Erik in the first place. They were all shouting at each other and hurling accusations, and the turbulent emotions were fraying everybody's nerves.

Colleen wished they'd all just stay out of it, but knew that was unrealistic for her large, close-knit and loving family. It was very possible that this situation would cause a rupture that would never heal, but would also strengthen her determination that no one would know about her pregnancy.

April left work early that afternoon, so Colleen was later than usual getting home. It was a hot, sultry day and she headed immediately for the shower. Afterward, she slipped a silky caftan over a pair of panties and padded barefoot to the kitchen in search of something to fix for dinner.

She was standing in front of the open freezer trying to decide between a TV dinner and a bowl of leftover stew when she heard a key turn in the door lock. She froze. Nobody had keys to the apartment except Erik and her. Was someone trying to break in?

She closed the freezer and moved quickly to the telephone to call security when the door opened, and a voice she recognized as belonging to the security guard on duty spoke. "Take it easy, Mr. Johansen, or you'll fall flat on your face."

She dropped the phone and rushed to the small entryway where she found Erik, dressed in hospital pajamas and robe, leaning against the wall with the security guard hovering nearby. One look at her husband's white, strained features convinced her that he was indeed going to collapse, and without thinking she rushed to him and put her arms around his waist.

His bandaged arms immediately closed around her and he slumped against her. "Erik," she cried in alarm, "what are you doing here?"

He rested his cheek on the top of her head. "You wouldn't come to me, so I came to you."

"But how did you get here? Surely the doctor hasn't released you from the hospital yet."

He shifted more of his weight to the wall, but tightened his hold on her. "No. When Dad gave me your message about seeing a lawyer I checked myself out, and insisted they call a cab for me. I couldn't stand it any longer, knowing what you were thinking and not being able to tell you the truth about what happened."

She shook her head against his shoulder. "I don't want to hear," she moaned. "I just want you to leave me alone."

He lowered his face to the exposed side of her neck and kissed it, sending tiny tremors all through her. "Don't lie," he murmured. "Your tongue will cleave to the top of your mouth." He shifted again. "Sweetheart, can you help me into the living room? I'm afraid I'm not very energetic."

The security guard stepped forward, and between him and Colleen they got Erik to the couch and seated him. He refused to release Colleen and pulled her down on his lap.

The embarrassed guard excused himself and left. She knew she had to get away from Erik before her resistance melted and she forgot everything but the exquisite pleasure of being in his arms again, of his solid flesh beneath her and his lips caressing the pulse points in her jaw and throat.

She shivered with the need to hold him even as she put her hands against his chest and pushed. His arms tightened around her, but his face blanched with anguish. "If you fight me you'll do a lot of damage to the burns on my arms and hands," he said hoarsely. "Incidentally, they hurt like hell."

She collapsed against him and knew she was beaten. She couldn't deliberately injure him or cause him pain.

"That's my girl," he said, and she felt him relax. "Oh, darling, I've needed you so. Why did you run away? They told me you came to the hospital, but left before I woke up."

She stiffened with remembered agony and sat up. "I left because you looked right at me and called for Brett."

Erik swore. "I'm sorry. I don't remember. I couldn't have been more than partially conscious, but if I called for Brett it was because I was frantic wondering if she was dead or alive. I didn't want her, I only wanted to know if she was all right. If I'd gotten her out in time."

It sounded reasonable, but there were still too many unanswered questions. "That doesn't explain why you drove Brett over a hundred miles from Detroit to a secluded cabin in the forest without ever explaining why or telling me goodbye," she said bitterly. "I was frantic with worry when you didn't come home. Your secretary said you'd left early that morning and hadn't expected to be back in the office that day. Then, hours later, when I was going out of my mind, I called Brett's apartment, and she wasn't there. I kept calling most of the night and still no answer. What on earth did you expect me to think?"

"I expected you to think just what you did," he said surprisingly. "That's why I feel responsible for the fire and Brett's injuries. Let me explain.

"I didn't take Brett anywhere. She called me shortly after I arrived in the office that morning, and she was frantic. It seems she and Paul Forbes had been spending several days together in a cabin he owned deep in the forest area north of Bay City. The night before they'd had a vicious quarrel and he'd walked out, taken the car and left her there alone. He hadn't returned and she had no way to get home. She wanted me to come and get her."

Colleen interrupted angrily. "She had a lot of nerve, expecting you to drop everything and cater to her. Why didn't she call him?"

"That's what I asked her. She said she'd tried but couldn't find him, and she didn't dare leave messages. Even though his wife has filed for divorce now, Paul is still politically vulnerable and Brett didn't want to damage his career."

Erik grunted. "Apparently Brett has finally met her match in Paul Forbes. He's taking all he can get from her, and giving little in return. She admitted that she'd treated me badly in the past and she couldn't blame me if I wouldn't help her, but she was really desperate. There was a storm coming up and the cabin was miles off the main road in an area that was totally isolated. I could tell she was scared and—well—I know now I should have handled it differently, but at the time it didn't seem all that big a deal. I figured it wouldn't take more than five hours to drive up there and back, and I couldn't very well leave her alone and stranded."

Colleen felt her anger waning, and her sense of relief was enormous. She knew Erik was telling the truth. How like Brett to think of no one's inconvenience but her own. Colleen couldn't blame him for going to her rescue. He was right, he couldn't have just left her there, but that didn't excuse him for not letting her know he was going out of town and might be late.

"Why didn't you let me know where you were going and why?" she asked. "I was away from the boutique a couple of times that day, but April said you didn't call."

"April's wrong," he said mournfully. "I called in the morning before I left to ask you to go with me, and again at noon when I stopped for gas before turning off the highway, but the phone was answered by a stranger who said you weren't there so I didn't give my name or leave a message."

Colleen thought back and remembered, belatedly, that they had been training a new sales clerk that morning. She'd apparently answered the phone while April was busy.

Before she could interrupt Erik continued. "Brett was right about the storm. By the time I got to the turnoff it was raining hard and the wind was blowing. The dirt road that led to the cabin was slippery and it was slow going. When I finally arrived Brett was nearly hysterical. The electricity was off so there was no heat or lights, and the phone was out of order."

He shifted uncomfortably, and Colleen knew he was tired and hurting. She put her arms around his neck and cradled his head against her breast. He sighed gratefully and rubbed his face in her softness. "Before I could get her things together and lock up, the rain turned into a cloudburst," he continued. "We couldn't start out in that, and when it showed no signs of letting up I built a fire in the fireplace to take off some of the chill. The cabin was situated in a grove of trees where little light or warmth could penetrate."

Colleen could feel the tension building in Erik again as he recounted the maddening events, and she knew he was telling the truth. It was too dramatically improbable to be anything else.

She kissed the top of his head and murmured, "Don't get upset, darling, I believe you. But how did the fire start in all that rain?"

He took a deep breath. "It didn't. The rain finally stopped, but the car was up to its hubcaps in mud, and the dirt road back to the highway was impassable. By then I was furious with Brett for getting me into such an impossible situation, and desperate to get to a phone so I could call you. I decided to walk to the main road and try to catch a ride to the nearest town to get help. Brett pleaded with me not to leave her alone, but she wouldn't go with me so I slammed out of the cabin and walked away." He shuddered. "Oh God," he groaned, "if I'd stayed with her as I should have she wouldn't have been injured. I never should have walked out on her."

Colleen finally understood why he'd called so insistently for Brett when he regained consciousness in the hospital; he blamed himself for the fire.

Her arms tightened around him. "Sweetheart, Brett's certainly old enough to take care of herself. Besides, I don't understand. If you left the cabin how did you get burned?"

"I went back," he answered. "I wandered for quite a while before I realized that it was getting dark and I could easily get lost in that unfamiliar place. Reluctantly I retraced my steps, and when I finally got within sight of the cabin I saw flames flying from the chimney and the windows. The fire started inside. I don't know how it happened, but by the time I got there the whole interior was aflame, and Brett was unconscious on the floor with her clothes on fire.''

Erik was trembling, and his voice was raw with pain. ''I grabbed her and pulled her outside where I rolled her in the wet, muddy pine needles on the ground. I remember that my lungs were about to burst from the smoke I'd inhaled, but I didn't know I'd been burned too until I woke up in the hospital with my hands and arms feeling like they'd been singed in hell. I kept asking for you, but you wouldn't come. I would have called you but I couldn't dial the phone, and besides, the painkillers left me pretty much unable to function. I was afraid that this time I really had lost you.'' His arms tightened around her. ''Colleen, for God's sake don't leave me.''

By this time Colleen was crying. Tears streamed down her pale cheeks, and her body was shaking with sobs. ''Oh Erik, my darling, haven't you learned yet that you couldn't get rid of me if you tried? I tagged you for my own when I was eight years old, and I've loved you ever since.''

For several minutes they sat quietly, holding each other and trying to piece together their shattered emotions. Finally Erik raised his head and looked at Colleen. He'd aged in the four days since she'd last seen him. His face was white and ravaged with grief and exhaustion, and there were deep lines at the corners of his mouth and his eyes. The knowledge that she'd been mainly responsible for his anguish brought more tears from the well of regret that tormented her.

Her fingers caressed his Nordic features, and she touched his lips with hers in a gentle kiss of love beyond passion. He smiled, and it went all the way to his eyes. "Would you be interested in putting me to bed?" he asked with a rueful glance at his useless hands.

She smiled back. "I might be. Do you promise to go to sleep?"

"Eventually," he said, and nibbled on her ear.

"Now," she insisted, and slid off his lap.

She helped him up, and walked beside him as he made his way unsteadily down the hall to the bedroom. He insisted he was all right, but she knew his store of energy had been seriously depleted by the extensive burns.

When they reached the bed he asked her to remove the pajamas and robe he was wearing. She unknotted the belt on the robe and opened it, then unbuttoned the pajama coat and slid them both carefully over his bandaged arms and laid them across the back of a chair. Next she untied the drawstring around the waist of the cotton trousers, and pushed them down over his muscular thighs. Those thighs were a potent temptation and she wanted to caress them, but she restrained the urge and helped him step out of the pajamas. He sat down on the side of the bed, and she plumped up the pillows as he twisted around and lay down. Colleen reached to pull the sheet over him, but he put his hand on her arm to stop her. "Now take off your dress," he murmured.

She started to protest, but the look in his eyes told her it would be useless. Instead she straightened up and pulled the gown over her head and flung it across the bottom of the big bed.

He watched hungrily. "The briefs, too."

She stepped out of the brief panties and left them on the carpet as she stood naked for his inspection.

His penetrating gaze was hot and exciting, and when he held out his arms to her she forgot her concern for his burns and went to him. She couldn't lie with his bandaged arms under her, so she climbed on top of him and stretched out full length against him.

He put his arms around her and held her there. "This is what I've been wanting, needing," he said huskily. "I'd have gone crazy if I'd had to spend another night without you." He lifted her chin and ravaged her willing mouth.

"I love you, my warm and cuddly little wife," he continued. "I wouldn't say it if I didn't. I waited a long time to tell you because I didn't want to love you so much. It scares the hell out of me, and leaves me wide open for torment I don't want to feel, so why do you find it so hard to believe? How can you think I'd want Brett when I have you?"

She laid her cheek against his chest and could feel and hear his heart pounding. She was sure her own was going to burst with happiness as she answered him honestly. "Because Brett was your first choice. You chose her for a wife, but got me by default. You never would have made love to me if I hadn't been there when you needed someone, and you wouldn't have married me if you hadn't gotten me pregnant. You even admitted you didn't love me when you asked me to marry you."

He muttered a sharp oath and caressed her other cheek with his bandaged hand. "I loved you, sweetheart. I've always loved you, but I hadn't yet realized that it had changed from the love of a young man for a child to that of a mature man for a woman. I was so used to thinking of you as Devin's cute little kid sister. I began to accept the fact that you were grown up when we started going out together after you graduated from college, but I wasn't prepared for the sexual feelings I felt for you. You were Devin's little sister, and off limits. I guess that's why I was so quick to take up with Brett when she appeared on the scene. She was older and had been around. The type I was used to, nonthreatening and available."

Colleen moved her head to tease his nipple with her tongue. "I'm nonthreatening and available," she murmured.

Erik groaned. "If that's a proposition I accept, but we have a problem." He raised his bandaged hands.

"No problem," she assured him and began to inch slowly down his hard muscular body, trailing kisses across his chest and stomach as she went.

He gasped and arched against her as her lips circumvented his pelvis and worried his hipbone before traveling on to his quivering leg. She made moist little circles on his rough skin with her tongue and felt his impaired hands clutch at her head as she stroked the inner side of his sensitized thigh.

"Sweetheart," he moaned. "If you don't come up here right now you're going to miss the main event."

She quickly repositioned herself over him and shivered with pleasure as she received him.

Later she lay sprawled over him, relaxed and marvelously content. Erik's hands rested on her bare buttocks, and she could feel his heartbeat returning to normal under her ear. She knew she should roll off him and let him sleep. He badly needed the rest, but he seemed as content as she was and she couldn't bring herself to leave him. Besides, there was still something she had to confess.

She took a deep breath and began. "Darling, I have something to tell you."

He rubbed his cheek in her hair. "It's about time," he whispered sleepily.

She blinked and raised her head. "I beg your pardon?"

He grinned and kissed her. "I've been waiting two weeks for you to tell me you're pregnant."

Her mouth dropped open in disbelief. "How did you know?"

His green eyes twinkled with amusement. "Honey, my second best subject in school was numbers. I can even count, and when we make love for six full weeks I figure it's time to start shopping for diapers."

"But you didn't say anything," she accused. "I thought you hadn't noticed."

His arms came up to circle her waist and cuddle her to him. "Colleen, my love," he said, "when are you going to understand that I notice everything about you? I was a little hurt when you didn't share your suspicions with me, but I figured you wanted to wait until you were sure."

"Then you're not angry?"

He kissed her forehead. "Concerned, yes, but never angry. What happened? I thought those pills were practically foolproof."

She felt a chill of apprehension. "They are, but I quit taking them."

He was silent for a moment. "Why didn't you tell me? Discuss it with me? The doctor said you shouldn't get pregnant again for at least six months."

She nodded. "I know. I was afraid you'd insist that we wait."

"If I had it would only have been prompted by concern for your health. You're very necessary to me, you know. Have you seen the doctor?"

"Yes. I had an appointment Friday. He said everything's fine. I was going to tell you Friday night, but you never came home."

"Oh God, sweetheart, I'm sorry." His voice throbbed with regret. "I really messed up good this time, didn't I?"

She nuzzled the hollow at the base of his throat. "That's all in the past, and we're going to forget about it," she said, and closed her eyes.

They lay quietly for a while until she whispered sleepily, "Erik."

"Mmmm?"

"You said your second best subject in school was numbers."

"Uh-huh."

"What was your first best subject?"

Erik chuckled. "The birds and the bees, of course. What else?"

AMERICAN TRIBUTE

Where a man's dreams count for more than his parentage...

Look for these upcoming titles under the Special Edition American Tribute banner.

LOVE'S HAUNTING REFRAIN
Ada Steward #289–February 1986
For thirty years a deep dark secret kept them
apart—King Stockton made his millions while
his wife, Amelia, held everything together.
Now could they tell their secret, could they
admit their love?

THIS LONG WINTER PAST
Jeanne Stephens #295–March 1986
Detective Cody Wakefield checked out
Assistant District Attorney Liann McDowell,
but only in his leisure time. For it was the
danger of Cody's job that caused Liann to
shy away.

AM-TRIB-1

AMERICAN TRIBUTE

RIGHT BEHIND THE RAIN
Elaine Camp #301–April 1986
The difficulty of coping with her brother's
death brought reporter Raleigh Torrence
to the office of Evan Younger, a police
psychologist. He helped her to deal with
her feelings and emotions, including love.

CHEROKEE FIRE
Gena Dalton #307–May 1986
It was Sabrina Dante's silver spoon that
Cherokee cowboy Jarod Redfeather couldn't
trust. The two lovers came from opposite
worlds, but Jarod's Indian heritage taught
them to overcome their differences.

NOBODY'S FOOL
Renee Roszel #313–June 1986
Everyone bet that Martin Dante and Cara
Torrence would get together. But Martin
wasn't putting any money down, and Cara
was out to prove that she was nobody's fool.

MISTY MORNINGS, MAGIC NIGHTS
Ada Steward #319–July 1986
The last thing Carole Stockton wanted was to
fall in love with another politician, especially
Donnelly Wakefield. But under a blanket of
secrecy, far from the campaign spotlights,
their love became a powerful force.

Silhouette Special Edition

COMING NEXT MONTH

THIS LONG WINTER PAST—Jeanne Stephens
Cody Wakefield was a temptation that Assistant District Attorney
Liann McDowell vowed to resist. He was intelligent, charming
and attractive... but he was a cop.

ZACHARY'S LAW—Lisa Jackson
Zachary's law partner was against him taking the case, but when
Zachary looked into Laura's eyes and saw the pain that so closely
mirrored his own soul, he knew he had to help her.

JESSE'S GIRL—Billie Green
Ellie had always been his "Little Peanut." Even when the trouble
started and Bitter, Texas, turned against him, Jesse didn't realize
that the girl standing beside him was becoming a woman—and
she was in love.

BITTERSWEET SACRIFICE—Bay Matthews
While searching for the surrogate mother who was now denying
him his child, Zade Wakefield found Lindy. Neither of them
knew that the bond they felt was the child they shared.

HEATSTROKE—Jillian Blake
Ten years had passed since Carey had been introduced to rock
star Tony Miles. Now she could discover if the sparks ignited that
night meant love, or were merely a flash in the pan.

DIAMOND IN THE SKY—Natalie Bishop
Taylor couldn't just walk away. Jason had transformed her from
an ex-model into a box-office smash. Now he needed help, and he
was going to get it... whether he wanted it or not.

AVAILABLE THIS MONTH

LOVE'S HAUNTING REFRAIN
Ada Steward

MY HEART'S UNDOING
Phyllis Halldorson

SURPRISE OFFENSE
Carole Halston

BIRD IN FLIGHT
Sondra Stanford

TRANSFER OF LOYALTIES
Roslyn MacDonald

AS TIME GOES BY
Brooke Hastings